WHEN WE WERE US

ELENA AITKEN

Ink Blot Communications

Also by Elena Aitken

Unexpected Endings - Short Story

Mistaken Gifts

Secret Gifts

Goodbye Gifts

Tempting Gifts

Holiday Gifts

Promised Gifts

Accidental Gifts

The Castle Mountain Lodge Collection: Books 1-3

The Castle Mountain Lodge Collection: Books 4-6

The Castle Mountain Lodge Collection: Books 7-9

The Castle Mountain Lodge Complete Collection

The Springs Series

Summer of Change

Falling Into Forever

Second Glances

Winter's Burn

Midnight Springs

She's Making A List

Summit of Desire

Summit of Seduction

Summit of Passion

Fighting For Forever

The Springs Collection: Volume 1

The Springs Collection: Volume 2

The Springs Collection: Volume 3

.

The Springs Complete Collection - Books 1-10

The McCormicks

Love in the Moment

Only for a Moment

One more Moment

In this Moment

From this Moment

Bears of Grizzly Ridge

His to Protect

His to Seduce

His to Claim

Hers to Take

His to Defend

His to Tame

His to Seek

Bears of Grizzly Ridge: Books 1-4

Destination Paradise

Shelter by the Sea

Escape to the Sun

Stand Alone Stories

All We Never Knew

Drawing Free

Sugar Crash

Composing Myself

Betty & Veronica

The Escape Collection

Vegas

Nothing Stays in Vegas

Return to Vegas

Halfway Series

Halfway to Nowhere

Halfway in Between

Halfway to Christmas

Chapter One

CHRISTY THOMAS TOOK a deep breath and then another.

It didn't work. She was still shaking and unable to focus on her reflection in the mirror.

With both hands planted firmly on the countertop, she squeezed her eyes shut and tried again.

One. Two. Three.

The counting technique her holistic healer had taught her was not working. Christy swallowed hard, opened her eyes, and stared at her reflection. Maybe it was the fluorescent lighting of the clinic's bathroom that made her look so puffy and old.

Maybe. But not likely. It was her.

Christy hardly recognized herself lately. *When had she become this worn-out version of herself?* The hot tears pricked at her eyes and threatened to spill over.

Again.

The worst part was she wouldn't be able to stop them. She'd always been an emotional person, but with all the hormones the doctors had her taking, it was next level, out of control.

She was exhausted.

And it wasn't over.

"Come on, Christy," she whispered to the woman in the mirror. "You can do this. Pull it together."

She tried her breathing exercises once more and pulled out her compact in a vain effort to cover the red blotches on her cheeks and the dark circles under her eyes. When she'd done the best she could, Christy snapped the compact shut, stood as straight as she could, and pasted what she hoped would pass as a smile on her face.

"There you are," her husband Mark said as soon as he saw her. He pushed up from the wall where he'd been leaning, tucked his phone into his back pocket and reached for her hand. "I was beginning to think you may have fallen in." He gave her a grin that was as equally fake as the one she wore on her own face. "Are you ready for this?"

How was she supposed to answer that question? Was she ready to lay on the doctor's examination table, like some sort of specimen, to see whether their latest round of in vitro fertilization and hormone therapies had worked, and they were finally, thankfully, mercifully pregnant?

Yes. She was ready for that.

But Mark's question was two-sided.

Was she ready to lie on that table, surrounded by doctors, nurses, and students and hear the news that once again the ultrasound revealed the treatments hadn't worked, and now, not only were they not pregnant, but they were completely out of options? Was she ready for that?

No.

Instead of saying exactly what she was thinking, Christy nodded and with cheer she didn't feel said, "Absolutely. Let's do this."

Mark's hand felt clammy in hers. Not the warm, strong support that he usually offered her with a simple touch.

When had that changed?

As they walked slowly down the hallway to Doctor Duncan's office, Christy snuck a look at her tall, strong husband. Even as teenagers, he'd always been a foot taller than her. The way he'd wrap his arms around her had always made her feel safe and protected, as if nothing bad could ever happen.

If only things were still so simple. If only she could be protected from sadness and bad news, with only Mark shielding her. But it wasn't like that anymore. How could he possibly protect her from the disappointment that radiated off him every time they found out the treatments hadn't worked? She knew he didn't mean to make her feel bad; he even tried his best to hide his feelings. After all, it wasn't her fault. Not entirely. A low sperm count and "tricky" eggs meant they carried *equal* fault with their infertility. But knowing that and *knowing* it were two very different things.

It was *her* body that continually failed to accept the embryos. It was *her* body that couldn't seem to manage to accomplish the very thing it was designed to do.

"I have a good feeling about it this time." Mark squeezed her hand. "It's different this time, isn't it?"

Different than the last two times? Only in the sense that instead of the overwhelming feeling of hope and anticipation, Christy —who was generally unwaveringly positive and optimistic to the point of occasionally being annoying to her friends and family—couldn't for the life of her find anything to smile at these days.

At least not genuinely.

"It is, isn't it?" Mark asked again.

She nodded and, like the good wife she was, smiled. "It is." She lied. Because it didn't feel any different than the last few times they'd been through the process. She didn't have any tingling in her breasts, no feeling of fullness or the miraculous twinge that signified that there was now a new life growing in her womb. None of the things that women described in her online forums applied to her. But then again, not everyone experienced a moment when they just knew. *Maybe she was one of those women?*

With her free hand, she crossed her fingers.

It couldn't hurt.

She wanted to tell Mark how scared she was that she'd let him down again. She wanted to talk about what they could do if they got bad news again. More than anything, she wanted to tell him that she loved him and they'd be okay. No matter what. But somehow she couldn't find the words.

"Do you feel pregnant?"

She opened her mouth to lie again but thankfully, Dr. Duncan's nurse, Amanda, greeted them. "Dr. and Mrs. Thomas. Welcome back." She smiled warmly, the way she always did. She'd likely been trained to always be optimistic and hopeful without giving patients a false sense of security that they would be receiving good news. "Let's take you right back and get you set up."

Christy followed Amanda numbly down the small corridor to the exam room she already knew too well. The last time she'd been there was to have their last three embryos implanted in her uterus. It seemed crazy that they were the last ones. They were the last three hopes she and Mark had for a baby.

Dr. Duncan had warned against a multiple pregnancy, but those warnings seemed a world away. Not that twins or even triplets would be anything to be warned against, but also because the idea that even one embryo would stick seemed so unlikely to Christy's battered heart there was no way she could conceivably imagine multiples.

Amanda gave her a gown to change into and left the room so she could have a moment of privacy with Mark while she got situated for the exam that would change their lives either way.

Mark bent and pressed a kiss to her forehead. "I love you."

The tears that had been threatening all day were suddenly gone. Ironically when she would have welcomed them the most. When she would have welcomed any feeling at all, except for the deep sense of emptiness that filled her.

MARK HELD tight to his wife's hand, willing her to be okay. He no longer wished for a successful pregnancy, although of course he wanted that. But more than anything, he just wanted Christy to be okay. More and more over the last few months, during this last round of IVF, he felt her changing, hardening somehow. Pulling away from him.

At first, he thought it was just the stress of the treatments that was causing the shift in his usual lighthearted wife. But more and more, he worried that it was something bigger.

"Good afternoon." Doctor Brian Duncan greeted them in the same welcoming way he always did. It must be a mixed bag to be a fertility doctor, as opposed to having a general practice like his own. Sure, Brian would have all the highs of helping people get pregnant and realize their dreams to start a family. But there would also be the flip side of that coin. Breaking hearts.

The way he'd done with them. Up until now.

Mark refused to think anything but positive thoughts. *This time was going to be different. It had to be different.* Mark himself had seen it in his own practice for years. Especially with the couples he'd referred to Dr. Duncan. In vitro fertilization was becoming more and more successful. The success rates were strong. It was more unusual for it not to work.

The statistics were in their favor.

It had to work.

Especially considering this last round had eaten up the last bit of their savings. IVF was expensive, and insurance wasn't much help. Mark didn't want to tell Christy that he'd had to cash in a retirement fund he'd set up as well as take out a line of credit in order to make the final payment for this treatment. She thought they'd been able to use their savings. Mark hated keeping things like that from her and it was the only time he'd ever flat out lied to her in their relationship, but it was only to protect her.

She had enough going on with the hormone treatments and the emotional madness that cycled through her on a daily basis. He couldn't worry her about the financial side of things.

Besides, it would pay off when they held their very own baby in their arms. It would more than pay off. And there was no way she could be mad at him then.

"How are you both doing today?" Dr. Duncan looked at them each in turn, but his smile faded a little as his gaze landed on Christy. "How are you feeling, Christy? Has everything been okay this round?"

She nodded and that same smile that Mark had seen a little too often lately—the one that didn't quite reach her eyes and create the cute little crinkle in the corners that he loved so much—slid across her face. "I'm a little tired, Doctor. But otherwise, I'm just fine."

The doctor patted her hand, but he still looked concerned. "Well, it's normal for you to be tired. After all, your body is working very hard."

Christy's smile dropped away. Mark knew what she was thinking. That her body wasn't working hard. Because if it were, they'd already be pregnant. He knew she blamed herself for their infertility. More than anything, he wanted to take that away from her. As a medical doctor himself, he *knew* that wasn't true. *But deep down, didn't he blame her? Just a little bit?*

Mark shook the thought away. He couldn't let himself think

that way. Besides, this was the time it was going to work. He knew it.

"Well, why don't we take a look at what's going on in there, shall we?"

It was Mark who answered with a simple nod of his head.

Dr. Duncan and his nurse Amanda kept up an easy line of conversation and chatter that Mark knew was designed to put them at ease, but he wasn't listening. He was focused on his wife's face. She'd been crying for the littlest reasons for months. Like toast that was slightly browner than she would have preferred, or just that morning the fact that there were no seeds in the raspberry jam. But now, lying on the exam table waiting for the news that they were going to be parents—or not, he had to remind himself—she was straight-faced, with no glimmer of emotion or…anything really.

He squeezed Christy's hand and she met his gaze.

I love you. He mouthed the words but she didn't respond. Instead, she squeezed her eyes shut as Dr. Duncan placed the ultrasound wand on her belly.

"It's going to be a little cool," he said despite the fact they all knew he heated the ultrasound gel, but no one said anything.

SHE'D KNOWN GOING in what the results would be.

No baby.

Not even one.

She wasn't pregnant.

Again.

Leaving the clinic felt final this time. They wouldn't be back. There were no more embryos and no more money. That was it.

Her final failure to be a mother.

Christy knew Mark felt it too, the sense of finality when the glass door swung gently shut behind them in a soft whoosh that felt incongruous with how she was feeling. Thankfully, after Doctor Duncan finished his exam, she was able to get dressed and they could leave. After all, there was nothing more he could say.

And then finally, mercifully they were back in the car, driving away from the clinic and the doctor who, despite his best efforts, couldn't give them what they so desperately wanted.

"We can go..." Mark let the sentence fall away unfinished. "Christy? Are you...are we..."

Numb, she tucked her hands between her legs to keep him from reaching for them. She couldn't stand the idea of being touched. Of being loved by him when she'd just failed so completely to give him what he wanted most. Not right then.

"I love you."

She forced a small smile. "I know. I love you too."

That was the hardest part. Their love for each other. It just didn't seem fair. They loved each other so much and they'd done everything right. They'd been safe in high school and all through college, using protection so they wouldn't start a family until they were ready and able to give their child everything he or she deserved. And then it was time. After they were married and settled back into their home town of Timber Creek, with a house of their own that had spare bedrooms to fill, it was finally time to start the family they'd both dreamed about since they were high school sweethearts and barely more than children themselves.

But it hadn't happened.

And now all they had was that love that had pulled them along all these years. *Would it be enough?*

She didn't want to cry. She wanted to stay numb so she couldn't feel the overwhelming sense of loss inside her, knowing she'd never be a mother. She swallowed hard to keep the tears down. She wouldn't cry. She couldn't.

"Christy." Mark's voice was soft, almost as if he knew if he spoke too loudly she would crack and break. "There are other things we can—"

"Can we just not talk about this right now?" She kept her eyes fixed to the road in front of them and the thick pine forest that lined the highway. She unrolled the window and inhaled the pine-filled air. It was a smell that never failed to ground her. "Let's just not talk about it for a few days, okay?" She looked at him then and could see the confusion on his face. Up until a few hours ago, it had been Christy who wanted to talk about other options, and Mark who'd wanted to wait. He was so sure the IVF would work that he didn't want to entertain any other ideas. Now the roles had flipped. Maybe it didn't make sense to him, but it did to her. She needed a break. Even for a few days of not having this dominate her every waking moment.

She'd tried to use the Timber Creek High School reunion party as a distraction, but that had been over for months. Besides, even when she filled her days with business to distract her, it was never enough.

It was always there. Right under the surface.

"I just need a few days, Mark. Please."

"Okay." He nodded and turned his attention back to the road but Christy could see the hurt lined on his face. It wasn't just her who this experience had taken a toll on. Mark was hurting just as deeply as she was. It wasn't just her who'd wanted parenthood.

She knew that. Of course she did. But knowing it and doing something about it were two very different things. And even though it made her sick inside, she just couldn't bring herself to reach out to him. With every minute that passed, she hated herself a little bit more for it.

Chapter Two

TWO DAYS LATER, Cam Riley, loaded down with an oversized bouquet of flowers, a bag of freshly baked cookies, and a bottle of wine knocked on Christy's front door twice before walking into the house. As the only other part of the foursome who made up the circle of best friends, who actually lived in Timber Creek, Cam had been dispatched to Christy's house to check on her, provide hugs, and pig out on cookies and wine with their friend in an attempt to let her know that she wasn't alone.

Cam had been desperate to get over to Christy's ever since receiving the simple, and painfully to the point text message two days earlier that their last round of IVF hadn't worked.

Not pregnant.

Her heart ached for her friend and Cam immediately replied with words of comfort, but she knew it wasn't enough. It wasn't near enough to ease the pain she knew her friend was feeling. Christy had wanted to be a mother as long as Cam could remember. She couldn't even imagine the hurt she must be going through.

Which was why she wasn't surprised when Christy hadn't

answered the door when she knocked. She also hadn't answered any of her phone calls or text messages. Cam had gone by the clinic to talk to Mark, and he'd told her that Christy had been lying in bed, mostly sleeping and staring at the television since they'd come home. Cam wanted to be respectful and give her friend space, but she also knew there was such a thing as too much space.

"Christy?" She called into the house as she made her way down the hallway into the kitchen. Cam was used to the smells of baking coming from Christy's oven, or at least plates of cookies and muffins on the counters.

She put her packages down on clean, bare countertops. Not only was there no trace of Christy's usual baking, there didn't seem to be a trace of anything.

"Christy?" Cam called again. "Are you awake?" She shook her head and muttered to herself, "If you're not, you will be soon." She made her way down the hall, fully prepared to wake her friend, get her outside and shower her with the love she obviously needed. But when she got to the bedroom door, knocked and pushed it open, she wasn't prepared to find Christy fully dressed, slipping into a pair of shoes and grabbing her purse.

Christy practically ran into her as she stepped into the room.

"Cam?" Her friend took a step back, but her smile didn't slip. "What are you doing here?"

"Checking on you." Cam looked around the room. The sun shone through the blinds, onto a perfectly made bed with nary a glass of water, let alone a crumpled tissue, in sight. It wasn't even a little bit the scene she'd expected to walk into. "How are you doing?" She looked back to her friend in question, trying to assess how Christy was *really* doing. "I was afraid you would be..."

"I'm fine." Christy slipped her purse over her shoulder.

"Fine?"

"Of course. Why wouldn't I be?"

Because of everything you've just been through, Cam wanted to say. *Because your dreams of motherhood were just crushed. Because…because you must be heartbroken.*

Instead, Cam reached out to her friend and said, "Because you've had a rough few days is all. I just thought you might want to talk. I brought cookies."

Christy was known for her bubbly personality, the way she never let anything get her down, and no matter what, always had a positive attitude, but…Cam could not reconcile her best friend with the person in front of her when Christy laughed. *Laughed.* And said, "Cam. I'm fine. In fact, I was just going to go out and see about getting my hair done."

"Your hair?"

Besides the fact that Christy's hair looked perfectly fine, it just seemed…strange. The Christy she knew would be hurting, crying, and reacting very, *very* differently.

"Are you sure you're okay? Did you hear me say I brought cookies? They're from the Dough Knot, and they were just pulled out of the oven. Still warm."

If there was one thing Christy loved, it was baking. Usually her own delicious creations, but no one in town would turn down anything Sylvie over at the Dough Knot pulled out of the oven.

To Cam's surprise, Christy shook her head and patted her stomach. "No more cookies for me. I'm afraid I have a few extra pounds that need to come off and cookies are definitely not diet friendly."

"Christy, you don't need to lose weight. You look great."

She shook her head and gestured past Cam to the hallway.

Unsure of what was going on, Cam led the way to the kitchen. "Do you want to at least sit and have a cup of tea?" she asked. "Or maybe a glass of wine? I know it's early, but…"

The wine was a long shot, because ever since Cam had come back to town in the spring, Christy had been participating in what seemed to be an ongoing round of fertility treatments and had been for quite a while and therefore was completely avoiding alcohol. But to her surprise, Christy picked up the bottle and laughed. "It's never too early for a glass, is it?"

She moved around the kitchen, looking for an opener and a few glasses, while Cam sat in kind of a stunned silence. She should be happy that Christy looked to be bouncing back from what had to be a crushing disappointment with so much ease, but it worried her. A lot.

"I wasn't sure if you were going to drink," she said when Christy handed her a glass. "Or if you were going to…"

"Have more treatments?" She raised her glass and Cam met it with a clink. "Nope." She took a deep drink. "That ship has sailed."

Cam choked on her wine and only barely refrained from spitting it out.

"Are you okay?" Christy put a glass of water in front of her and sat down next to her at the table. "Here, drink this."

Cam did as she was told and once the coughing subsided, drank a little more water in order to give herself a moment to pull her thoughts together. *Surely, Christy was in shock of some kind?* She'd heard about that happening when something terrible happened and this situation must rank pretty high on the terrible scale for Christy and Mark.

"I'm fine," Cam said after a moment. Before Christy could stand up and slip away again, Cam reached for her hand. "Sweetie, I just want you to know that it's okay to feel any way you need to about this. I know you must still be in shock about how things went the other day, but it's okay."

Christy's smile slipped a little, and just for a moment, Cam thought she might have gotten a glimpse of what was really going on with her friend. But then the moment was gone.

"I'm okay, Cam. Really." Christy turned her hand over and squeezed it. "I know it probably doesn't seem like it, but I really do have a handle on things. If I'm being honest with you, it's actually a relief."

"A relief?"

"For sure." Christy nodded, her blonde ponytail bouncing. "I mean, trying to have a baby was so all-consuming for so long that I don't think I bothered to actually look ahead to what it would mean if we actually had one, you know?"

She didn't know, but she nodded dumbly and let Christy keep talking.

"So anyway, it's kind of a nice feeling to not have to worry about all that stuff. Does that make sense?"

Christy didn't wait for an answer before she jumped up from her chair and grabbed her glass of wine. She took another long sip. "I almost completely forgot what wine tasted like." She closed her eyes and savored another sip. "So good, right?"

Cam nodded and assessed her friend. She wasn't convinced by Christy's act, not by a long shot, but she also knew she wouldn't get anywhere by pushing her.

"Well, I'm glad you're feeling okay," she said instead.

Christy smiled, but even from where she was sitting, Cam could see it didn't reach her eyes. "I am," she said and Cam knew without a doubt that her best friend was lying to her. And more troubling—to herself.

IT'S NOT that Christy was lying to her best friend. Not really.

She did feel okay. As okay as she could be expected to.

Whatever that meant. She'd spent the last few days lying in her bed, feeling sorry for herself, reliving the last few months and everything she'd been through.

Was it her fault that the IVF hadn't worked?

Could she have rested more? Gotten more sleep? Maybe she forgot to take her vitamins. What had the doctor said about exercise?

She'd been over every angle in her head. What she could have done differently.

Everything.

Nothing.

It hurt her head to keep thinking about it. But not as much as it hurt her heart, which was why that morning she'd made a decision. No more wallowing in bed thinking about what could have been, or should have been or…*no*. No more.

She'd been determined to get up, put on a happy face, and get herself a new haircut and maybe a new outfit or something to mark this new beginning. Her entire life, Christy had been unfailingly positive. She was the one out of all her friends who could always find the bright side of things, something to smile about on a rainy day, and always the good in people.

Her mother had always told her, "Fake it till you make it, darling. Smile and the world smiles with you. Cry, and you cry alone." It had become a mantra that had become part of who she was. So, with her mother's words ringing in her ears, Christy had pulled herself out of bed, jumped in the shower, and carefully applied makeup to mask the dark circles under her eyes and was just about to face the day when Cam ambushed her.

It's not that she didn't love her friend. She really did. No one knew her better than her best friends. With the exception of Mark. But that was the problem. She didn't want to be around anyone who knew her really well. Not right now. Not until she was feeling better.

And she was about to take the first step in feeling better and moving on the best way that she knew how.

Cam had sounded surprised when Christy said she was going to get her hair done, as if that was going to make her feel better. But it was. Christy knew it would make her feel better. If only because it couldn't make her feel any worse.

She'd gone straight down to Main Street the moment she was able to convince Cam that she was fine. Christy knew Cam wouldn't want to go to the Crop Shop with her, not since her fiancé, Evan Anderson's, ex-girlfriend worked there. The last time Cam had her hair done at the Crop Shop, Stephanie had taken liberties with Cam's hair. Sure, it was passive-aggressive, and Cam ended up with a much shorter haircut than she'd wanted, but it still looked amazing. Because Stephanie was a talented stylist. Which was why Christy was there.

"Hi, Christy." Stephanie waved at her across the shop as soon as she stepped inside. The smell of the chemicals used for perms and colors, combined with a sweet, almost fruity shampoo smell, mingled in the air. "I'll be right with you. Take a seat."

Christy nodded, grabbed one of the hairstyle magazines off the table and perched on the end of a chair. The minute she sat, she wished she hadn't. It was a thin plastic chair. The kind that was designed more for style and the trendy way it looked in a waiting room than for comfort or durability.

The chair tilted forward the instant she sat down and she had to quickly shoot her legs out in front of her to keep from falling off. The chair slammed down as she regained her balance and there was an audible cracking sound.

Christy wanted to die. *Had she seriously just broken the chair?*

Her face flamed with the heat of the embarrassment. She wanted to melt into the floor and disappear. Instead, she stood and took a quick step away from the chair, putting distance between herself and the offensive object. Her eyes locked with a woman sitting on the other side of the waiting area, and Christy immediately averted her eyes from the look of judgment the other woman was giving her.

"Hey there." Stephanie's friendly voice distracted her from her moment of mortification. "What's wrong?" The smile slipped from Stephanie's face when she saw Christy's.

"I broke the…I think maybe…" She gestured to the chair and fought the tears that were threatening.

Seriously? After everything she'd been through, she was going to cry about a stupid chair? Christy blinked hard and shook her head. She would *not* lose it over a stupid chair.

"What?" Stephanie looked between her and the chair and finally made the connection. "The chair? Oh my goodness, Christy. Don't worry about it. These stupid chairs are always breaking. I just can't wait until they're all finally garbaged so we can get some new ones in here." Stephanie took her arm and gently steered her into the shop. She led her to her stylist's chair, where Christy sat with relief in the much sturdier seat.

"Now…" Stephanie lifted her hair out over the protective cape and let it flutter over her shoulders. "What are we going to do today?"

"I need a change." Christy looked directly into the mirror at her reflection. At the lifeless blonde hair that fell limp around her chubby face and down her back, the lines under her dull eyes that hadn't been there last year. She was only thirty-four years old, but she looked at least ten years older. To say that the last few years had been hard on her was a huge understatement.

They'd destroyed her.

It had all been worth it, though. At least, that's what she'd told herself through the countless treatments as she watched the extra pounds add up, dealt with the almost constant headaches, the overwhelming fatigue that left her feeling wrung out and lifeless. It would all be worth it once she had a baby of her own in her arms.

And it would have been. *But now...*

She swallowed hard and squeezed her eyes shut against her reflection before she opened them again with a new resolve. "Cut it all off."

Chapter Three

"DO YOU LIKE IT?"

Christy heard the hesitation in the other woman's voice as she stared in the mirror at her new hairdo and completely new look, but she couldn't bring herself to answer. Her hand drifted up to her head. She fingered the much shorter, much redder strands and still couldn't formulate any words.

"Christy?" Stephanie bent so her head was closer to hers. "Say something. I know you wanted it to be different, but I hope this isn't too different. I mean, I think you look—"

"Amazing." The word came out as a whisper of incredulity. Christy squeezed her eyes shut and opened them again but the reflection was still the same. "Like a completely different person."

She didn't recognize herself. She'd asked Stephanie to cut it all off, and although the hairstylist had used restraint in that regard, she'd still taken at least five inches off the length, leaving Christy with a sassy, shaggy cut that just brushed her shoulders. But as incredible as the cut was, it wasn't the biggest change.

Not even close.

While she'd been sitting in the chair, Stephanie had mentioned something about putting some highlights in for something different. Christy couldn't remember the last time she'd ever had a color of any kind in her blonde hair. There was once a time where she regularly got things brightened or lifted or even got some fun temporary colors when she was younger, but it had been years since she'd allowed herself the indulgence. After all, some people thought that it wasn't safe to color your hair while you were pregnant. And even if there was no truth in it, Christy wasn't going to take that risk while she was even trying.

But that was no longer a problem.

She vaguely remembered telling Stephanie to do whatever she wanted and the end result was…

"Amazing," she said again, louder this time. Christy ran fingers through her hair, now a striking shade of red and laughed. It was the first real laugh she could remember in way too long.

"You really like it?"

Christy met Stephanie's gaze in the mirror. "More than anything. It's exactly what I didn't know I wanted."

Stephanie laughed at that. "Good. I'm glad. I kind of got the impression you wanted something totally different and well…"

"This is different." In all the right ways.

"That it is." Stephanie pulled the cape that was protecting Christy's clothes off, and let down her stylist chair so she could step out.

"It's perfect." Christy followed the stylist to the front and paid her bill, including a healthy gratuity.

She left the salon feeling lighter and better than she'd felt in months. It was just hair; Christy knew that. It was just a small thing, but definitely a step in the right direction. She'd intended to go home after her appointment, but she just couldn't bring herself to go back to the big, quiet, lonely house. There'd once been a time she loved nothing more than spending time in her home, decorating each room, picking out just the right colors, and furniture for the family she would soon have. Every day had been exciting and full of anticipation.

Not anymore.

Determined not to let sadness creep over her again, Christy turned around and headed instead for Dress Up, the nicest boutique shop in town. It was pricy, so she usually reserved shopping at Dress Up for special occasions, but if a fresh start wasn't a special occasion, she didn't know what was. Besides, she deserved something new and more importantly, something that would match her new hair.

She giggled a little at herself and swung open the glass door of the shop where she spent the next forty-five minutes selecting new outfits. She'd put on a few pounds since fertility treatments started and at first she was discouraged with her increased size. But the salesgirl, Beth, showed her some things she never would have considered that actually accented her new curves instead of trying to hide them. She tried on dresses and tops she never would have considered and pants that hugged her backside instead of the oversized jeans she had been wearing to cover herself. By the time Christy left the shop, she had two bags bursting with new outfits and a hefty credit card bill, but more importantly, she felt fantastic about her new look.

Before she left, she changed into one of her new purchases —skinny jeans, with blinged-out rear pockets, and a low-cut black top that flowed over all her trouble spots but made her feel ridiculously sexy—and left her worn-out baggy jeans and old t-shirt in the dressing room.

If she hadn't wanted to go home before, Christy really wasn't in the mood to be alone after her mini makeover. She glanced down the street at Daisy's Diner, her favorite coffee shop, but coffee or tea wasn't what she was in the mood for.

Her lips twitched up into a grin, and once again she changed directions, heading for the end of the block and the local pub, the Log and Jam. What she needed was a drink to toast her fresh start.

It was still early afternoon, and there were only a handful of people in the pub yet, but that was perfect as far as she was concerned. As confident as she was feeling, she still wasn't sure she was ready for a lot of faces. Not yet.

Christy slipped onto a stool at the end of the bar. A moment later, Ben Ross, the owner—who also happened to be one of her best friend's brother-in-law, and one of the many guys she went to high school with—appeared to offer her a drink.

"Hey, welcome to the Log and Jam. I'm Ben." He put a paper coaster down in front of her. "Can I get you a —Christy?"

His mouth fell open in surprise and Christy laughed. She couldn't help it. She'd known Ben most of her life, and they were good friends.

"You look...wow..." He shook his head and joined her in the laugh. "I'm sorry, I didn't recognize you," he said after a moment. "You look totally..."

"I needed a new look." She saved him from trying to find something appropriate to say. "It was time."

"Well, you look great. Can I get you a coffee or something?"

His question wasn't totally unexpected considering it was pretty unusual for Christy to order anything alcoholic in the pub. There'd been a few times between treatments, but it definitely wasn't the norm.

"I'll take a glass of white wine actually, Ben."

"Really?"

She smiled and nodded. "Absolutely."

"One glass of white coming up." Ben left to fill her order and Christy turned on her stool to take in the pub. There were a few people at the tables, but more interesting was the activity in the far corner of the room. Ben sometimes brought in bands on the weekend, and it looked as though one was setting up a few days early. Christy watched with interest while the two men attached cords and speakers.

Ben brought her the wine and disappeared again before she could ask him who was playing that weekend. She and Mark would often come down to listen to the bands, but she didn't recognize the guys setting up. She sipped the wine, letting the cool liquid slide over her tongue and down her throat.

She closed her eyes and savored the taste before opening them to see she was no longer alone. She jumped a bit, shocked to see a man on the stool next to her. Her cheeks flushed with embarrassment for the way she'd been enjoying her drink.

"Sorry," the stranger said. "I didn't want to interrupt. You seemed to be having a moment." He grinned at her and nodded to her wine.

His smile was genuine and so disarming that Christy laughed. "I was," she said. "Maybe a little too much."

"No such thing." He waved away her explanation. "My name's Jamie." He extended his hand. "Jamie Morris." She shook his hand and looked into his green eyes that flashed with…something. "I'm with the band." He laughed and ran his hand through his shaggy dark hair. "Sorry, that sounds like a pretty bad line."

Was it a line? The thought hit her hard. It had been so long since she'd been on the receiving end of a pick-up, she didn't even know what it looked like. Which was why there was no way that's what it could have been. She almost laughed at herself.

"I'm Christy. Not with the band."

"Nice to meet you, Christy Not With The Band." He extended a hand and when she took it, a spark coursed through her body, startling her, but she didn't drop his hand. Not right away.

Jamie grinned at her, and she couldn't help but return his smile. The attention felt nicer than she would have expected. After a moment, she tipped her head to the side and looked wistfully at the setup. Her eyes landed on the microphone. There'd been a time when she'd secretly wanted to be a singer. Well, the fact that she liked to sing wasn't a secret, but only Mark knew that she'd actually dreamed about being on stage and maybe one day actually being famous. It was a childhood dream, and in no way rooted in reality, but there were still times when she yearned for it.

"Do you sing?"

Jamie's question took her off guard. She shook her head and looked back at him, away from the stage area. "No. Well, not really. Not anymore."

"But you do sing?"

"Not like that." She shook her head and took another sip of her wine.

"Like what then?"

He was watching her with his intense green eyes and instead of making her nervous, it had the opposite effect. Maybe it was her new hair, or new outfit, or maybe even the wine in her hand, but she was feeling uncharacteristically bold. "I sing like in the shower, or the car. Not on a stage."

Jamie contemplated the answer for a moment and tapped his fingers on the bar. "Have you ever sang on a stage?"

She laughed. "Not since the high school talent show."

"Would you like to?"

She studied him, trying to figure out whether he was being serious or not. But there was nothing in his expression that told her he might be joking.

"Well?"

Christy took another, bigger drink of her wine. "Yes. I would."

AS ONE OF the only doctors in town, Mark's practice was busy. He liked it that way. It kept him busy and he truly enjoyed getting to know each of his patients and their families. It hadn't taken long for them to feel like part of his own family as well. It did make for full days, and although there was a time when that would have been problematic, for the last few days, Mark had craved it.

Immersing himself in other people's problems allowed him to check out of his own. And he was smart enough to know it wasn't a long-term solution, nor was he pretending it was, but it was a short-term coping strategy.

In a few days, he'd be okay. Or better, at least. Besides, there were a lot worse ways he could be dealing with the disappointment and pain of everything they'd been through. He didn't drink excessively, he didn't gamble, and he loved his wife more than anything else in the world. Even if he felt like he barely knew her anymore.

The last few days had been...strange. He'd expected Christy to cry, to lash out about how unfair everything was. More than anything, he'd wanted to talk to her. Together they could figure out what to do next. There was adoption, and maybe even surrogacy. They had options. But if they didn't talk about them, they had nothing. But Christy hadn't wanted to talk. She hadn't wanted anything to do with him at all.

It was hurtful and confusing. *Did she not think he was in pain, too?* That he was equally sad and disappointed and…he couldn't tell her any of that. How could he confide in her about his sadness, when she seemed to be…well, he wasn't sure what she seemed to be.

"Dr. Thomas?" The intercom on his desk beeped to life, distracting him from his thoughts. He neatly stacked the files he'd been looking at and picked up the phone.

"Yes, Sarah?"

"I'm sorry to bother you, Doctor Thomas. I just wanted to check to see if I could make you a tea or something? The kettle is warm."

Mark had missed Sarah's attention to detail while she'd been on maternity leave. Christy had filled in for her a few days a week and he'd enjoyed having her around, but her heart wasn't in the work, and it was good to have Sarah back.

Even if she did come with a desk full of pictures and daily stories about her new son, Nick. It hadn't bothered him, not at first. Especially considering he'd been so sure that the last round of IVF would work and he'd soon have his own stories and pictures to share.

"I'm good right now," he said into the phone. "Thank you, though."

"No problem, Dr. Thomas." Her voice was laced with just a shade of the exhaustion that plagued all new moms, but she'd never let it show. "You just let me know if you need anything."

"Will do."

"Shall I send your next patient in? He's here a few minutes early."

Mark checked his watch and nodded, despite the fact that she couldn't see him. "Sure. Send him to room two. I'll be right there."

He took a moment to stretch in his small office before he headed down the hallway to the exam room. It had been awhile since he'd gone for a decent run the way he had that morning; he probably shouldn't have pushed it so hard. He'd be sore tomorrow.

But it wouldn't stop him from doing it again.

He chuckled at himself and paused outside exam room two long enough to pull up the chart on his tablet. The office had recently upgraded from paper files and Sarah had them all using tablets and an electronic charting system. He hadn't been too sure about the change, but it did solve the problem of him not being able to read his own handwriting. So that was a distinct benefit.

He clicked through the steps and opened the file for the patient waiting behind the door.

No.

He read the patient's name again and turned to look down the hallway toward the reception area, as if that would clear things up. He scrubbed his hand over his face and knocked once on the door before he twisted the door handle.

Mark hadn't seen Eric Ross in years. More than he could remember. They'd gone to school together, but it was Ben, Eric's little brother, who'd been Mark's age, so Mark didn't actually know Eric very well at all. He'd seen him a few times over the years since one of Christy's best friends, Drew, married him, but they'd moved away and as far as he knew, didn't come back to visit very often.

In fact, Eric hadn't even come back for the big school anniversary party that had been held that past spring. To say he was surprised to have Eric Ross in his exam room would be an understatement. But as surprised as Mark was to have Eric there, he was even more surprised to *see* him.

"Eric? Hi." Mark's voice dipped when he saw the other man who he'd remembered as tall, strong, and broad like his brother Ben. Not the emaciated, shell of a man who now sat in front of him. Mark called on his training and moderated his voice and facial expression to match. "It's good to see you."

"Hey, Mark. Or should I say Doctor—"

"Mark's fine." He took a seat on the stool and set his tablet down. "I know it can be a bit weird for people I knew when I was a kid. Whatever you want to call me is fine by me."

"If you don't mind, I'll call you Mark." Eric's smile was weak. "I've had my fill of doctors for the last little while. No offense."

"None taken." He hadn't had time to read through Eric's entire file, but he didn't need to in order to see that Eric wasn't well. Not at all. "It's good to see you, Eric. What's it been…"

The other man shook his head and managed a small smile. "Too long. That's for damn sure."

"What brings you back to town?" Mark almost hated to ask the question, because it was clear by the look of him, and the expression on Eric's face that told him everything he needed to know, but he was a professional and he needed to hear it from him.

Eric nodded to the tablet on the counter. "You read my file?"

"Not all of it," Mark answered honestly. "I thought maybe you'd want to tell me."

"There's not much to tell," Eric said with a sigh of resignation. "Not anymore."

CHRISTY WAS BURSTING with excitement by the time she finally got home. After leaving the Log and Jam, she'd made a quick stop at Timber Trade to pick up a few things to make Mark dinner and tell him her news.

She'd sung. A full song.

Sure, it wasn't on stage in front of people. Not unless you

counted the rest of the band that was still setting up, Ben, and the few customers he had at the time. But it didn't matter if it was for one person or a hundred—she felt amazing.

Never in a million years did Christy think she'd ever get up with a microphone in her hand and put herself out there like that. There was that one time at karaoke, but that was different because she'd been drinking and…this had been different.

Something about Jamie and his encouragement had propelled her to go for it, which was crazy because she had never met him before and had no idea who he was. But maybe that was the point?

Whatever it was that had made her get up there and hold on to that microphone, it didn't really matter because the point was, she'd done it and it had felt great.

Jamie had nothing but supportive things to say about her attempt and even offered for her to come and rehearse with the band if she wanted to. He'd given her his number, and maybe if she was younger and single she might have considered the idea that he was hitting on her. Because he *was* hitting on her. But she wasn't young *or* single, so she chalked it up to him just being nice. But she didn't throw his number away like she should have. Even after she got home, she pulled out the napkin and stared at the numbers written there and wondered…

What? She didn't know. *Would she call him? Would she actually rehearse with his band?* The idea was completely insane. There was no way she could entertain either the idea of Jamie or singing with a band. That wasn't who she was. No matter how good the attention had felt.

Still, she'd kept the number. And it made her feel a little… naughty? Guilty? Excited? Maybe a little of all three.

It didn't matter though, because Christy couldn't wait to tell Mark about her singing—she'd leave out the part about Jamie because she wouldn't want him to get the wrong idea—

and have a nice dinner. Maybe they could finally share a bottle of wine and spend a little time together, just the two of them, without the weight of everything between them. Maybe, just for one night, they could pretend that everything was okay.

Yes. It was going to be a great evening.

"I WASN'T sure you'd be up for this today." Aaron Owens picked up his pace to match Mark's strong stride. "Clearly, I was wrong."

"Yep." Mark was sick of talking about everything he and Christy had been through. He was tired of people asking him whether he was okay, how Christy was, and what they were going to do next. He was sick and tired of all of it.

He knew his friends and family, and even his patients and random people in town, were asking from a place of care and concern, but frankly he didn't give a shit. Maybe he'd be ready to talk about it some other time. But it certainly wasn't now.

And after the afternoon he'd had, seeing Eric Ross in his exam room...he was more than ready for a run.

All he wanted to do was feel his feet on the pavement, the breeze in his hair, and the burning in his lungs as he pushed himself to run faster and farther. Because when he was running, he didn't have to think about anything else except putting one foot in front of the other.

Aaron, his best friend, who also happened to be his first cousin, was thankfully smart enough to pick up on Mark's need to ignore that part of his life and matched him step for step.

They ran in silence for a few minutes before finally Aaron called for mercy. "I need to slow down, man. You're killing me."

Mark laughed but he slowed his pace and let Aaron catch his breath.

"That's better," Aaron said. "I haven't seen you run like that since…well, ever. Usually you're the one trying to keep up with me. What's gotten into you?"

Mark wiped the sweat from his brow and slowed his pace even more until they were walking. "I was just thinking that maybe I'd like to sign up for a few races this year." He glanced at his friend. "Like the old days." Truthfully, he hadn't been thinking of it at all, but the moment the idea sprang into his head, it seemed like a good one. A *really* good one.

"Really? Like proper races or get up late on a Saturday and finish with a beer, races?"

"T-shirts and medals." Mark laughed. "But I'm more than happy to finish with a beer." Years ago, the two of them signed up for as many races as they could, and the joke was that they were trying to build up their wardrobes with free race t-shirts and decorate all the door handles in their homes by hanging the medals from them. Together they ran every race, from community fun runs to a few marathons and even one ultra-marathon. It was a busy few years until finally Mark's medical practice started demanding more of his time and energy and Aaron turned his attention to taking over the Creekside Inn that his father owned. They'd scaled back their training to daily morning runs, sometimes together, but more often on their own time. Although they had committed to meeting once a week for a longer run and to catch up, even that had fallen off until their time together was more sporadic than regular.

Mark missed it.

He missed a lot of things.

His medical practice had taken up so much of his time and when they'd started fertility treatments…well, he couldn't decide what had felt like more of a job. Either way, running with Aaron again felt good and it would take his mind off everything else in his life.

Or at the very least, it might help to take the edge off his total and complete failure to give Christy the one thing she wanted more than anything else. The failure was magnified by the fact that he was a doctor. He should *know* what to do, how to fix it. His whole life, whatever he'd wanted, he'd worked his ass off for and earned. This was different. Infertility was so very different. Intellectually, he knew that Christy didn't blame him, at least not intentionally. But it was his job to protect her and no matter what he'd tried, he could not manage to protect her from the hurt of not getting pregnant. He'd failed. More than once.

"How many races are you talking about?" Aaron's question broke through his internal diatribe. They'd reached the parking lot where they'd left their vehicles. Aaron grabbed a bottle of water from the back of his truck and tossed one to Mark. "And what distance? What are we talking about here?"

"I don't know." Mark tipped the bottle back and drank deeply. "Maybe we can start out with a 10K and move into an ultra by fall."

Next to him, Aaron spat out his water. "An ultra?" He stared, mouth open, at Mark. "You want to *move into* an ultra?"

Mark nodded.

"By fall?"

Mark nodded again. "I mean, I haven't given it much thought," he lied. "But I don't see why not. We're both in good shape. It gives us a goal."

"A goal?"

"Right." Mark drank again and wiped his mouth on his arm.

"An ultra is not a goal, it's a destination."

"Exactly. The Polar Peeks is exactly that. It's at the end of September."

"That's not enough time to train, man." Aaron shook his head and laughed. "We haven't done anything serious like that in years."

"We can handle it."

Aaron must have sensed the need in him because instead of protesting the way Mark was sure he would, he closed his mouth and simply nodded. "Okay."

"Okay? Just like that?"

"Well, not *just* like that." Aaron chuckled. "We're going to have to work some things out. Most notably, a training schedule." He shook his head and grabbed his ankle as he pulled his leg into a stretch. "But…sure. Why not?"

Mark let out a whoop that surprised even him. He hadn't realized how badly he wanted it until that moment. But the prospect of spending the next few months focused on a new goal excited him more than he expected.

They spent the next few minutes stretching out their legs while Mark briefed Aaron on the ideas he had for a training schedule. It was rigorous, and it would keep them busy, but that was the whole idea.

"How does Christy feel about all of this?"

Mark avoided his cousin's gaze and busied himself with stretching out his calf muscles. A muscle group he'd already attended to. "She's fine with it."

"Really?" Aaron eyed him.

"Well, not really." He came clean. "I haven't told her yet. But honestly, I think she'll be okay with it." Another lie, but not such a big one because the truth was, he had no idea how Christy would feel about it. He had no idea how she felt about anything these days.

"That would be a bit of a change, wouldn't it?"

It *would* be a huge change. Aaron remembered, just like he did, how Christy felt about him training for ultra-marathons. She didn't mind the long runs once or twice a week when he was training for a marathon. But the length of the runs and the time commitment changed drastically when you start talking about running an eighty- or ninety-kilometre race. Fifty miles was a lot longer than twenty-six, and the training increased appropriately. The last time Mark had trained for an ultra, Christy hadn't liked it. At all.

He'd been gone a lot. Early morning runs, all day on Sundays—it was a lot for her and they'd spent a lot of time apart.

But maybe that was a good thing right now. And maybe that's what she would think, too.

He scrubbed a hand over his face in an effort to clear the thoughts from his head. He didn't need to be thinking thoughts like that. Not right now. Mark was sure Christy felt it, too. The need to spend time apart and maybe…well, he didn't know exactly what she was thinking. But he did know there was no way it could just be him feeling the distance between them. Something had shifted during their last treatment. She'd pulled away, and he couldn't blame her. How could she *not* be disappointed in him?

"You okay, man?" Aaron surprised him by putting a hand on his shoulder.

He jumped a little, yanked from his thoughts.

"I mean, I know you…well…is everything okay?"

Mark nodded and forced a smile. "As good as can be expected." He dropped his leg out of the stretch he was still holding and clapped his hands together. "We should get moving. I need to be at the clinic in an hour."

Aaron didn't push, and that was one of the things Mark appreciated about him. He knew if he needed to talk, his buddy would be there. But the last thing Mark wanted to do right then was talk.

It was easier to run.

———

BY THE TIME Christy heard the front door open, she had an Alfredo sauce bubbling on the stove, fresh pasta ready to go, and a big fresh salad, with a homemade Italian dressing she knew Mark preferred. The table was set and the bottle of wine was breathing. She'd stopped short of lighting candles. It seemed like overkill and a little too cheesy, but the mood was definitely set without it. *Maybe they would even make love later?*

The idea of having Mark lying next to her, his body touching hers, just because they loved each other, and not for the purpose of trying to make a baby, excited her. And scared the hell out of her. How long had it been since they'd made love simply because they'd *wanted* to?

She gave the sauce one last stir before wiping her hands on her apron, untying the strings and tossing it onto the counter before going to greet her husband. "Hey there." She walked into the living room. "You're home a little later than I expected. Busy day?"

Mark was on the couch, his elbows on his knees and his head in his hands. He looked up, startled, when he heard her voice. "I didn't think you'd be out of—Christy?"

She grinned and touched her hair tentatively. "Do you like it?"

He nodded, but she couldn't read the look on his face. "It's…wow…"

"Is that a good wow?" For the first time, she was starting to feel a little uncertain about her new look. She'd just assumed Mark would like it, because to be honest, she hadn't really thought at all about what he'd think. He always liked how she looked. At least, he'd never said otherwise. "I mean, I wasn't really planning on going red, but it just seemed like a good idea. I went in for a trim, or actually a major cut, but…" She was vaguely aware that she was rambling, but she really needed the look on his face to change. He was starting to worry her. "And then Stephanie asked me if maybe I'd like to try a color since I haven't been able to dye my...well, just because I haven't had anything different lately," she amended quickly. There would be no talk about pregnancy or babies or any of that. Not tonight. "So, I thought...what the hell. I mean, it's just hair, right?" She took a breath and swallowed hard, forcing herself not to cry. "You don't like it?"

As if a switch was flipped, Mark jumped to his feet and crossed the room. He reached for her hair and let the strands slide through his fingers. "Honey, I like it. I do. It's just different. You took me off guard."

"You're sure you like it?" The need to please him surprised her with its intensity.

"I do." He kissed her on the cheek. "And this is a new outfit, too." He stepped back and took in her complete transformation. She spun around and put a little wiggle in her behind as she did so. "It's cute."

Cute wasn't totally what she was going for. More like sexy, or hot. But after almost twenty years of being together, she'd take it.

Christy took her husband's hand and led him toward the kitchen. "I made dinner. I thought maybe we could..." *Could what?* She couldn't use the word celebrate. That didn't feel right. "Mark this day," she finally settled on.

"What's special about today?" He sat at the table, and once more, Christy had trouble reading his expression. He looked tired, but there was something else there too.

She poured two glasses of wine and handed one to him. "Today is a new start, I guess. I can't really explain it, but I was lying in bed and I had this realization that...well, that I just needed to get up and then—"

"Get up?"

She nodded. Christy didn't have the first clue about how to explain to him what had propelled her to get out of bed that morning, undergo a transformation, and ultimately put a microphone in her hand. But despite the fact that she couldn't articulate any of it, she still wanted to toast. She raised her glass. "To getting up." It seemed easier not to explain at all.

He gave her a strange look and raised his glass to hers. They clinked and each took a sip. She had to go slow or if she wasn't careful, she'd get tipsy. It had been so long since she'd enjoyed a few glasses, and after the one she'd had earlier in the day, she needed to be aware of how much she was drinking.

"Dinner's almost ready." Christy turned back to the stove and carefully wrapped her apron around her new outfit before getting to work. "I made your favorite. Homemade pasta with a creamy Alfredo sauce and a big salad."

"Oh, honey, that sounds great, but we might have to scale back on the heavy foods. I kind of have my own *get up* moment to let you know about, too."

She turned, spoon in hand. "What's that?"

For the first time since coming home, his smile was genuine. "I was thinking of signing up for the Polar Peeks Ultra this fall."

The spoon fell to the floor with a clatter. Sauce splashed on her new pants and she cursed but didn't bother picking up the spoon. "You're signing up to do a what?"

"An ultra."

"An ultra?"

"An ultra-marathon," he explained as if she were stupid and had no idea what he meant.

She knew what he meant, all right. She knew all too well what he meant.

On some level, Christy realized she sounded like an idiot, but she simply could not believe her ears. The last time Mark had trained for an ultra-marathon, she'd barely seen him. To say it had been hard would be a massive understatement. They'd both sacrificed a lot for him to achieve his goal. And he had. *So why now?* She asked him as much.

"I don't know," he began. "It just seemed like kind of good timing with the...well, with the changes and everything going on around here."

"Changes?"

"You know what I mean."

She nodded and looked down at the floor, to the spoon sitting in the congealing sauce, the white splatters on her new pants, her own puffy feet that were in desperate need of a pedicure and all she could feel was a deep sense of *whatever*.

Maybe she should have cared more about his decision. Maybe she should have told him no, that it was selfish and they needed to focus on each other and their relationship now more than ever. That the last thing they needed was for him to be off every night running for hours. But she didn't. Instead, Christy bent down, picked up the spoon and dropped it in the sink.

"Okay," she said after retrieving a fresh spoon. "If that's what you want to do." Even to her own ears, she could hear the lifelessness in her voice and she hated herself for not telling him how she really felt. But with everything else...with everything she'd already disappointed him with...she couldn't disappoint him by objecting to the race. It wasn't fair.

She didn't look, but she knew instinctively that he was probably watching her carefully, waiting for a sign that she in fact was not happy with him racing.

"And...you're sure you're all right with this?" He was hesitant, but Christy could also hear the twinge of excitement behind the question. He desperately wanted her to be okay with his decision.

She was not okay with it. Not at all. She wanted him home. She *needed* him home with her, rebuilding what had been broken. *But maybe that wasn't what he wanted? Maybe he...*

"Yup." She lied. "It's fine." She only wanted him home if he wanted to be there. She wasn't going to force it. Christy still didn't turn around. She busied herself putting pasta in the boiling water.

"I know it takes a lot of time," he said. "Maybe you could join a book club or something."

A book club?

Christy turned then and pasted the biggest smile she could on her face. "I'll find something to keep me busy, don't worry." An image of Jamie holding his guitar, watching her closely with those deep green eyes of his while she'd sang into the microphone, flashed in her mind and she immediately felt guilty.

But excited too.

Mark had his running to keep him busy, but it wasn't as if she were without options. She still had Jamie's number *and* his invitation to sing with the band. Christy had been so excited to tell Mark all about it, but now, in light of his own news, she no longer felt like sharing.

They sat down to the meal she'd prepared, and Christy tried not to notice how little pasta Mark ate. But she couldn't help but see that most of his plate was covered in salad, with very little dressing. She refused to let it bother her. Instead, she poured herself another glass of wine and tried to change the subject to anything but Mark's rekindled desire to race.

"How was work? Anything exciting today?"

She knew he couldn't talk about his patients, not really, but he'd usually tell her general details, leaving out anything specific and every once in a while he'd let something slip.

Mark's face changed. The stress lines around his eyes deepened at the mention of work. "It was a…it was a hard day, actually." He put his elbows on the table and rested his chin in his hands.

"Hard?" She put her fork down and focused her attention. "How so? Is everything okay?"

He shook his head slowly. "Not really. But you know I can't—"

"I know you can't say anything." It was obviously not one of those situations where he was going to share information. "But if you want to talk, you know—"

She was interrupted by her cell phone ringing. "Sorry, Mark. I'll just go turn it off." She jumped up to put her phone on silent. They had a strict rule about no cell phones at the dinner table, and she usually remembered to turn it off. "It's Drew." She reached for the switch that would silence the ring. "I'll just call her—"

"You should get it."

"What? But it's dinner time. I'll just call her back after."

"No." He shook his head. "You should take the call. I think I know why she's calling. Take the call, Christy."

He looked so sad and serious all at the same time, Christy did as he suggested and hit the button to accept the call.

Chapter Four

AFTER A NIGHT of tossing and turning, Cam wasn't feeling rested and she certainly wasn't feeling any better about the news she'd received the day before. She dragged herself to the shower and stood under the hot stream of water for longer than she needed to, before dressing and heading out to the kitchen where her fiancé, Evan, and teenage daughter, Morgan, were already at the table.

"How are you feeling?" Evan greeted her with a kiss on the cheek and a mug of coffee. "Did you manage to get any sleep?"

She shook her head and accepted the coffee gratefully.

"I'm sorry, Mom." Her teenage daughter squeezed her in an uncharacteristic hug. "Evan told me about your...well...I'm sorry. I don't really know what to say."

"Thanks, sweetie." Cam walked to the window that overlooked their yard and her new photography studio. "And it's okay. I don't really know what to say either. In fact, I don't think there is really anything we can say in these situations. We just need to be there for our friends."

"Speaking of friends." Evan came up behind her and put his hand on her back. "When are the girls coming by?"

Drew Ross, one of her best friends, had called unexpectedly the night before to tell her she was back in town. It had only been a few months since Drew had come back for the big reunion party. Cam hadn't expected another visit so soon. But what she really hadn't expected was for Drew to tell her that they'd moved back to Timber Creek so her husband Eric could live out his last days. *Her husband was dying.*

The news had slammed into her. Eric was only a few years older than she was. Drew and Eric were high school sweethearts and now...he was dying? It didn't make sense.

But whether or not it made sense, it was happening and in only a few minutes, Drew would be sitting at her kitchen table and she'd have to...what? Cam didn't know what she'd have to do.

"Soon." She leaned into Evan's touch. It hardly seemed fair that just as Cam and Evan were rediscovering their love for each other, Drew was losing her true love. It wasn't fair at all.

"Do you want us to be here?" Evan tucked a stray hair behind her ear.

Cam considered Evan and Morgan, who was still watching with worried eyes, and shook her head. "No," she said after a moment. "I think it would be best if it's just us girls. I can't imagine any of this is easy for Drew, and she'll need us to be strong for her. I don't want her to feel like she can't let go because people are around, you know?"

"It's cool." Morgan cleared her dishes to the sink and came to give her mom a hug that Cam accepted readily. They'd had some rough times, but things seemed to finally be settling down for Morgan now that they'd been in Timber Creek for a few months. "I have to head to work." Cam squeezed Morgan tight. "I really am sorry, Mom."

Cam smiled at her daughter before she turned away. She really was turning into a kind, considerate young woman.

"I'll drive you, Morgan," Evan said. "I think I'll head over to Ben's house and see how he's doing with all of this." Ben was Evan's best friend, but also Eric's little brother. The two brothers had been more or less estranged for the last few years, not spending much time together at all after Eric and Drew got married and moved away. If you asked Ben, it was because it was hard to keep in touch when there was so much distance between them, but anyone who knew Ben well knew it was because he had been in love with Drew since they were kids. And even though Drew never knew how he felt, it had killed a little something inside Ben when she'd chosen his older brother over him.

"He must be devastated." Cam moved to the counter and popped a piece of bread in the toaster. She wasn't really very hungry, but she should eat something before the girls arrived. "I can't even imagine…"

"I know." Evan ran his hand through his hair. "And if I know Ben, he's probably not really dealing with it all. It's a lot to process." Evan gave Cam a kiss on the cheek and promised to call her later before he and Morgan left out the front door, leaving her alone.

But she wasn't alone for long. Cam had barely had time to eat her toast, forcing it down past the lump in her throat, before there was a knock on the door followed by Christy's voice.

"Can you believe this?" Christy greeted Cam with a hug, pulling her in for a tight squeeze. "I've been thinking about it all night. I can't even…"

"Christy? What?" Cam detached herself from her friend's grip and stared at her friend. "Your hair?" It wasn't just her hair, though. Christy was dressed in distressed jeans and a bright-green v-neck top that made her newly red hair shine. "You look so…"

"Do you like it?"

"I do," Cam said truthfully. "It's different. But I like it."

"Oh, good." Christy looked visibly relieved. "Mark said he liked it but I'm not really sure if he meant it and—"

"Hello?"

At the sound of Drew's voice at the door, Christy and Cam exchanged glances. Cam nodded and together they went to greet their friend.

It was always good to be back together in the same room, but given the circumstances, there was no celebrating.

Cam settled them around the kitchen table and poured everyone a cup of coffee. She'd dug a box of cookies out of the pantry and placed them on a plate in the center of the table, but no one was eating.

"I wish Amber were here." Christy looked to be on the verge of tears, and Cam silently hoped she wouldn't cry. It was going to be a hard-enough morning.

"Me too," Drew said. "But I'll call her later. I feel so fortunate that the two of you are here. I mean, I never thought I'd be moving back to Timber Creek." She looked down into her coffee cup. "And I certainly never thought it would be because my…"

She let the sentence drift off, and no one pushed for more.

Finally, it was Christy who asked, "Is it cancer?"

Drew nodded. "Pancreatic cancer. It's been…" She shook her head. "It's been a crazy year."

"A year?" Cam stared at her friend. "You've known about this for a year and didn't say anything?"

"Drew." Christy reached across the table and took her friend's hand. "Why didn't you say anything? Oh my God, you were just here and…that's why Eric didn't come."

Drew nodded.

"I thought maybe you were having problems." The words sounded dumb even as Cam said them. "I meant...you know what I meant."

Drew smiled a little. "I know you all would have totally been there for me, but the truth is, we didn't want to tell anyone. When Eric was first diagnosed, we were optimistic and didn't think anyone needed to know. Eric was convinced he could beat it. I mean, he was young, fit, strong."

Cam didn't miss the use of the word *was*. She flinched a little and hoped Drew hadn't noticed.

"And then when it became clear that maybe it wouldn't be as easy as he thought it would be, well, we didn't really know what to say. Eric insisted on not worrying anyone. He was still so sure he could...well, let's just say that it took him a little longer to accept what was happening to us."

"But now?" It was Christy who asked.

Drew nodded. "Now he's closer to accepting it. I mean, he has but I think he still holds out hope."

"I guess you'd have to," Cam said.

"I guess." Drew shrugged. "I mean, don't get me wrong. I still pray every night for a miracle that will keep my husband here with us." A tear slipped from Drew's eye. She didn't bother to wipe it. "But I think I'm a little more practical. I also know the survival statistics aren't good and we've tried almost everything. We need time to get things in order and to...well, time to just be without the drug trials, the treatments, and the hospitals. You know what I mean?"

Cam nodded, although she really had no idea. She simply couldn't imagine what Drew was going through. Her friend still looked so composed and self-assured. She knew Drew must be a mess on the inside, but she'd always been strong. Physically, she reminded Cam of a porcelain doll, but they all knew better. Drew was tough. Even so, no amount of toughness or inner strength could possibly prepare a person to go through the pain of watching your husband die.

IT HAD BEEN A HARD NIGHT. After the phone call that had interrupted the dinner Christy had so clearly put extra care into, just for them, whatever mood they'd been trying to recreate had been ruined.

The fact that it hadn't been *just* the phone call that had ruined their evening, but also his news about the ultra-marathon, didn't seem an important detail anymore.

Mark had debated with himself all night whether he'd done the right thing by encouraging Christy to answer Drew's call. Obviously he'd known what Drew was calling to tell her. He could have encouraged her to let the call go to voice mail so they could have spent the evening together, and maybe he should have. Maybe they would have been able to talk about his decision to run, and maybe she would have pushed back a little more. Truthfully, he'd *wanted* her to push back a little more. He'd wanted her to care; maybe even part of him wanted her to tell him not to do it, to spend the time with her instead. But she hadn't.

So he'd let her answer the phone.

He was used to dealing with life-and-death situations. Not that it got any easier, but he was stronger in that way than Christy was. He should have known she'd be distraught at hearing the news about Eric.

But whether he should have let her ignore the call or not, Mark knew she wouldn't be able to avoid the topic. Even so, when she left to meet the girls for coffee, Mark went straight to the store to buy her a big bouquet of flowers. It was his way of trying to tell her that he appreciated the gesture of the dinner the night before, he loved her and…well, hopefully she wouldn't think they were just guilt flowers.

Just to be sure, he scratched a quick note:

Can't wait to see you tonight.

Love, Mark

HE PROBABLY SHOULD HAVE COME up with something a little more original, but it was the truth and he'd never been very good with words.

Office hours didn't start for another few hours, and despite the fact that there was a "honey-do" list on the fridge that had more than enough chores on it to keep him busy for a morning, he changed into his running clothes, tied up his runners and went to burn off some energy. Running had always allowed him the opportunity to think things through, and after Eric had come into his office the day before, informing him that he needed Mark to act as his respite care doctor and allow him to die as easily as possible, he had a lot he needed to process. Never mind everything else going on.

Besides, he was now officially in training. Although that seemed a whole lot less important at the moment.

It only took Mark a few minutes to fall into his stride. Just as he had been the last few times he'd been out running, he pushed himself to go faster, run harder and farther.

The burn in his lungs and the ache in his muscles as he demanded his body to push harder felt good. It made him feel alive.

Alive.

He shook his head and tried to push thoughts of Eric from his mind. The man had asked him to help him die gracefully and ease him through as many days as he had left. However many that was. And he'd do his best, too. Eric was a friend, and even if they weren't close, their wives were and that made them practically family as far as he was concerned. He'd do anything and everything he could to help because he couldn't imagine how hard it would be not only for Eric, but also for Drew and their little boy.

Maybe the one thing that was worse than not actually being a father was being one and knowing that in only a few months you'd be leaving your son fatherless.

The thought spurred Mark on, and he pushed harder in his run. He was breathing so hard, his eyes blurred with sweat, he hardly noticed the woman sitting on the grass next to the path. He ran past her before his brain had a moment to register what he'd seen—a woman holding her foot, obviously in pain. He took a couple strides to slow his pace before turning around and jogging back toward her.

"Hey there," Mark called before he was too close. He didn't want to spook her by sneaking up on her. "Are you okay?"

He slowed to a walk as she looked up. She was clearly a runner as well, her athletically toned body dressed in only tights and a sports bra, her long blonde hair pulled back in a ponytail. His eyes drifted to her foot. "Are you hurt?"

"Hi." She dropped her hands in frustration. "It's my stupid ankle. It's been giving me a little trouble lately, and then wouldn't you know it, I was totally lost in thought and got too close to the edge of the path here."

Mark glanced down to the path. There was a definite edge where the concrete met the grass. He'd come close to slipping off it a time or two himself.

"I can take a look if you like. I'm a doctor. My practice is on Main Street. Timber Medical."

"I know it." She leaned back on her hands, sticking her leg out for him to examine. "I'm sure it's just a sprain. But...since you're here. If you wouldn't mind."

"Not at all." Mark eased his six-foot-five frame to the

ground and knelt in front of her. She had the long, lean legs of a serious runner. He lifted her foot gingerly and palpitated the ankle, looking for signs of something serious. "Does this hurt?"

"No."

"How about this?"

The way she flinched and tried to pull her leg back was answer enough. "Okay," he said. "I won't do that again." He moved his fingers slowly, asked her to bend her foot, which she could do, curl her toes, which she could also do and finally, the exam was done.

"I think you're right. It's just a slight sprain." He looked up at her pretty face. Her lips turned down in a frown at his announcement and her bright-blue eyes dimmed. For the first time, he looked at her like a woman, and not a patient.

She was younger than him by a few years, but maybe it was just her sporty look that made him think that. Mark caught himself looking at her a moment too long before he remembered himself and put her leg down on the ground as gently as he could.

"I thought so." She dropped her head back and looked up at the sky.

"At any rate, you should try not to put too much weight on it for a day or two. Ice and elevate. It should be fine in a few days, but I'd recommend that you start taping it up to make sure it's as strong as it could be if you're going to keep running."

"Thank you." She shook her head. "I think my friend has some crutches I can borrow. If I can make it home."

"Where do you live?" The second it came out of his mouth, Mark realized the question probably sounded a bit creepy. "I mean…that's not what I mean."

"It's okay. I parked over by River Park."

"That's not too far." Mark wiped his hands. "I'll help you to your car."

She gave him a smile of thanks and groaned. "This is just so annoying. Last week, I committed to a huge race. This is the worst timing."

"Well, at least it's not broken." Mark stood and helped the woman up. She balanced on her good foot and he supported her with an arm around her slender waist. He tried to ignore the closeness, and the fact that she smelled vaguely like oranges. "Besides," he said. "It could always be worse."

She laughed, a light, refreshing sound. "I suppose that's true. I could have broken my leg, I guess. You're right."

Still supporting her, he held his other hand out. "My name's Mark, by the way."

She took it. "Alicia."

"What's your training plan?" he asked as they started to make their way slowly in the direction of the parking lot. "I just started training for an ultra-marathon."

"No way." Alicia whipped around so fast she almost lost her balance. "An ultra? Which one? I just signed up for Polar Peeks."

"That's the race you committed to?" Mark shook his head. "Me too."

"Are you kidding?" She laughed again, and deep inside him, Mark realized how much he liked the sound and how her laughter made him want to smile. "What are the odds."

He helped her the short distance to her car as they compared training notes and strategies.

"We could maybe get together sometime," Alicia said as she unlocked her bright-blue Jeep. "To train, I mean."

"Oh." Mark waved her suggestion away, but the idea appealed, probably more than it should have. "I actually have a running partner."

"Really?" Alicia made a show of looking around for Aaron, who obviously wasn't there. "I don't see anyone."

"Well, I don't run with him all the time."

She smiled and once again it surprised Mark that he noticed the way it made her face light up. "Maybe for those times you don't run with him," she suggested. "My running schedule can vary but I'm for sure here every Tuesday and Thursday night at seven. Keep it in mind." She sat in the driver's seat and unrolled the window. "Thank you for helping me out, Mark. It was nice to meet you."

"You too, Alicia." He shifted from foot to foot, oddly nervous. "You take care of that ankle." He shifted into doctor mode. "Make sure you don't push yourself to start running again, and tape it up just to be safe."

"Will do, Doc." She smiled again. "And maybe I'll see you out here again."

As she drove off, Mark stared after her, stunned. *What had just happened?* He couldn't remember even one time since he'd been with Christy feeling the way he just had about another woman. Especially not a woman he'd known for all of ten minutes. It had to be stress. Stress and all the pressure he'd been under.

And there was only one sure-fire way Mark knew to relieve pressure. He watched as the Jeep rounded the corner and disappeared before he turned back to the path and once again started to run.

AFTER SPENDING the morning with Drew and Cam, Christy was wrung out. She'd done her best not to cry when Drew explained the way they'd discovered Eric's diagnosis and how for the last few months they'd tried every treatment available to them, including a number of experimental drug trials. The thing that sat with Christy the most wasn't the devastation of the original diagnosis, but the subsequent roller coaster of emotional highs and lows that Drew had been on for the last twelve months.

With each new drug trial, or treatment option, she'd been hopeful and excited, thinking only the best thoughts because she had no other option except to be positive about the outcome. And when ultimately the treatment didn't work or the drugs failed to make a noticeable impact on the cancer, she'd been plunged into depression and devastation that she couldn't even dwell in because she had little Austin to think of.

Austin.

The thought of Drew's little boy made Christy want to cry all over again because as much as she'd done her best to control her own emotions, she'd mostly failed. She felt guilty for being sad, but Drew wouldn't hear of it.

"You're allowed to feel whatever you need to feel," Drew told her. "I know this isn't just about me. It affects all of us. It's okay."

Her friend's understanding only made her feel worse. After all, she wasn't the one losing her husband.

She still had hers.

Even if some days it didn't feel like it.

After she left Cam's house, Christy contemplated just going home and spending the afternoon baking cookies or puttering in her garden the way she used to. Pulling weeds from her flower beds always made her feel better. But for some reason, the thought of going home only unsettled her. She wandered aimlessly up the street away from Cam's house before reaching into her purse for the piece of paper with the phone number on it that Jamie had given her the day before.

She still didn't believe she was actually good enough to rehearse with them. He'd just been nice so he wouldn't hurt her feelings. She knew that.

But still.

Christy ran her fingers over the piece of paper and she traced the numbers Jamie had written down.

"Oh, what the hell?"

Before she could change her mind, she pulled her cell phone out and typed in a quick message.

It's Christy. From the Log and Jam yesterday.
Were you serious about rehearsing?

She punched in the number and sent the message before she could chicken out. She watched as the text bubble changed colors on her phone, indicating that the message had been sent. Christy stared at the screen for another few seconds before she laughed at herself and put her phone back in her purse. She was a grown woman; she couldn't stand in the middle of the street, staring at a phone like a teenager.

But a moment later when her phone beeped, she snatched it up quickly and squealed when she saw Jamie had texted her back.

Of course.
We're rehearsing right now.
201 Elm Drive

AN ADDRESS? He'd given her an address. He actually wanted her to rehearse with them. *For real.*

Christy bit back the urge to squeal again. But she couldn't stop the grin that spread across her face.

There were so many reasons why she shouldn't go running off to an address that a stranger had sent her. Hell, there were a *million* reasons why it was a terrible idea. Nonetheless, now that the idea was in her head, there was no way she could get it out again.

After a quick consultation with her cell phone and the map feature, she was on her way. Less than ten minutes later, she stood outside a garage, the muffled sounds of a band practicing on the other side of the wall, pulsing through her.

What would Mark say about her singing with a bunch of strange men?

Christy almost laughed at the idea. Mister Straight-laced play by the rules. Mark would stare at her as though she had three heads and tell her that there was no way she should even consider going into a strange man's garage.

He could be a serial killer.

But he wasn't strange and he *definitely* wasn't a serial killer. He was Jamie.

Not that she knew much more than that. But she'd always been a decent judge of character and Jamie seemed like a nice guy. Decent. There was nothing about him that had sent up any red flags for Christy. Quite the opposite. Besides, he had nice eyes.

"Hey."

Startled, she spun at the sound of the voice behind her.

"You came."

As soon as she saw it was Jamie, a guitar case in his hand, her stomach fluttered, but oddly enough, she relaxed a little too.

"I didn't think you'd come." He smiled.

As he approached, Christy almost started laughing at herself. There was no way this man with the intensely kind eyes was a serial killer. The way he looked at her made her feel something, that much was for sure, but threatened definitely wasn't it.

"Here I am," she said. "But I have to be honest, I almost didn't come. I mean...you can't really be serious about me rehearsing with you guys." She hated the doubt that she heard in her own voice. She wasn't usually so insecure. Of course, she didn't usually expose herself by singing to strangers, either. In fact, never before had she put herself out there so vulnerably.

"I'm totally serious." When Jamie smiled, the skin around his eyes crinkled.

Definitely not a serial killer.

"You have real talent, Christy. And as it turns out, our lead singer just had a family emergency and he's going to be gone for a bit. We actually could really use someone right now."

"Someone to sing for you?"

"No." He laughed and at once Christy felt stupid for making assumptions. "No. We need someone to sing *with* us. Interested?"

Interested?

Hell yeah, she was interested.

"I can't." She shook her head. "I have to…" *What? What did she have to do?*

Nothing.

The answer hit her like a brick. She had absolutely nothing to do. The only thing waiting for her at home was pulling weeds from a garden no one would see, or baking cookies that no one would eat. She could spend her days puttering around her big house, dusting rooms that should have held babies. But for what? Her temporary work at Mark's clinic was done. She had nothing.

She was thirty-four and she had nothing. Everything she'd worked her entire adult life for hadn't materialized. *And it never would.*

The unexpected sadness hit her like a wave. If she allowed it to, it would take her under and she would drown.

But she wasn't going to let it. Christy shook her head. "You know what," she said before she could chicken out. "I would love to."

Jamie's smile instantly made her feel good about her decision. She followed him into the garage, where he introduced her to the other guys who she hadn't officially met the other day—Josh on drums and Caleb on bass guitar. Christy instantly felt at home with the guys. They were quick to crack a joke, tease Jamie—who was late to rehearsal—and they made her feel welcome right away.

"Grab a mic," Caleb told her. "Jump right in and get warmed up. We mostly sing popular covers. If you're even half as good as you were the other day, you'll pick it up in no time. Even if you do prove Jamie right. He couldn't stop going on about your talent."

He'd talked about her? He'd said she was good?

It was ridiculous that Christy needed outside validation from total and complete strangers, but ridiculous or not, she beamed with pride. It was just the confidence boost she needed to pick up the mic and jump right in with the guys.

She was nervous at first and her voice shook a bit but it didn't take long for her to find her rhythm. They moved from song to song until finally, Josh beat out a quick rhythm on the drums, clashed the symbols, and declared rehearsal over.

Christy looked around, as if she were seeing the space for the first time. She felt light-headed and disoriented, as if she'd just woken up from a long nap. "What…what time is it?"

Jamie laughed kindly and handed her a bottle of water. "Come sit." He guided her to a beat-up couch sitting against the back wall. "It's exhausting, isn't it? Do you feel like you've been working out?"

Christy laughed so hard, she almost spat out the water she'd just sipped. "Well, I don't have the faintest clue what working out actually feels like, so…"

"We're not all muscle heads, man." Caleb punched Jamie's shoulder as he walked by.

Christy laughed because the last thing Jamie looked like was a muscle head. He was lean and fit, and his arms filled out his t-shirt in a way that she probably shouldn't have been noticing. Just like the way she'd noticed him looking at her again in that way that felt like more than it should have been. Her laughter cut abruptly and she jumped up from the couch.

"I should go."

"You don't have to." Jamie stood and put his hand on her arm.

The touch froze her to the spot. She stared at his hand. She'd just spent hours singing her heart out, which for her was something so incredibly intimate, that a simple touch shouldn't spook her.

But it did. It spooked her in a way that had nothing to do with singing and everything to do with how this man made her legs go a little weak, and her breath come a bit faster.

Christy pulled away and grabbed her purse, holding it in front of her like a shield. "I really should be going." She turned and practically sprinted to the door.

"Christy, you were great today."

Jamie's voice was so full of sincerity that she stopped and turned around.

"Really," he said when their eyes met. "Your voice is fantastic. We'd love it if you'd rehearse with us again. Maybe even play a show? We have one coming up at the Log and Jam."

She looked around the garage, but they were alone. The other men had vanished and she hadn't even noticed. Christy let her eyes drift back to Jamie, but still she couldn't answer.

"Think about it," he said. "You have my number."

She bit her lip and nodded before turning and fleeing to the warm summer afternoon.

She wasn't doing anything wrong. She knew that.

But then, why did it feel like she was?

Chapter Five

IT HAD BEEN a few days since Christy's rehearsal session with Jamie's band. She realized she didn't even know what they called themselves, but she couldn't help but think of them as Jamie's Band. Hell, she couldn't stop thinking of Jamie.

Christy had tried to put the experience out of her head. After all, there was no point dwelling on it. *It's not like it could happen again. What was the point?* She wasn't really a singer. She was just a bored housewife with nothing else going on in her life, and Jamie was just indulging her.

Wasn't he?

Maybe she was good?

Maybe that was the real reason he'd encouraged her to come back?

Or maybe it was because he really was flirting with her. Either way...the attention felt good. She couldn't deny that.

More than once over the last few days, Christy had pulled her phone out, composed a text message to Jamie, and then deleted it. She was nervous.

Whether it was because she was singing or because of the fact that despite herself, there was a little part of her that was attracted to Jamie when she knew how wrong it was—she didn't know. But every time she thought about Jamie and the band, her stomach flipped and she felt as if she were doing something illicit.

It was probably only because she hadn't told Mark about it yet. She'd meant to, at least until he'd told her about his race. And then again, later, after her rehearsal with the band, she was going to tell him. But for whatever reason, it just never felt like the right time. In the mornings, he got up early to go for a run, and even some evenings, he was running again after work. In between his training, they'd talked a little bit about Drew and Eric and how terrible their situation was, but beyond that, they hadn't spent much time together at all.

There'd been a few days before when she'd tried to surprise Mark at his office by bringing him lunch. She'd thought they could go sit by the river and have a picnic the way they used to when he'd first opened his practice. But when she'd arrived five minutes before his usual lunch time, Sarah, his receptionist, had informed her that he'd already left for a meeting with a pharmaceutical rep.

Disappointed, Christy had thought about leaving him a note, but then decided against it. Sarah would tell him she'd stopped by. Although, when Mark got home that night, he hadn't mentioned it, so either Sarah hadn't said anything, or he'd forgotten.

In another attempt, she thought that maybe after a long week at work, cuddling in front of the couch with a bowl of popcorn and a good movie would be a good way to unwind, and when Christy had suggested it, Mark agreed. The fact that he'd fallen asleep ten minutes into the show only meant he was exhausted, nothing more. At least that's what she told herself while she was finishing both bowls of popcorn. But it was becoming harder and harder to ignore the distance that just kept growing between them.

Somehow the week slipped by and now it was Saturday

morning, a time that was usually reserved for the two of them to spend a leisurely morning cooking brunch together before eating it in front of the television, where they streamed old cartoons from the eighties and laughed at the terrible graphics and even worse theme music.

But Mark had gone running, opting instead for a protein shake and a quick kiss on the cheek.

Christy finished her coffee and pushed up from the kitchen table. She rinsed her mug at the sink and grabbed a banana. It didn't seem worth it to make a big brunch just for her.

I wonder if Jamie is a pancake or waffle man?

She should have been surprised by the way Jamie randomly infiltrated her thoughts. But she wasn't, because Jamie had slipped into her daily thoughts more and more since their rehearsal session. She couldn't stop thinking about him. And the way he'd smiled at her, encouraged her, touched her arm.

Would things be different if she was married to Jamie? Would she be a mother by now?

The thought slammed into her and she almost lost her balance at the sink.

It was terrible. She should definitely not be thinking anything remotely like that. And she definitely shouldn't be having feelings about another man. Even if they were innocent.

Mostly.

Innocent or not, it wasn't okay. Her focus should be her husband. Always.

And wasn't that the real reason she hadn't told Mark about her singing with the band?

She put both hands on the countertop and dropped her head as she exhaled, long and slow.

Christy stood that way for a few moments.

She didn't want to be thinking of another man. She wanted to be thinking of Mark. She loved him. She'd always loved him and that hadn't changed. Thinking about anyone else felt wrong.

What didn't feel wrong was the way she felt when she held the microphone in her hand and sang her heart out.

Christy lifted her head, empowered by recreating the feeling in her mind. Nothing else had felt quite so amazing in a very long time.

A smile crept across her face as she remembered the sensation of the air pushed from her lungs as she belted out song after song. A few minutes later, with a new focus, she felt dramatically calmer. But she still needed to get out of her head.

In an effort to focus on something else, Christy quickly changed out of her pajamas into one of her new outfits and headed out the door to Daisy's Diner for another cup of coffee. She didn't know what she would do from there, but maybe wandering around Main Street, doing some window-shopping, would take her mind off everything. At the very least, it would get her out of the house that more and more was starting to feel like a prison.

Main Street was unusually quiet for a Saturday afternoon in July, and Christy didn't run into many people she knew. But as she approached Daisy's Diner, she saw a familiar petite brunette standing outside, looking at the notice board full of community announcements.

"Good morning," she said to Drew. "Interested in taking piano lessons, are you?" She gestured to the piece of paper Drew was holding.

"Hey." Her friend looked startled as her dark eyes focused on Christy. "I was just…" She looked down at the paper in her hand. "No," she answered with a shake of her head. "I don't know why I have this. I meant to grab this one." She reattached the piano lesson announcement with an available thumbtack and pointed instead at an announcement for a rental house. "We need a place to live. We can't stay at Eric's parents. Not while…" She didn't finish the thought, but she didn't have to.

"I was just going to grab a cup of coffee," Christy said softly. "Why don't you join me?"

Drew nodded, clearly thankful for the reprieve. "Yes." She smiled, but it didn't reach her eyes. At that moment, more than anything else in the world, Christy wanted to take her friend's pain away.

A cup of coffee would have to do.

They ordered their drinks from Morgan, Cam's daughter who'd recently started working part-time, and found a table in the back of the busy diner.

"How are…I mean…well…" Christy chuckled uncomfortably. "I don't know what to say."

"It's okay." Drew's lips twitched up. "I get it. No one knows what to say when your husband is dying. It's okay." She shrugged. "Neither do I. But actually today is a good day. He took Austin to the river this morning with his dad. Honestly, most of the days are good days right now. That's the craziest part. It's so hard to look at him and think that in a few months…well, it's hard to reconcile one thing with another."

Christy nodded sympathetically.

"He's so young, and besides being way too skinny, he's actually still really full of life. It's like he just won't give up."

"That's a good thing."

Drew nodded, but she didn't look convinced. "It is," she said after a moment. "I mean, obviously. I don't want him to give up on living, of course not. But…"

"It's okay, Drew." Christy reached her hand across the table and laid it over Drew's. "We're friends. You can tell me anything."

"I know. Thank you."

"Of course."

"It's the craziest thing," Drew said after a moment. "I

never thought I'd be sitting here telling you this, but I actually want my husband to talk to me about what's going to happen after he dies." She shook her head as if she couldn't even believe she'd said it out loud. "Doesn't that sound insane?"

In any other situation, Christy would have agreed with her friend, but they were not in any other situation. They were talking about Drew and Eric, and as terrible as it was, it was their reality.

"No," Christy said. "It's not insane. You guys should be talking about that stuff. I mean…"

"It's going to happen," Drew finished for her.

They sat in silence for a moment. Their lattes were delivered to the table, and they each sipped thoughtfully before Drew spoke up again.

"I know things haven't been super easy for you either lately. I'm really sorry I haven't asked about the treatments."

Christy put her coffee down and waved her friend's objection away. "Forget it. Seriously, you have enough going on without worrying about my baby problems."

Saying the word *baby* caused the same familiar spark of pain in her chest, but it was nothing compared to what her friend was going through, so she ignored it and wrapped her hands around her mug.

"It's just not time for us right now," Christy said. *Maybe if she said the words enough, she might start to believe them.* "Maybe we'll try again later." There'd be no trying again. She knew that, and likely Drew knew it too, but if she did, she was kind enough not to say anything. "I'm fine." Another lie. "In fact, I've decided to try something new."

The words slipped out before she could stop them. Maybe the need to talk about her singing was greater than she realized.

"That's great." Drew's smile was genuine. "You mean

something new besides your new look?" Her friend raised her eyebrows. "That's a pretty huge change. I love it, by the way."

"Thank you." She reached for her hair subconsciously and smoothed it back. Christy kept forgetting that her hair was now a vibrant red. There'd been a few times over the last few days when she'd caught her reflection in the mirror and been surprised. In a good way. She loved her new look, and it was definitely part of trying something new. "But no, I meant besides my new look. Do you remember how I used to like to sing?"

"Like in high school?" Drew nodded. "Totally. You sang in the talent show and then the musical that one year."

"I did," she said, proud that Drew remembered.

"Don't tell me you've decided to do a musical?"

"Not a musical." Christy was practically bouncing in her seat. It felt so good to talk about her secret. Well, not all of it. There was no way she was going to tell anyone, not even her best friends, that she'd had any thoughts, no matter how innocent, about another man. But the singing part. *That* she was going to talk about. At least with Drew. "But I have been singing with a local band. It's so silly. I don't even know what they call themselves and it's nothing serious. But I thought I'd try it out, and I really like it and they need someone to rehearse with, so it's worked out perfectly. I mean, not that it's worked out. Nothing's worked out really. It's only been a few times. One, really. It's just so—"

"Christy," Drew interrupted her with a chuckle. "That's awesome. I can see how excited you are. I think it's great. No matter if it's serious or not, if you're enjoying it, that's what matters."

Christy nodded as Drew's words sank in. "Yes," she said slowly. "That is what matters. And I do enjoy it."

"Good." Drew sat back in her chair and swirled her finger

through the foam of her latte. "I'm so glad you've found something you love. What does Mark think about it?"

"Mark?" She looked down and took a long drink of her latte so she wouldn't have to answer right away.

"Yeah." Drew gave her a pointed look. "Mark. What does he think about you singing? You have told him, right?"

"Well, here's the thing…"

"Christy." Drew sat up and stared at her until finally she put her mug down.

"No," she admitted. "I haven't told him. But it's not because it's a secret." That was a lie and judging by her friend's face, she wasn't the only one who knew it. "It's just that Mark's been really busy for the last few days and he's been running a lot. Did I tell you he's decided to do another ultra-marathon?" She tried to force a smile but Drew just shook her head.

"Tell him. He loves you and he'll be excited for you. You know that."

Christy did. But she still couldn't tell him. Not yet. And she couldn't even begin to explain to her friend why she wanted it to stay a secret from him. Especially when she couldn't put it into words herself.

"I'll tell him. But not yet." She held her hand up to ward off the objections she knew Drew would have. "But only because it feels kind of cool that this is my little secret. Like it's extra special. Does that make sense?"

"No."

"Don't tell him," she pleaded. "Please."

"I won't." Drew picked up her mug again. "It's not my story to tell. But can I tell you something, Christy? Something I've only just recently learned?"

Drew's face changed. The easy smile was gone again, replaced by the curtain of sadness that hung over her most of the time. Christy nodded, and Drew continued.

"All of this with Eric…it's just made me realize how lucky

we are. And not just Eric and me, but you and Mark. Cam and Evan. All of us. Love isn't guaranteed and living a long life with the one you love is even less of a guarantee. I know you guys have been through a lot of stress lately as well and—"

"It's not like—"

"We're not comparing here, Christy," Drew cut her off. "It doesn't have to be the same. Stress is stress and it's hard on a relationship. But the one thing I've learned is that you need to cherish every moment, even the stressful ones with the one you love. Because...well, you just never know how much time you have."

MARK ONLY INTENDED on going for a short run around town that morning, but as he ran past River Park, he couldn't help but notice the same bright-blue Jeep in the parking lot. Before he realized what he was doing, he changed direction and headed toward the parking lot and the familiar blonde head.

"How's the ankle?"

Startled, the woman jerked up from where she'd been tying her shoe and looked around. When she saw Mark, her face morphed from a mask of worry to a brilliant smile.

"Hey there," she said. "The ankle's doing fine. Thanks... Mark, right?"

He nodded. "Alicia?" *As if he didn't remember her name.* He remembered, all right. And for some reason, that felt completely wrong but all at the same time, very exciting. Alicia's face had popped up in his mind more than once over the last few days. Just remembering her smile put one on his face, too. "I'm glad to hear your ankle's feeling better," he continued when she confirmed her name.

"It's been a frustrating few days." She finished tying her

shoes and stood straight. "But I'm finally ready to get back out there and see if it will hold up."

"Is this your first run on it?" The doctor in him kicked in and he was instantly concerned. Ankles could be tricky and despite the fact that he barely knew the woman, he didn't want to see her hurt it again if it wasn't ready for a run. "Did you have it checked out?"

She laughed. "No, Doc. I didn't. But there was barely any swelling and it hasn't even remotely bothered me for the last twenty-four hours. I think I can handle a slight jog."

Mark wasn't convinced, but he knew all too well how frustrating it could be to be sidelined from an injury when you were keen to get training.

"Would it make you feel better to examine it yourself?"

"It actually would." He laughed and nodded to the ankle. "May I?"

Alicia leaned back against the car and lifted her spandex-clad leg so he could take it in his hands.

Mark did a series of basic manipulations, and just as she'd said, it didn't seem to be giving her any trouble at all. Gently, he put her ankle down and shrugged. "I think you might be right," he admitted. "But I really do think you should take it easy for a few more days. Don't try to get too much distance."

"I can live with that." Alicia pulled her leg up into a quad stretch and Mark had to look away. There was something about the woman that made him nervous, slightly off-kilter. "Are you finishing or starting?"

"Starting what?"

She laughed. It was soft and almost musical, like wind chimes. "Starting your run?"

"Oh, no." He looked behind him as if the pathway he'd arrived on held the answers. "I'm kind of halfway through, I guess." It was a lie. He was almost done with his planned run. He'd only intended to go for a short one so he could get home and cook waffles with Christy. She'd just woken up when he'd left, but they always cooked brunch together on Saturdays. He didn't want to miss it. "What's your route?"

Was he really asking to run with her? He hadn't said the words outright, but it sure sounded that way.

"I mean, I'm not…"

"You're not what?" She put her hands on her hips and grinned. "Asking to run with me?"

Mark was about to admit that he was in fact looking to join her, when she spoke up again. "If it will make you feel better about me running on my ankle, okay."

"Okay?"

She stretched her arm across her chest. "Please join me. After all, I wouldn't want to get hurt again, Doc." She took off down the path in a gentle jog.

Mark watched her for a second before shaking his head. He pushed down the objections he should have been telling himself about how he should be home with his wife and not running—literally—after another woman, and sprinted to catch up with her.

They ran in silence for a few kilometers. The quiet gave Mark a chance to think about what he was doing. *Was running with another woman wrong? More importantly, would Christy think it was wrong?*

Christy didn't run; she never had. In fact, she mostly blew off any type of exercise at all. She'd never cared before when he ran with Aaron; why would she care now?

That was different.

The only thing that made it different was that Alicia was a woman.

And that was a big difference. But it wasn't the only one. And he knew it.

He didn't want to be, but Mark couldn't help it. He was attracted to Alicia.

Not that he would ever act on it. Attraction was one thing. Love was a different one. And he loved Christy. More than life itself. She was his entire world and he would never do anything to hurt her.

And maybe that was why it felt so wrong and at the same time so good to be running next to Alicia. This woman didn't know him. Didn't know his failures or his disappointments. He hadn't let her down. It was fresh and easy.

"Are you usually so quiet when you run with someone?" Alicia's voice burst into his thoughts, a welcome distraction because he was only going around and around with trying to decide on what his level of guilt should be in regards to the woman next to him.

"No." He laughed. "But I only ever usually run with my buddy Aaron. What about you?"

"I don't usually run with anyone at all."

"Really?" He couldn't stop himself from adding the next question. "What about your husband?"

She laughed so hard, her pace slowed.

"What's so funny?"

"Was that your way of asking if I was single?"

Her question hit him hard and he came to a sudden and complete stop. He froze to the spot; his mouth fell open and he stared unseeing in front of him.

It took Alicia a moment to realize he wasn't right next to her before she stopped and turned around. "I'm sorry." She made her way back to him. "I wasn't trying to—"

"No." He held up a hand. "I'm the one who should be sorry." He dropped his head and shook it back and forth for a moment. *He was being an idiot.* The moment Alicia thought he might be hitting on her, everything had felt a little too real. *How could he even be out here, entertaining the slightest thought about this woman instead of his wife? What did he think he was doing?* Yes, it was innocent. But at the same time, it wasn't. Not at all. And if he didn't put an immediate stop to it, it really would be wrong.

"I didn't mean anything by the question," he said. "I mean, if I did, I shouldn't have. Really. I was just making conversation, and—"

"Hey." Alicia put her hand on his arm and he jumped back. "Sorry, Mark." She tucked her hands behind her back. "I didn't mean anything. I just thought maybe you were flirting and—"

"Flirting!" His face fired up with embarrassment. *Was* that what he was doing? The idea that he was flirting with anyone was laughable. He'd never been a flirty guy. Even with Christy, they used to joke about how little game he had and how if she hadn't made the first move when they were teenagers that they'd probably still be eyeing each other across the room instead of being actually married.

Married.

"I'm married." He said the word as if it were a shield that would protect him from any thought of flirting.

"That's great." Alicia's smile was genuine. "I really didn't mean anything by the comment. If you still want a running partner...or does your wife run?"

"No." He shook his head. The flush was starting to fade as if just by mentioning his wife to this other woman, he was suddenly absolved of any thoughts he may have had that might be considered inappropriate in even the remotest way. "She's not a runner at all."

"And would she mind if you had a running partner? I mean...another one?"

"No." Mark shook his head, suddenly feeling foolish with the entire conversation. "She wouldn't. She's always been really supportive of my goals and I know she's not super excited that I signed up for another ultra, but she's still supportive of what it takes for me to get there." He gestured lamely between them. "Including running partners."

Alicia nodded and narrowed her eyes to give him a look that said she wasn't totally convinced. "Okay," she said after a moment. "So…should we keep running?"

Mark thought about it for a moment. He had been enjoying the pace they'd set and despite the awkwardness there'd been, it was a good run and he did like her company. Now that the awkwardness had been sorted out and he didn't need to feel guilty… "Yes. Let's keep running."

Chapter Six

CHRISTY HAD GIVEN a lot of thought to what Drew said about appreciating what you had because you never knew what life could throw at you. In fact, after they finished their lattes and had gone their separate ways, Christy went straight home. With a plan.

She had no idea how long Mark would be out running. The last time he trained for an ultra-marathon, his training sessions escalated until finally he was out all day, trail running in the middle of the woods. But he'd just started, so surely he wouldn't be gone longer than a few hours.

That's what she was betting on.

There'd been a time, not that long ago, when Christy spent almost all of her free time on her home. She'd taken a certain level of pride in decorating each room just right, making the bed with crisp sheets and all the throw pillows placed in the perfect positions. She spent a great deal of time picking out the perfect essential oil combinations to diffuse in each room to suit the mood or the weather, or any emotional ailment she or Mark might have. Her home was her career and she excelled at it.

Things had changed after the big high school reunion earlier that spring. She couldn't quite pinpoint when the tipping point happened, but one day she woke up and just stopped caring as much. If she was being really honest with herself, she knew exactly when it was. During the last IVF cycle, she'd been worn out. Somehow, she just knew it wasn't going to work and the effort was pointless.

And if she didn't have a family to fill her beautiful home then…what was the point?

But all of that was about to change.

The moment Christy walked in the door, she took a moment to walk around and open all the windows she could to get the fresh air circulating. She opened curtains that had been closed and let the bright sunlight shine in.

In the kitchen, she tied her favorite apron around her new blouse and set to work, whipping up a batch of Mark's favorite granola bars that he'd enjoyed the last time he trained for a major race. When they were in the oven, she turned her attentions to the bedroom, where she stripped the sheets and made the bed with a fresh set. She turned her diffuser on with a combination of essential oils that were known to be seductive and then she changed into a silk negligee she had hiding in the back of her lingerie drawer. It was one of the only pieces she had that still fit after her weight gain. It was a little snug in the chest, but it fit pretty well, and with any luck, she wouldn't be wearing it long once Mark got home.

It was only mid-afternoon, and probably too early for wine, but this was a special occasion, so Christy popped a bottle of white in the fridge to chill and set two glasses out.

The granola bars out of the oven and finished with her preparations, Christy didn't know what to do with herself while she waited. She'd toyed with the idea of leaving him a note to come to the bedroom and find her, but she had no idea when he'd be back, so she discarded the idea in case she fell asleep.

That wouldn't be very sexy. And she was definitely going for sexy.

How long had it been since they'd made love?

If she pulled out her calendar, she'd know exactly the last time they had sex. Because despite the fact that they'd been trying IVF, they still secretly hoped it would happen naturally and therefore Christy kept a strict calendar of her ovulation dates and ideal days for conception. It was probably the least romantic thing she'd done.

And quite possibly, it had been one of the hardest things on their relationship.

But that had been sex for the sole purpose of conceiving. This was different.

Very different. Because she was going to seduce her husband and—

Christy's thoughts trailed away as she heard the familiar click of the doorknob, followed by Mark's footsteps. She leaned against the doorjamb, with one arm on her hip and the other up the wall in a way she hoped was more seductive than it felt because it felt completely ridiculous. When Mark walked down the hall, he was looking at the sports watch he wore that recorded all of his statistics during his run. He was so intent on pushing buttons and deciphering whatever data his watch had recorded he didn't look up until he was almost directly in front of her.

"Christy! Hi. I...well, hello." His demeanor and voice changed the moment he realized what she was wearing and why she was standing there. "This is a surprise." He dropped his arm, the watch and its data forgotten.

"Isn't it ever." She hoped her voice sounded seductive and not silly. "And that's not all...come with me." She crooked her finger and turned, hoping he would follow. A moment too late, she realized she should have kissed him. She'd fix that right away, Christy decided. First, the wine.

"I know we missed brunch, but I thought maybe we could spend the afternoon…"

"Watching cartoons?"

It was a joke. She knew it was, but still the words stung considering what she was wearing, and that watching television was definitely not on her mind. She flinched inwardly but was determined to brush it off.

"No," she said sweetly as she opened the fridge and grabbed the wine. "I thought we could spend our afternoon together. In bed."

For whatever reason, she was embarrassed to look at him while she made the suggestion, which was silly because they were never embarrassed around each other. But it had been so long. Too long since they'd been together just because they *wanted* to be. It felt…different somehow.

"Come on." She picked up the glasses and led the way to the bedroom. Before she could chicken out, she put the glasses down on the nightstand and spun around into her husband's arms.

Christy pressed her lips to his and instead of the chaste kiss routine they'd fallen into in recent months, she deepened it and slipped her tongue into his mouth. It took him a few seconds to catch up but once he did, he kissed her back and Christy sank into the familiar taste of him.

His arms slipped around her and her skin tingled with his touch.

How long had it been since he'd touched her like this? *Too long. Way too long.*

"Hmmm…this is nice." Mark pulled back enough to look in her eyes.

"It is, isn't it?"

He nodded and smiled. "But I'm all sweaty, Christy. I need a shower."

"A shower?" Her heart sunk. "Now?"

He nodded again and released her from his embrace. "It was a great run and I'm really sweaty."

She was determined not to let it get her down. "It's okay." She stepped forward and ran a hand down his arm. "I like you sweaty. Besides, we're just going to work up a sweat together anyway."

She blushed with her choice of words, but she'd come this far—she wasn't going to back down now.

Mark turned and gave her a strange look. "Seriously, Christy. It'll just take a minute."

He couldn't leave. She had a whole plan and if he left, it wouldn't be the same. "Why don't we have a glass of wine and—"

"I'm in training, Christy." He turned toward their ensuite bathroom and pulled his running shirt over his head without looking at her. "I'm not drinking right now."

She wanted to cry, or scream, or… She shook her head and grabbed the bottle of wine as Mark disappeared into the bathroom.

"I'll be right back, honey," he called. "I really like the way you surprised me."

"Yeah, right," she mumbled under her breath and climbed up on their king-size mattress with the bottle in one hand and a glass in the other. She poured herself a healthy glass as she heard the shower turn on.

There was a time when Mark would have jumped her at the first sight of her standing in a negligee. A few years ago, he never would have opted for a shower first, no matter how sweaty he was. She took a long drink of the wine, letting the crisp coolness of the liquid soothe her hurt feelings.

"Just wait till I get out there," Mark called from the shower.

She shook her head and drank deeply again. Christy knew him too well. He was just trying to cover his butt because he realized he'd been a bit of an ass by putting her off.

She took a deep breath and refilled her glass. She wouldn't let it derail her. She had to remember what Drew had said. Love isn't guaranteed. And life definitely wasn't. They loved each other and they had each other. That was the most important thing.

Christy could feel the effects of the wine start to flow through her body. She was feeling more relaxed and almost a little too relaxed by the time Mark appeared in the bathroom door. But when she saw his hard chest, dripping with water, and nothing but a towel slung around his slender hips, Christy sat up so quickly, she sloshed a little wine on the comforter beneath her.

Her body may have changed over the years, but Mark's had only gotten leaner, harder, and sexier with each passing year. *Maybe all that running wasn't such a bad thing after all.*

HE FELT like an ass the second he stood under the hot water.

When was the last time Christy had met him at the door wearing only a negligee?

Never.

But he'd been caught off guard and he needed a minute to pull himself together and wash his run away. Not to mention the whole misunderstanding he'd had with Alicia that had him feeling like a jackass.

Even after they'd finished their run, he still felt bad about having even the smallest thought about Alicia in any way that wasn't perfectly innocent. It wasn't right and he needed a moment to compose himself before he went to join the woman he loved.

He lathered up and as he rinsed the soap off, the guilt hit him. *He'd been a total jerk to Christy. She'd obviously gone to a lot of effort for them and he'd…*

"Just wait till I get out there," he called out to her from the shower. He could almost see her rolling her eyes. He never talked like that.

Shit.

As quickly as he could, Mark finished rinsing, turned the water off, and grabbed a towel.

"Hey there."

She was lying on the bed, a glass of wine in her hand and a frown on her face. When she saw him, she jumped up and wine splashed out of the glass.

"Here." He tried to take the wine, but she pulled it back.

"Hold on." She tipped the glass to her mouth and drained it before handing it to him. "Now you can have it."

She smiled and scooted back on the bed. "Come here." She crooked her finger and beckoned to him.

He wasn't about to put her off again. Mark crawled up on the bed over to his wife and kissed her firmly on the lips.

She tasted like wine.

Christy's arms came up around him and held his head while she deepened the kiss. Her tongue slipped into his mouth and sloppily tangled with his.

He should have been turned on. His wife hadn't been so forward in years, but something was off. Something didn't feel right. It felt forced, different, not like Christy at all.

He pulled back a little to look at her. Her eyes were closed, but when she opened them, they were glazed and unfocused.

"Are you drunk?"

"What?" Christy's mouth fell open in objection. "No. I'm not drunk, Mark. I had a glass of wine while I waited for you."

He looked to the nightstand and the half-empty bottle and back at her.

"Okay, maybe two."

Mark sat back and put a little distance between them. "I was only in there for five minutes." He'd never seen her drink so quickly. In fact, she'd barely had more than the occasional glass for the last few years while they were undergoing treatments. *But half a bottle in only a few minutes?*

He shook his head and tightened the towel around his waist. "You're drunk."

"I am not drunk." She pushed up to her knees; her negligee pulled tight over her chest and one breast threatened to pop out altogether. She had to be drunk—otherwise, the Christy he knew would have been tugging at the fabric to adjust it back in place, or at the very least, covering it up. "I was waiting for you." She pointed at him and raised her voice. "Because I wanted to *seduce* you."

Her words were definitely slurring.

He shook his head a little and tried to decide what to do. He wanted to be with her. He *needed* to be with her. It had been so long. But not like this. Not with her drunk. It wasn't right.

None of this was right.

Mark tried to back away, but Christy lunged forward and grabbed his arm. "Where are you going?"

"Christy." He tried to untangle himself from her. "I think you should—"

"Kiss you."

She pushed him back and straddled his chest with her legs before smashing her mouth to his.

Despite what his brain was telling him, his body responded at once to the feel of his wife on his chest and he kissed her back.

"See?" She sat back and looked at him. "I'm not drunk, I'm just trying to…" She must have seen the doubt on his face because whatever she was going to say was lost. Instead, her eyes filled with tears. "I'm not drunk," she repeated. "I was just trying to…oh, God." She covered her face with her hands. "I'm so embarrassed."

She tried to swing her leg off him so she could slip away,

but he caught her hips with his hand. "No." With one hand, he reached for her face and pried one of her hands away so he could see her. "Don't be embarrassed. Christy, please. This just all got started wrong."

To his relief, she dropped her other hand and looked into his eyes. "I'm not drunk."

He nodded, although he still wasn't convinced. If she wasn't drunk, she was definitely tipsy.

"I was just trying to… I just thought it would be nice for us to…"

"I know what you mean," he said softly. "And I agree."

Her lips twitched up into a tiny smile. "You do?"

"Of course." Mark laughed a little and wiped a tear from her cheek. "How could I not want to have sex with my gorgeous wife?" Something in her eyes flickered. The smile disappeared and he wondered again whether he'd said the wrong thing, but then the smile was back. "Can we start over?" he suggested.

It took her a moment, but she nodded.

"Okay." Mark released her hands and slid off the bed. "You stay right here." He pointed to her. "Don't move."

He disappeared into the bathroom for a moment but then turned right around and returned to the bedroom.

"Hey there, beautiful." He took a moment to properly admire Christy in her nightie before crawling into the bed with her. And then he was next to her, kissing her.

There was so much hurt between them. So many broken dreams. So much blame. He knew she blamed him for the lack of their family—how could she not? There were too many things left unsaid, and he tried to kiss it all away and focus on the love between them. But something had shifted in her.

She kissed him back, but the enthusiasm from earlier, no matter how misguided, was gone. He used his hands to caress her and she reached down to touch him. A few moments later, he was on top of her, inside of her and instead of being the reconnection they so desperately needed, he'd never felt further away from her.

Afterward, Christy rolled over and fell asleep even though it was only mid-afternoon. Mark lay next to her, watching her. More than anything, he wanted to pull her close and kiss away all her pain and everything that was fractured between them. Instead, he quietly slipped out of bed, dressed and let her sleep.

Chapter Seven

"I DON'T KNOW." Cam looked down at her notebook again, before looking up at Evan. "It just doesn't feel right, you know?"

She hadn't been in a hurry to get remarried after her disastrous divorce, but with Evan it didn't feel like a hurry at all. It felt as if they'd been waiting their entire lives to finally move forward together. After they'd officially become engaged, they'd tossed around a few ideas for a wedding, including eloping, just the two of them, with only Morgan in attendance.

But Evan had never been married before and he really wanted the big party with all their friends in attendance, dancing into the night and celebrating the two of them.

They'd planned to hold the wedding in September, right when the leaves started to change and it was a bit cooler, but not too cool to have an outdoor reception. They even had a venue picked out. But now, with the news of Drew and Eric, it just didn't seem right to be celebrating the start of a new life together while one of her best friends was facing the end of her own love story. She'd spent the last few days debating with herself and finally, almost a week after Drew had shared her sad news, she knew she had to say something to Evan about it.

"I know what you mean." Evan stood behind her and rubbed her shoulders. "I've been struggling with that for the last few days, too." He leaned down and pressed a kiss to her cheek.

Cam reached up and put her hand on his and squeezed. "I want to marry you."

He laughed. "Babe, I know that. And you're not going to get rid of me that easily, just by postponing the ceremony."

"So you do think we should put if off for a bit?" She twisted around in her chair and examined him. Part of her, the selfish part, wanted him to insist that they shouldn't postpone their nuptials, but the other part of her, the more sensible part, knew that's exactly what they should do.

He nodded, the way she knew he would. "I do. I just don't know how I could really completely enjoy the day knowing that…well, I just don't know if it's the right time. I'm sorry, babe."

Cam stood and went into his arms. Hugging Evan always felt like home. She could hardly believe they'd been apart for sixteen years. It felt as though they'd always been together. "Don't be sorry," she said. "It's the right thing to do. And it's not like it's going to make any difference to us."

"That's right."

"But it could mean the world to Drew and Eric. I really think we should focus this time on them. In fact, I was going to invite Amber out for an extended visit. I think she should be here as well."

Amber was the fourth of their quartet, and a self-described workaholic based in San Francisco. Miraculously, she'd come back to town for the reunion party a few months earlier, but Cam was pretty sure Amber didn't take any regular holidays at all. "She's up for a big promotion," Cam told Evan. "So it might not be perfect timing for her to come, but…"

"She will," he finished for her. "And before you ask, of course she can stay here."

"Thank you." Cam grinned because Evan knew her, and her friends, so well. Amber's father still lived in town, her mother having passed away years earlier when they were teenagers. But he was a cantankerous old man, and although Amber made a point to visit him, she refused to stay in her childhood home because it was too draining. Cam couldn't blame her. "You're awesome."

"I know it." Evan kissed her again before he moved to the fridge. "Hey, speaking of awesome, it's pretty cool about Christy, don't you think?"

"Christy?"

Wedding issues forgotten, Cam stared at her fiancé. "What are you talking about?" Surely he wasn't talking about the fact that Christy and Mark's latest attempt at having a child hadn't panned out. That wasn't cool at all. "Her hair?"

"Her hair? Why would I be talking about her hair?" Evan looked at her as if she'd just spoken in German, and Cam almost laughed. Typical that he wouldn't have noticed Christy's dramatic new hairstyle. She shook her head, and he continued. "No, I meant her singing."

"Singing?" It was Cam's turn to look confused. "What are you talking about?"

"She didn't tell you?" Evan put a plate of sandwiches on the table and went back to the counter to grab the rest of the lunch he'd been preparing.

Cam grabbed some glasses and a pitcher of water out of the fridge. "She didn't tell me anything," she said. "Not about singing anyway. What are you talking about?"

"I was over at the Log and Jam yesterday, and Ben said Christy had been rehearsing with the Lumber Kings."

She turned and stared at her fiancé. "Rehearsing? With the Lumber Kings? You realize that sentence didn't make any sense, right? Who are the Lumber Kings?"

Evan laughed. "I keep forgetting that you haven't lived in Timber Creek for the last sixteen years." She shot him a look and he smiled. "But you're here now."

"Yes, I am." She playfully punched his shoulder as she moved past him to sit at the table. "So…who are the Lumber Kings?"

"They're a local band that plays fairly regularly at the Log and Jam." He picked a ham sandwich off the plate in front of them and took a bite.

Cam loved these lunches together when Evan wasn't working and she could sneak away from her home photography studio in the backyard. It was a little thing, but it made her happy.

"They sometimes play in some of the nearby towns," Evan continued. "But that's about it. They're really good. We should go check them out sometime."

Cam nodded and assessed her own sandwich. "Sure. But I still don't understand what it has to do with Christy. She's been rehearsing with them? Like singing? In a band?"

"Yup. That's what Ben said." He chewed thoughtfully. "I thought you knew."

"Nope." It was strange that Christy hadn't said anything to her about it, though. She'd just talked to her on the phone the day before and she hadn't mentioned anything at all about any singing. Come to think of it, Christy hadn't said much at all. Nothing of substance anyway. Her friend was definitely acting strangely, and it wasn't just the new hair and new clothes. She was different.

"I'm sure it just slipped her mind." Evan looked at her thoughtfully. No doubt he could see the concern all over her face.

"Maybe," Cam agreed, but she didn't believe it. Something like singing in a band was not something that would have slipped Christy's mind. Her friend intentionally hadn't told her. And she was going to find out why.

CHRISTY WAS NERVOUS, which was ridiculous, but when Jamie had texted her and asked whether she could meet the band at the Log and Jam for a rehearsal, the initial excitement she'd felt had been immediately followed by nerves. It had been a few days since her last rehearsal and as much fun as she had, she hadn't thought that it would become a regular thing. Not really.

She'd taken extra time getting ready that morning. She didn't usually wear makeup at all unless it was a special occasion, or Mark was taking her out for dinner or something, but she'd taken care to apply eyeliner and even lipstick. Christy tried to tell herself it had nothing to do with the fact that every time she saw Jamie and he smiled at her, she felt a special warmth inside that she hadn't felt in a very long time. But if she allowed herself to be honest with herself, she knew that feeling had a lot to do with why she'd taken extra care getting ready.

As usual, Mark hadn't even asked what her plans were for the day, so she hadn't told him. And she didn't even feel bad anymore for keeping her singing from him. After all, if he wasn't going to ask, why should she volunteer the information? He clearly didn't care how she spent her day. There was a growing list of things that Christy was pretty sure Mark didn't care about anymore.

Ever since her sort of failed, somewhat salvaged attempt to seduce him a few days earlier, the strangeness and awkwardness between them had only grown more intense. She'd really tried not to dwell on it, or overthink anything, but whenever she remembered Saturday afternoon, and the epic fail of a seduction, she felt sick inside. *How had they become so lost that they couldn't enjoy an afternoon of no-pressure sex?*

When had it happened?

She knew Mark had tried to save the situation, but by then, it had gone too far and she hated herself for going along with it anyway and having sex with him, in the hopes that the enthusiasm and desire she'd felt earlier would reappear.

It hadn't.

When it was over, she pretended to be asleep so she could be alone. As soon as he left the room, she cried for everything that was broken between them. Because she had no idea how to fix it.

Christy had spent the rest of the weekend keeping busy with various projects around the house, and finally it was Monday and Mark went back to the office. The next few days passed in kind of a fog, with both of them pretending nothing had happened. It wasn't until Tuesday when Jamie's text came in, asking her whether she would rehearse with them on Thursday afternoon. She'd spent the next forty-eight hours focused on the feeling of having the microphone in her hand again, her eyes closed, and the music coursing through her. The excitement of it all had pulled her through the last few days, given her something to focus on and look forward to. It had been way too long since she'd felt that type of anticipation.

When she pulled into the parking lot of the pub, the beat-up black truck she now recognized as Jamie's was in the parking lot. She parked a few spots over, grabbed her purse and with a deep breath, left the safety of her car behind.

There was a poster on the front door advertising live music. *The Lumber Kings.*

Christy paused and examined the poster before laughing at herself as she made the connection. The Lumber Kings must be Jamie's band. She still hadn't asked what they called themselves. It hadn't seemed important.

Live at the Log and Jam — July 26

That was tonight.

Why would Jamie want her to rehearse with the band if they had a—

Her mouth fell open as she connected the dots in her mind. Still in shock, she pushed through the heavy wooden door into the pub. She'd been coming to the Log and Jam ever since Ben Ross opened it almost ten years earlier. The rough, exposed logs that made up the walls gave the pub a cozy feel and the artifacts and antiques from Timber Creeks' early days as a logging town gave the place charm and character. But it wasn't just the atmosphere that made the Log and Jam feel like home for Christy. It was the fact that the place was always filled with friends. No matter what else was going on, she knew she would see a friendly face there.

"Hey, Christy." Ben Ross greeted her with a smile and a wave as if to prove the point she was feeling. "Are you here for lunch today? Michael made a mean chili for the special this afternoon."

Michael, Ben's chef, was amazing, and the aroma coming from the kitchen was tempting, but that wasn't why she was there. "I bet it's delicious," she said with a smile as she looked around the space, letting her eyes grow accustomed to the dimmer light inside. "But I'm actually here for…"

"Oh, that's right. You're singing tonight."

She spun around and stared at her old friend. "Singing? Tonight?"

"Yeah, with the Lumber Kings. Jamie said something about—"

"Jamie must have been drunk." At that moment, her eyes locked on Jamie's across the room, where he was plugging cables into a speaker. "And if you'll excuse me, I should probably go make sure he's not drinking right now."

She could hear Ben laughing behind her as she crossed the room to confront Jamie.

He was smiling and looking at her in that easy way he had that made her feel like the only woman in the room. It made her stomach flip in a way it hadn't since she was a teenager, but it also gave her confidence, which was exactly what she needed if she was going to hold that microphone in her hands and sing her heart out. She let her gaze flick to the microphone stand before she focused back on Jamie.

"Hey, Christy. I'm glad you came today."

She nodded, momentarily forgetting the sign she'd seen on the door. "For rehearsal? Because we are just *rehearsing* today?"

Jamie shrugged, but didn't meet her eyes.

"Right, Jamie?"

"Well, we do rehearse before…"

"A show?" She put her hands on her hips but had no idea why she was feeling defensive. "Do you have a show tonight?"

Finally, he looked at her with a slightly apologetic smile on his face. "We do. And I was kind of hoping that you might fill in for our usual lead singer. Remember, I told you that he'd had some family issues to deal with and I think things are a little more serious than we thought and he might not be back for a while. Having you rehearse with us has been awesome, so I guess I kind of figured it wouldn't be too much of a stretch."

A show? He wanted her to sing in a show. In front of people.

Intellectually, she'd known it the second she saw the concert poster on the door. But to hear him say it…that made it real.

Very real.

The thought bounced through her mind for a few moments. She expected to immediately reject his offer but as the reality of what he was asking settled in, Christy realized she didn't totally hate the idea. In fact, she might actually even like it.

A lot.

"So?"

She blinked and looked into his green eyes. "Do you know that up until a few minutes ago I didn't even know what your band was called?"

Jamie laughed, but not at her. "Well, I guess that's a good thing since we can't really be the Lumber Kings with a female singer."

"Did she say yes?" Caleb, a drum in hand, walked up to the stage area and smiled at Christy. "Tell me you said yes?"

She looked around. They were setting up for a show. They *did* need a singer. She looked between the men and finally laughed. "You were pretty confident I was going to say yes, weren't you?"

Jamie answered by raising his eyebrow.

"He said you'd do it," Caleb said. "Or we would have cancelled the show."

"So that's an official yes?"

"Yes." She nodded and a thrill ran through her body, electrifying her. "I'll do it."

IT HAD BEEN A LONG WEEK. And it was only Thursday. Mark almost never took a day off, but not for the first time that day, he considered rescheduling his Friday patients and taking a long weekend.

Maybe he could take Christy out for a special dinner, or better yet, to Seattle for a romantic weekend. In fact, it's what he *should* do. But a quick glance at his schedule for the next day told him it would be next to impossible to reschedule everyone.

Healthy baby checkups, yearly physicals, and some ingrown toenails may not be on everyone's crucial list, but for his patients, those things were crucial, which was why they were important to him. It's what made Mark such a good small-town doctor.

He cared.

He needed to start applying that same amount of care to his marriage. He knew it. In a deep, soul-touching way, he knew his marriage needed extra love and attention.

He just didn't know where to begin. Which was a terrible reason for not doing anything; he knew that. But maybe they were just going through one of those rough patches that lots of couples went through. *It would pass. Of course it would pass.* They were Mark and Christy. High school sweethearts, the loves of each other's lives. *Yes, this phase would definitely pass.*

"Doctor Thomas?"

Sarah's voice over his loudspeaker startled him. He scrubbed his hands over his face and pressed the button to talk to his receptionist. "Yes, Sarah."

"Eric Ross is here for his check-up. I sent him to exam room three."

"Thanks, Sarah." He was about to get up when he had a thought. "Oh, and Sarah?"

"Yes, Doctor Thomas? What else can I do for you?"

He hated asking Sarah to make personal arrangements for him, but… "Would you mind terribly making a reservation for two at the Riverside Grill for Saturday night?"

He could hear the smile in Sarah's voice when she answered. "It's no problem at all. Should I tell them it's a special occasion?"

"Just that I want to take my beautiful wife out on a date."

"Sounds special enough to me. Consider it done."

Satisfied that a romantic dinner would go a long way in bridging the distance between himself and his wife, Mark picked up his tablet and quickly logged into Eric's file.

It had been almost two weeks since Eric had arrived and asked him to be his respite care doctor. Mark had talked at length with Eric's oncologists from the city and learned everything he possibly could about Eric's case.

The prognosis wasn't good.

But of course, everyone already knew that.

He took a deep breath and went to exam room three. Hands down, the hardest part about his chosen profession was when he lost a patient. It was never easy, of course, but it almost seemed harder when it was a chronic illness that he could do nothing to stop. He'd become a doctor to help make people better, not to watch them die.

"Hey, Eric," he said as he knocked on the door and pushed it open. "How are you doing today?"

He tried not to let the shock show on his face as he saw his old friend. In only two weeks, Eric's condition had clearly deteriorated. He was thinner, if that was even possible. His clothes hung on him, and despite the hot summer day outside of his office, Eric was dressed in long pants and a knit sweater, no doubt in an effort to preserve whatever body heat he could.

"Doc." Eric managed a smile. "It's not a terrible day."

"It's not a great day." Mark turned to see Drew, Eric's wife, sitting across the small room in the chair reserved for family members. He hadn't noticed her. "Hi, Mark."

"Drew." He offered her a smile and a nod. "Now, why isn't it a good day? What's going on?"

"I'm dying. That's always a day wrecker." Eric's attempt at lightheartedness fell flat.

Drew's lips pressed into a thin line. "Eric."

The tension in the room was palpable. Mark couldn't even begin to imagine what Drew and Eric were going through, and it made his difficulties with Christy seem insignificant and petty. They were both healthy. He didn't have to watch his wife face his own mortality day after day.

"Why don't we start with an exam," he suggested. Mark

went through the motions of blood pressure, listening to Eric's lungs and taking all the various vitals to fill out his charts.

"I don't know why you do that, Mark," Drew said when he was finished. "None of it matters."

"It does matter—"

"No," she cut him off. "What we really need to know is how I can ease his pain when he's screaming out in the middle of the night because it hurts just to lay in his bed." She stood and clutched her purse to her. She looked both much smaller than Mark remembered, and much stronger, too. As if there were an iron rod running through her, holding her up. "I need to know how to explain to my son why some days Daddy can take him to the river when the next day he might be too weak to even stand up for more than five minutes, let alone walk anywhere." A tear slipped down her cheek, but she was angry, not sad. "I don't need to know what his blood pressure is, Mark. I need to know how to help him die."

"Drew." Eric reached out to her from the exam bed where he was perched. "Babe. It's okay."

"No." She shook her head. "It's not." She turned to Mark. Her eyes were a stormy mix of sadness and determination. "Absolutely none of this is okay." She dropped her chin to her chest for a moment before she looked up. "I'm sorry, Mark." The last thing he'd expected was an apology that wasn't necessary. "It's not your fault. I'm sorry I yelled. It's just…well, it's been a bad day. Will you excuse me for a moment?"

"Of course." Mark reached for her hand and squeezed gently. "There's never any need to apologize to me, Drew. You know that, right?"

She answered with a smile so sad it cracked his heart before she squeezed past him in the tiny room, kissing Eric on the cheek and slipping out of the room.

The two men sat in silence for a moment before Eric spoke

up. "I told her today that I want her to remarry after I'm gone."

Mark stared at the other man.

"That's why she's upset. She doesn't usually get so emotional. But I think it's finally all sinking in, you know?"

Mark didn't know. No amount of medical school or losing past patients could have prepared him for this situation.

"I mean, we've known for a while, of course," Eric continued. "But for the longest time, there was hope and now…well, now I need to make sure they're okay after I'm gone. That's the most important thing. Not the pain. Not the cancer. None of that. I need to know the Drew and Austin will be okay. Maybe not right away, but eventually. Which is why I'm going to need you to take care of something for me."

Eric pulled a folded envelope from his back pocket.

"What's that?" Mark didn't take the envelope right away. Eric had already signed all of the necessary paperwork at the hospital with his medical wishes.

"I need you to give this to Drew after I'm gone." Eric held up one hand to ward off Mark's protests. "It's not a will or anything like that. I've taken care of all of that and trust me when I tell you I've spent a lot of time writing letters to everyone I love. And recording videos." Eric laughed, but it was a choked, strangled sound. "Remember that old movie from the nineties with Michael Keaton? The one where he makes a bunch of his videos for his unborn son?"

Mark nodded numbly. "I do. I remember taking Christy to see it. We both cried."

"Yeah, there's nothing funny about cancer, that's for sure." Eric winked at him and Mark couldn't help but smile.

"But if you've done all that, then what's in the envelope?" He took it gingerly from Eric's fingers as if it might explode on him.

"It will all make sense for her when you give it to her. But here's the thing—promise me you won't give it to her until I've been gone a year."

"A year?"

Eric nodded as the door opened and Drew reappeared, looking much more put together and in control of her emotions.

"Does that sound good, Doc?"

Drew looked between the men as Mark instinctively tucked the envelope into his jacket pocket. "Does what sound good?" She directed the question to Mark.

"Eric was just asking me for an increase in his pain medication. And something to help him sleep at night." Mark looked at Eric, whose lips quirked up into an approving smile. "And that sounds perfectly good to me, Eric. I'll write out the prescription and make a note in my files about the date."

"That's all I can ask for, Doc."

———

"YOU'RE SOUNDING GREAT, CHRISTY," Josh called out from behind her. She turned to see Josh tuck his drumsticks to the side, stand and stretch his long body. "But I think that's enough of a free show for today, don't you? We go on in a few hours. Let's grab some food and take a break."

"I hate to admit it." Caleb lifted his guitar strap over his head and stuck it in the stand off to the side of the small stage. "But the man has a point. Besides, I'm starving and Ben said something about chili."

After an afternoon of rehearsal, where she ran through all the songs in the Lumber King's set list, Christy was just getting warmed up. She was energized in a way she couldn't remember ever feeling before. Or at least, for a very long time. It was amazing to hold that microphone in her hand and belt out the lyrics but it was different than before because this time there were a few more people in the pub listening. Almost an audience. And later there'd be an actual audience. The idea was exhilarating. She never wanted to quit. She spun around in a circle, but Josh and Caleb had already started to make their way to the bar.

"I guess it's break time," Jamie said, noticing her reluctance to leave. "Besides, you should probably rest up those vocal cords. You were giving them a pretty major workout." He tucked his own guitar off to the side, flipped a couple of switches to shut down the gear and took Christy's hand to help her off the stage. She tried to ignore the flash of heat in her palm where he touched her, but then he released her and it was gone. *Maybe she imagined it?*

"I guess I could use a glass of water." It's not as though she had a choice anyway, so she might as well take a breather and rest. For the first time in the last few weeks, she found that she didn't want a glass of wine. She was too fired up from the high of singing.

They joined the others at the bar and ordered their drinks before taking a table close to the stage. "You're doing really great," Jamie said when they were settled. "I can't believe you've never performed before. Are you nervous?"

Nervous? She was nervous about a lot of things. And if she let herself really think about it, the nerves might overwhelm her, so instead she shook her head. "No. Not really. At least, I'm going to pretend I'm not." She took a deep drink, letting the cold water soothe her throat. "But truthfully, I'm totally freaking out."

Jamie laughed. "I knew it. But you hide it well."

"It's the craziest thing." She put the glass down hard and squirmed in her seat, energized once again. "The second I hold that microphone in my hand, it's like something comes over me and I feel…"

"Feel what?" He had one leg crossed, his hands behind his head while he watched her closely.

"Unstoppable." She nodded slowly. "Absolutely unstoppable."

"Well, whatever it is," Jamie chuckled and tipped his beer to his mouth, "you're doing awesome. The crowd is going to love you tonight. So just relax and go with it. You're going to rock it."

Rock it.

Never in her life had she done anything that could be described that way. She was in completely uncharted territory when it came to her life. And she was loving every minute of it.

She felt a flicker of guilt for not telling Mark about her singing, but at the same time, whenever she thought of telling him, it seemed wrong and the energy and enthusiasm was gone. As if just by bringing her husband into her new pastime, she was killing the part of it that made her feel alive.

No. She'd keep it a secret for a bit longer.

"Do you have anyone coming to watch?"

"What?" Jamie's question took her off guard. "Like watch the show?"

"That's usually how it's done. We play, people watch."

"Very funny." She shot him a look. "But considering I didn't even know I'd be singing tonight…no. I don't." It was a convenient excuse. Also, it was plausible.

"It's not too late." Jamie finished his beer and stood. "I have a few things to take care of, but I'll be back. Do you want anything to eat?"

Her stomach grumbled, but she was too excited to eat. "No." She shook her head. "I'm good. Thanks. I have a few things to take care of too."

As soon as Jamie left, Christy took her cell phone out of her purse. Two missed calls and a handful of text messages.

A few texts from Mark. They were pretty normal. Just asking about her day.

She fired a quick one back.

My day is good. I hope yours is. I won't be home for dinner. Enjoy your run.

He'd mentioned going for a long run with Aaron after the office, so she shouldn't feel too bad that she wouldn't be home. In fact, she didn't feel bad at all. Christy looked to the rest of her texts.

From Cam: *Call me. Now!*

From Drew: *Are you around later?*

Followed by another one from Drew: *I just spoke to Cam. Call me!*

Both missed calls were from Cam. She didn't bother listening to the voice mail, but instead called her friend directly.

"It's about time you answered me," Cam said as soon as she picked up.

"I called *you*."

"Whatever. Where are you?"

Christy looked around the pub. It shouldn't be a secret. In a few hours, it was most definitely not going to be a secret. "Well…you're not going to believe this, but—"

"Are you singing with the Lumber Kings tonight?"

"What?" Christy's mouth fell open and she immediately spun around in her seat as if there were a spy watching her and reporting on her every move. Her eyes landed on Ben and it all made sense. Not a spy. *Just a small town.*

"Well?" Cam said. "Are you actually singing tonight? Like with the band?"

Despite all the things she was thinking and everything she should be feeling, Christy smiled. "Yes." She whispered the word into the phone at first and then, louder, said it again. "Yes. I am singing. Can you believe it?" She stopped just short of squealing like she had when she was sixteen and landed the lead in *Grease*.

"No." Cam laughed. "I totally can't. I mean, I can. You were always super talented. But...wow, Christy. I had no idea you were singing again."

"I wasn't. And then I did and then...well, I can't even believe I'm singing tonight." She shook her head and for the first time let that fact sink in. *Really* sink in.

"I'm coming."

"No." Her focus shifted again to the phone and her friend on the other end. "You can't come."

"Yes, I can. And I am. We'll be there in time for the first set. Ben's saving us a table."

"Of course he is." Christy shook her head, but couldn't keep from smiling. Maybe it would be nice to have some friendly faces in the audience.

"Is Mark coming?"

A hot flash of guilt pierced her gut. She shook her head and then, realizing that Cam couldn't see her, said, "No. He won't be here. He has a long run tonight. I told you he was in training again, right?"

Cam ignored the question. "He's really not coming?"

"No. But it's fine." She didn't bother telling her friend that she still hadn't mentioned to her husband that she'd been singing with a band, let alone that she was performing that night. The truth was, if Mark knew about it, he wouldn't miss it and for some reason that she couldn't fully articulate, she didn't want Mark there. It was almost like if he were in the audience, it would be too real. And that was the last thing she needed. She was enjoying her little escape from reality way too much. Singing allowed her to forget about every terrible thing in her life. Having Mark in the audience would only remind her.

Across the bar, she saw Jamie. *Was he part of the reason that she didn't want Mark to come?*

In her heart, she knew he was. It wasn't fair and she shouldn't be thinking of Jamie like that, but she couldn't seem to help it. And if Mark came to watch and saw Jamie…would he be able to guess that they'd been flirting?

And that's all it had been. *Flirting.*

Harmless. But harmless or not, she enjoyed it. His attention made her feel good and she wasn't ready for that to end yet. Even if it was wrong.

As she watched, Jamie was joined by the other guys and Christy felt the pull to join them. "I should run, Cam. But I'll see you later, I guess."

"I'm looking forward to it."

Warmth and a genuine happiness spread through her. "So am I," she answered truthfully.

Chapter Eight

CAM HADN'T BEEN able to take her eyes off the stage, or more specifically, off Christy. From the moment the band struck up the first chord of the first song, she'd been riveted to her best friend standing in front of a full crowd, holding the microphone as though she'd done it every day of her life. She was a natural.

It wasn't until there was a short break between songs that Cam allowed herself to exhale the breath she must have been holding in anticipation and sit back in her seat.

"She's so good," Cam said to Evan, who raised his bottle of beer in agreement.

"I can't believe she's so calm up there," Drew said.

Cam had been thrilled when Drew and Eric had agreed to join them for the evening. Drew had warned her that they wouldn't be able to stay all night, but she was happy to get Eric out of the house and have a bit of normalcy. Not that Eric looked very normal, bundled up in a thick sweater and knit cap on a hot summer night, but it was good to see her friend's husband with a smile on his face as he enjoyed the music, too.

"I would be totally freaking out," Drew added. "I think I *am* freaking out for her."

"Me too." Cam laughed. "I didn't know I was so tense. But she's doing amazing."

"Right?"

The women quieted as Christy started singing again up on the stage.

Cam twisted in her seat so she was once again facing the stage and settled in to enjoy the entertainment. The Lumber Kings were great and she wasn't just being partial because it was Christy on the stage. They played a wide variety of songs everyone could sing and clap along with.

Christy looked stunning in her dark jeans and jade-green top that fluttered around her chest. The color accented her hair beautifully, and Cam couldn't remember the last time she'd seen her looking so confident.

She closed her eyes as she belted out the lyrics and Cam's heart swelled with pride. Cam was watching her friend so intently, she didn't miss the briefest moment when Christy opened her eyes and looked directly at the guitar player. Christy's lips twitched up in a coy little smile and she looked quickly away. It happened so quickly, Cam wasn't sure it had actually happened at all. But then she started paying attention, and it happened again. And then there was a wink from the guitar player.

Concerned, Cam glanced around the table at Evan and the others. *Had any of them noticed the interaction?* It didn't seem as though anyone else were bothered. She was likely overreacting. But Christy *had* been acting so strangely. And even more bizarre was the fact that Mark wasn't in the crowd to see his wife's big debut.

She was probably just seeing things, or it was part of a stage act. After all, Cam didn't know the first thing about performing on a stage. It was probably nothing. Even so, she made a note to talk to Christy as soon as she had a chance. With everything her friend had been through in the last few months, with the infertility treatments and the latest result, Cam should have been a better friend and paid closer attention to what Christy was going through.

However, Cam didn't get her chance to say anything during the intermission because after Christy came over to the table to say a quick hello and receive everyone's praise, she disappeared to sit with the rest of the band and go over the next set list.

"She's so great," Evan said as soon as Christy made her excuses and left them alone. "I'm so impressed. Who knew?"

"We knew." Drew laughed. "I mean, we all knew in high school. Remember when she sang the lead in the play? What was it again?"

"*Grease.*" Cam remembered well. "She was Sandy."

"How could I forget?" Drew smacked her forehead and laughed again. "Miss Sandra Dee. She was amazing."

"But not like this," Evan said. "This is awesome. What do you think, Eric?"

"Well, I don't remember the play. But I'm very impressed with this." He looked around the pub. "All of it."

Cam watched as Eric's gaze drifted to the bar where Ben, Eric's little brother, was tending bar. It was easy to forget that Eric and Drew hadn't been back to Timber Creek much since marrying and moving away. Eric had probably only been in his brother's pub a handful of times over the years.

"Your little bro did a pretty good job here, didn't he?" Evan asked.

"He really did." Eric nodded slowly. "I'm proud of him."

"You should tell him." Drew covered her husband's hand with her own. "I bet he'd like to hear it."

Cam watched the exchange with interest. The brothers weren't close. They hadn't been in years, but it hadn't always been that way. Growing up, they'd been tight despite the two-year age difference. Along with Evan, who'd spent more time with the Ross family than his own, the boys had spent all of their free time fishing, camping, and skiing in the back country. Things had changed during Eric's senior year, when he started dating Drew. Evan had recently confided in Cam that Ben had been in love with Drew since the second grade and as his best friend, he'd been sworn to secrecy, especially when Eric started to date her.

As one of Drew's oldest and best friends, Cam remembered well when Drew first started crushing on Eric and how she'd begged Ben, whom she'd only ever seen as a good friend, to please talk to his older brother about asking her out. Ben did as she requested; Eric asked her out, and they'd been together ever since.

Now, knowing that Ben had been in love with Drew, too, the distance between the brothers made sense. At least it *had* made sense. Now that Eric was home, and terminally ill, they still didn't seem to have mended any bridges between them. At least not in any kind of real way. Cam could see the concern in Drew's eyes.

They were running out of time.

"You're right." Eric smiled sweetly at his wife. "As usual, sweetie. And I will."

"He looks pretty busy," Evan said. "But I'll go see if he can spare a few minutes and—"

"No." Eric stopped him. "Not tonight. Not here. It's Christy's night."

"But you *will* tell him. Right, Eric?" Drew looked straight into her husband's eyes, and Cam couldn't help but feel as if she were intruding on a private moment between the two of them.

She turned to Evan and gave him a kiss on the cheek. Not for the first time since Drew and Eric had come back to town, she found herself more and more thankful for Evan and the love they shared together. Watching her friend's long, painful good-bye was heartbreaking, and Cam vowed never to take a single day with Evan for granted.

———

"THIS IS AMAZING." Christy tried to play it cool, but the second she walked into the staff room behind the kitchen, during their set break, she bounced up and down like a little girl. "I've never felt…I can't believe…did you see the crowd… how are you guys not freaking out?"

Josh laughed and handed her a bottle of water. "You're pretty cute. It's always like this."

"Well, not always," Caleb said. "Remember that time when no one showed up and we played to like three people?"

"Three?" Christy looked at the guys in horror. She just assumed that a packed room was normal. She thought she'd be nervous, but she was anything but. The crowd had fired her up. Invigorated her and given her the energy she needed. "I would die with three."

"You wouldn't die." Josh laughed. "But you are doing great. I don't know, guys…maybe if Grant doesn't sort out his stuff pretty soon, we might have a replacement singer."

Christy almost spat out her water. "Really?" She looked between all the guys. "Are you serious?"

Jamie nodded with a grin and Caleb agreed as well. "I mean, if you're up for it," he said. "We have some more dates planned and it would suck to cancel them because Grant's not available."

"It would," Josh said. "And I don't want to put any pressure on Grant. His dad's pretty sick," he said to Christy. It was the first time she'd heard a real explanation as to why the lead singer was missing. "Are you up for it, Christy?"

Was she?

"Absolutely!" She didn't even have to think about it. For the first time in months—hell, maybe years—she felt alive in a way she'd never felt before. For once she didn't have to think about babies or ovulation schedules, or temperatures, or injections, or any of the other details that had consumed her life. She didn't have to be Christy the patient, or Christy, Dr. Mark Thomas's wife. She could just be *Christy*. "I'm totally up for it."

They all raised their water bottles in a cheers and after a few minutes of discussing the details of the upcoming set, Josh and Caleb excused themselves out to the pub and she was alone with Jamie, who, up until that point, had been completely quiet about her joining the band.

They stood in silence for a few moments after the others left. An energy filled the air between them. Christy wanted to chalk it up to the excitement of the show, but she knew in her heart there was something more going on.

Finally, after what seemed like an eternity, Jamie spoke. "You really are fantastic out there." He held her gaze in a way that felt very intimate. She blinked, but didn't look away. "I really like watching you," he continued. "You came alive out there. Incredible. Really."

He looked away first, focusing on his water bottle.

"And you think I'd be a good addition to the band?" she asked. "I mean, not permanently…but…just to fill in, like Josh said."

Jamie nodded slowly, his eyes once more locked on hers. "You're perfect." He reached out and put his hand on hers. "In fact," he said. "I think you're—"

"You two ready to go?" Caleb burst into the staff room and Christy jumped back in surprise.

She ran her hand through her hair and nodded. "Totally. Just give me five minutes in the restroom." Before Jamie could say anything, or she could be left alone with him again, she turned and squeezed past the men and into the refuge of the ladies' room.

She didn't have much time to compose herself and she definitely didn't have enough time to figure out what had just happened between her and Jamie. But *nothing* had happened. That was the thing. The only thing she needed to focus on.

By the time she fixed her hair and touched up her makeup a little, she was calmer. At least calm enough to go back out there, forget about the not-really moment she'd just had with Jamie, and sing her heart out for the second set. And that's exactly what she did.

Christy surprised herself with the amount of energy she had to perform all night. She'd watched plenty of live acts before, and she'd always been impressed with the singer's stamina, but now she finally understood. It wasn't stamina at all; it was the pure excitement of entertaining for other people that drove her. By the time they'd sang their last song and then another when the remaining crowd demanded an encore, Christy was sure she still had more in her left to give, but Jamie and the other guys insisted that she would crash as soon as she sat down.

They insisted on sending her home right after the last set, instead of helping them tidy up. They'd return the next day to gather their equipment, so there wasn't much to do anyway. At least that's what Jamie told her.

She wasn't in a position to argue; besides, there was something lingering between them and she didn't think that one in the morning after such an emotionally charged night was a good time to figure out what that might be. So she gathered up her purse, said her good-nights and walked out to the parking lot with Cam and Evan, who had stayed until the very end.

"You were so amazing." Cam squeezed her tight into a hug. "I know I keep saying it, but you really were." She released her and Evan pulled her into a hug next.

"I am completely blown away, Christy." He gave her a quick squeeze before he stepped back. "Super impressed. Hopefully next time Mark can come down too?"

Christy blanched, but if either of her friends noticed, they didn't say anything. "Who said there'd be a next time?"

"Oh, I have a pretty good feeling there will be." Cam smiled. "Are you good to get home?"

"Of course." Christy opened her car door and put her purse inside. "Thank you both for coming. I'll talk to you soon, Cam." She blew them a kiss, before climbing into her car and driving home.

The house was dark when she pulled into the driveway, just the way she knew it would be. Mark would have fixed a quick plate of leftovers after his run, grabbed a shower and likely fallen asleep watching a documentary on Netflix. She sat in the driveway for a few minutes and stared at the sleeping house. As soon as she went inside, the high from the night would disappear.

She'd just be Christy again. *Barren wife of Doctor Mark Thomas.*

The idea made her want to cry in frustration.

She waited as long as she could. It was doubtful that any of her neighbors would be out and about at that time of night, but if anyone happened to see her sitting in her driveway, it would look strange.

With a sigh, she grabbed her purse, quietly shut the car door behind her and made her way up the walk to the front door. She didn't turn on any lights. She crept as silently as she could down the hallway to the master bedroom. She paused in the doorway and stared at the sleeping form of her husband illuminated by the moonlight from the open window.

She had loved Mark ever since she could remember. They'd gone through school together, starting in preschool, but it hadn't been until they were lab partners in grade eight biology that she looked at him in any way besides a school mate. She'd been terrified of dissecting the frog that was pinned to the board in front of them. She'd been stressed out about it for days, barely sleeping for fear of having nightmares of the poor creature jumping off the table.

The day of the lab assignment, Mark saw how freaked out she was and moments before she plunged the scalpel into the frog's puffy belly, he'd put his hand over hers and stopped it from shaking.

"I'll do it," he said.

"But…we're both supposed to—" She was mortified by the hot tears that threatened to spill over her cheeks.

"Don't worry," he whispered. "I'll take care of it. I like this type of thing."

"You *like* it?" She dropped the scalpel and stared at him. "Seriously?"

He nodded and grinned, his mouth full of shiny braces. "I'm going to be a doctor." He was so proud of himself, and so confident that Christy believed him. "I'll do all the cuts when Mr. Muldoon isn't looking. Don't worry. You just take the notes."

Christy smiled, relieved, and looked at him with new eyes as he expertly handled the specimen.

She'd been looking at him with those same eyes ever since.

Until now.

As she stood in the doorway to their bedroom, watching the man she loved, for the first time, she realized that things had changed. *Really* realized it. She was no longer looking at Mark the same way she always had.

She'd disappointed him in the most devastating way. He'd sacrificed so much for her, for them, to have the lifestyle they had. He'd worked so hard so she could be the mother to their children and spend her days raising his babies, and she hadn't been able to give him that. The emotion crashed through her and she covered her mouth with her hand to stifle the cry that finally threatened to burst from inside her.

It killed her to know that she'd never feel his child growing inside her. He'd never have the chance to teach his son how to throw a ball. They'd never be able to look down at the tiny face and wonder whether their child was going to get his smarts from his dad or inherit her mother's gift for baking. *He deserved more.*

Her body ached with the need to feel his arms around her. More than anything, she wanted him to tell her that it would be okay and that he loved her. Yet she couldn't go to him.

But why?

Despite her best efforts to stop them, a cry escaped her throat and Mark shifted in the bed.

"Christy?" He pulled himself up to sitting and ran his hands through his hair, still mostly asleep. "What are you doing?"

She stared at him while a tear slipped down her cheek.

"Come to bed, honey. What time is it?"

She took a step into the room. "I need to tell you something."

He sat up straighter and reached out for her. She didn't take his hand but sat on the mattress close to him. "What's going on? You're scaring me. Christy, what's going on?"

Tears fell unchecked now. "Mark, I'm so sorry."

"For what?" He reached for her, but she shook her head.

She needed to tell him everything she was feeling inside before she burst. It was long past time. He deserved to know.

"I'm sorry I can't give you a baby." The words felt like knives to her soul. "I'm sorry I failed. That my body—"

"Stop." He took her hands in his and squeezed. "You know this isn't your fault. You know—"

"No." She cut him off. It didn't matter how many times the doctors went through their history, and the challenges they both faced. They could tell her a thousand times, but it didn't change the fact that it was *her* body that had failed to carry any of the pregnancies. It was *her* who had failed. It was her fault. And living with that was killing her. "You deserve better. You deserve to have a—"

"Stop." He was angry now, the sleepiness gone completely from his voice. "I won't listen to you talk like that. You know better, Christy." He shook her hands a little until she looked at him but she immediately had to look away from the hurt in his eyes. Even if he didn't mean to, it was there. He didn't have to say it; she *knew* how disappointed he was in her. "You know that's not how this works. We're in this together and there are other things. We can talk about—"

"No."

"No?"

She shook her head. "No," she said again. She'd been thinking about their "options" but they all felt so daunting and there were still no guarantees. They could spend thousands of dollars and years of their lives and still never have a baby. And it would still be her fault. Logical or not, the blame was intense.

Mark didn't wait for her to elaborate. Instead, he pulled her into a tight embrace. "Christy, I love you. I don't blame you for any of this. It's not you, honey. It's just…it's just not fair. I'm sorry, baby. I am."

She let him hold her as her tears soaked the t-shirt he always wore to bed. But instead of feeling comforted by his arms, they only made her feel worse. He stroked her hair and murmured comforting words in her ear but none of them made any reasonable impact. She still felt empty inside and miles away from how she'd felt earlier that night on stage when life and vitality coursed through her. It was the perfect time for Christy to tell Mark about her singing. She knew she couldn't keep it a secret from him much longer anyway. But still, she couldn't bring herself to share with her husband.

How could she possibly tell him that the only time she felt okay anymore was when she was pretending to be someone else? How could she possibly look into his eyes and tell him that whenever she was with him, all she felt was an over-whelming amount of pain and disappointment?

She couldn't.

So instead she lay down next to him, still in her clothes, and let him hold her while the tears that wouldn't stop falling soaked the pillow beneath her head as she drifted off to sleep, only inches away from her husband in body but miles away in her heart.

Chapter Nine

THE NIGHT before had been intense to say the least. After Christy woke him up and confessed to him how much guilt she was feeling, he hadn't been able to sleep. No matter what he'd said to her, it hadn't seemed to make any difference and it killed him inside. Their infertility *wasn't* her fault.

Did he make her feel like it was?

How could she be holding so much hurt and blame and he didn't even know?

Because she wouldn't talk to him. He'd tried more than once to talk to her about everything they'd been through, but she'd kept putting him off.

After Christy finally had cried herself to sleep, Mark had laid there with her in his arms, going over all the ways he could make it better for her. For both of them. And despite a sleepless night, the only answer he could come up with was just letting her know how much he loved her and always would.

Together, they could get through anything. Even this. He'd given her the space she'd wanted, but no more. He needed to close the distance between them and they'd work through this rough patch—together.

More than anything, Mark had wanted to cancel his patients and spend the day with his wife, talking over everything, but he couldn't. His day had been packed with back-to-back patients, a number of phone consults with experts, and various other things that Sarah had scheduled for him. He'd tried calling Christy a few times throughout the day, but she never answered. He'd left voice mails telling her that he loved her and everything would be okay.

By the time his last patient left, he was more than a little anxious to get home to Christy. They had so much to talk about and despite the fact that he'd seen her in the middle of the night—she'd still been sleeping when he'd left for work—it felt like way too long since he'd seen her face.

Sarah had managed to make them reservations for the next night at Riverside Grill and he wanted to talk to her about his idea of heading out of town for a little romantic escape. They were long overdue for a little time together, just the two of them. It would be good to get away from everything so they could focus on the hurt and start to take the steps they needed to in order to work through it.

"Honey?" Mark left his computer bag at the front door and moved straight into the kitchen. "Christy? Are you home?" The house was oddly quiet. Christy's car was in the driveway, but there were none of the usual signs of her. Normally the sounds of the radio filled the house, or the delicious smell of one of her baked creations.

She wasn't in the kitchen. A spark of worry flickered to life in his gut, which was ridiculous because he had no reason to be worried about her. Except…he was. Especially after everything she'd said to him the night before. Just another reason why a weekend away was such a good idea. They needed the reconnection more than ever.

"Christy?" Mark moved down the hall into their bedroom and froze in the doorway. "What are you doing, honey?"

She was sitting on their bed, her back to him, staring out the window. She didn't move when he walked across the room. He laid his hand on her shoulder and sat next to her. "Christy? You're scaring me. What's going on? Are you okay?"

She turned to look at him. She'd been crying. *Maybe she hadn't stopped from the night before.* The thought hit him hard.

Her eyes were red and her cheeks were blotchy, the way they always got when she was worked up about something.

The flicker in his gut roared to a full flame. *Something was definitely wrong.*

"Talk to me, Christy. What's going on?"

She shook her head a little. "I can't do this anymore, Mark."

"What? What can't you do?" *Babies?* They didn't have to talk about their options right away. He'd respected her need to wait. Until the night before, he hadn't brought it up at all. It wasn't important. They could wait until the time was right. He told her as much. "We don't have to try for a baby right now, Christy. We don't need to even discuss it. There are no timetables on these—"

"No," she interrupted him. "I can't do *this*." She lifted a hand and pointed to him and then back at herself.

Still, Mark was confused. Nothing made sense. "This?"

"Us, Mark." She squeezed her eyes shut for what felt like forever. "I can't do *us* anymore. At least not right now. I think we should take a break from…well, from everything."

"A break?" He wasn't hearing her properly. The room spun and a roaring white noise filled his ears. "From us? That doesn't make sense, Christy. We're great. We're—"

"Are we?" She turned on the bed and stared at him. "Are we great, Mark? Because I don't think we are. I'm not." She shook her head and stood, walking to the window. "I'm not great, Mark. I can't breathe. I feel like I'm suffocating. Nothing is how it's supposed to be and the worst part is, I don't even know anymore what that's supposed to be."

"Christy, don't do this." His entire body was numb as he watched her. He couldn't feel his hands. *This couldn't be happening. She was the love of his life and…sure, they'd been a little distant lately. But the night before they'd… She wanted a divorce? A separation? A…what?* "We can figure this out," he pleaded. "Together. Let's go to counseling. I know there are a few great therapists in town and together we can…we don't need a *break.*" He shook his head as he said the word. It was unthinkable.

"No, Mark. I'm sorry." She clasped her hands together in front of her. "I don't think this is something we can figure out together. At least, not yet. I know it's hard to understand. But I need to figure things out for myself. I need to get to know myself again and I don't think I can do that with you here. At least not right now."

"You want me to leave?" He stood but didn't walk toward her. "My house?"

"*Our* house, Mark. And I think it's best. But if you want me to leave, I will. I'll go stay with—"

"No." He held up a hand. "I'll go. If that's what you want, I'll go." Like a zombie, completely detached from his body, he turned and walked to the closet, where he pulled out a duffel bag. "I don't understand what's happening, Christy. I love you," he said after he'd packed a few things. He wasn't even sure what he'd put in the bag. It didn't matter. Nothing mattered but the woman in front of him.

"I'm sorry, Mark." Tears streamed down her cheeks now. "I love you, too. So much."

"Then why?" He dropped his bag and ran to her. He clasped her arms with his hands and shook her a little until she looked at him. "If you love me, why are you doing this? There are other—"

"There's no other way, Mark. I don't know who I am anymore when I'm with you."

Her eyes were so full of pain, Mark wanted more than anything to take it away for her. But he couldn't. Because even if she'd let him, he realized, he had no idea how.

He dropped his arms. Not because he was giving up, but because he had no idea what else to do. "I love you, Christy. And that's why I'm going to leave. But you need to understand something."

She nodded.

"I love you more than I love myself, so I'll give you some space if that's what you think you need. But I'm not quitting. I'm not quitting on you or me. And I'm definitely not quitting on us. Because one thing I know for sure is that no matter what, I'll love you. We've been through a lot and I understand if that's been unsettling to you—how could it not be? But there's one more thing you need to remember."

She looked at him.

"None of this is your fault, Christy. I can't make you believe it, but I hope to hell you do." Her eyes squeezed together, as if she couldn't even bear to hear him say it. "Take your time, and rediscover yourself if that's what you need. I'm still going to love you like crazy."

Christy was sobbing by the time he finished talking.

They stood like that in their bedroom, the room Christy had decorated so lovingly just for them. Where they'd made love more times than he could count. Where he'd held her in his arms night after night. Where they'd tried and failed to make a baby. Their room.

Finally, Mark dropped his chin to his chest and took a breath. "I'll leave," he said softly. "But I'm not going anywhere."

HE HAD no idea where to go, but somehow Mark found himself parked in front of the Creekside Inn. It was the only hotel in town, but that's not why he was there.

Mark left his bag in the car and walked into the timber-framed lobby. Normally he spent a moment admiring the place. The hand-stripped log beams that ran the length of the ceiling never failed to impress. Aaron's grandfather had hand-built the hotel when Timber Creek was still an active logging town, determined to create a beautiful building that blended into the landscape and could be the focal point of town.

He'd done that.

But Mark wasn't looking around today. He wasn't looking anywhere except the check-in desk, where thankfully Aaron was talking to an employee. As if his friend had sensed his presence, Aaron looked up and straight at Mark. He must have looked as terrible as he felt because a moment later, Aaron was around the side of the desk and grabbing Mark's arm.

"What's going on? Are you okay? Is Christy okay?" He led Mark to one of the overstuffed couches that sat next to the large stone fireplace at the opposite end of the lobby. "What happened, Mark?"

"She left me."

"She what?" Aaron blinked. "Christy? She left you?"

"No." Mark shook his head. "She didn't leave me. She kicked me out."

"Kicked you out? You're not making any sense."

"Yes." Mark nodded, his movements mechanical and stiff. "She asked me to leave." He blinked until Aaron came into focus for the first time. "I don't know what happened, Aaron. I came home from the office. She was sitting on the bed, crying. And then she told me she needed a break from everything."

Aaron didn't answer right away. He scrubbed his hands over his face. "I don't understand."

"*You* don't understand?"

Mark stared into the fireplace at the stack of logs that was ready to light on a cold night. He couldn't make sense of anything. He couldn't formulate a single thought that made any amount of sense of the situation he somehow found himself in.

"What am I going to do, Aaron? She's my life." He dropped his head to his chest, and right there in the lobby of the Creekside Inn, started to sob as the reality of what had just happened hit him.

"Come on." He'd only been crying a few seconds, when Aaron pulled him up by the shoulders and led him through the corridors to the suite at the back of the building that Aaron called home. "Sit down."

Mark did as he was told.

"I'm going to give you two choices, man."

Mark looked up.

"We're going to get blind drunk. Or go for a hard run. Your choice."

More than anything, Mark wanted to drink and he wasn't a drinker. He couldn't remember the last time he'd had more than a couple of beers, let alone gotten drunk.

"Drink."

"You're sure?" Aaron raised his eyebrows. "I'm game if you are."

"No." Mark shook his head. "Let's run."

It was the right choice.

Aaron nodded. "There's nothing saying we can't do both."

It was a sad attempt at a joke and Mark didn't laugh. But the tears stopped. He swiped at his face, annoyed and disappointed in himself that he'd cried in front of his buddy. Not that Aaron would care. In fact, Christy would have told him that it was a good thing to show emotion in front of his guy friends.

Christy.

He shook his head. Everything reminded him of her. How could it not? She literally was his entire life. But he needed to stop. He needed to put her out of his head, at least for a few minutes. Long enough to work up a sweat and burn off some energy.

Ten minutes later, that was exactly what they were doing.

Mark pushed his body and ran fast and, just as Aaron promised, hard. He'd chosen a hiking trail on the edge of town that led almost straight up a mountain to a waterfall. It was a sharp incline that had Mark's muscles screaming.

It was perfect.

He didn't slow his pace but put his head down and pushed through the discomfort of his quad muscles, the noise in his head that kept repeating his last conversation with his wife, and the intense pain in his heart that threatened to stop him in his tracks.

The trail was too intense for talking, which was perfect because there was nothing Aaron could have said to him. Just his presence was all Mark needed. If he could think of anything but his crumbling marriage, he would have been able to appreciate his friend and Aaron's total lack of complaining for being pushed straight up a mountain trail at such a blistering pace.

Finally, they reached the top and Mark collapsed onto himself, bending at the waist and gasping for breath.

Aaron appeared next to him and handed him a water bottle. "Drink. Now."

In his haste to get out on the trail, Mark had completely forgotten about hydration. Another reason that Aaron was literally the best friend a guy could ask for.

Mark did as he was told. When they'd both caught their breath and stretched out their muscles enough so they wouldn't seize, they sat down on the cool grass by the waterfall.

He watched the water hit the rocks below and swirl into a

pool at the bottom before spilling out into the stream a little farther down.

"That was intense," Aaron said after a moment. "Do you feel better now?"

His muscles ached, his heart was still beating hard in his chest, and his mind hadn't stilled at all. "No." Mark didn't hesitate. "Let's get drunk."

Chapter Ten

"YOU DID WHAT?" Cam stared at her friend. It was a few days after Christy's singing debut at the Log and Jam and the women were doing a little shopping. But after what Christy had just told her, Cam was pretty sure they both needed a glass of wine more than they needed a new outfit.

"I asked him to leave."

Christy turned so Cam couldn't see her face, but she didn't miss the waver in her friend's voice.

"You're going to need to back up a beat." Cam took the blouse out of Christy's hand and placed it back on the rack before she turned to look at her friend. "You asked him to leave? Mark? Your husband, Mark?"

"Yes."

"The love of your life, Mark?"

Christy sucked her bottom lip into her mouth. "Yes."

"The man you've loved since the eighth grade, Mark?"

"Yes." She squeezed her eyes shut and tried to turn away, but Cam grabbed her arm.

"What the hell, Christy? What's going on? Did something happen?" The only reason Cam could possibly conceive of for

Cam to ask Mark to leave was if he was unfaithful, or God forbid— "Did he hurt you? So help me, if he laid one hand on—"

"No!" Christy shook her off. "Of course he didn't hurt me. You know him, Cam. Do you really think he'd ever touch me like that?" She shook her head, but Cam wasn't letting her off the hook.

"Of course not," she said. "But I know you, too, and I never thought I'd ever hear you say the words that you asked him to leave, Christy. What the hell is going on? He wasn't unfaithful, was he?" Even as she asked the question, Cam knew the answer. Mark would never cheat on his wife. He loved her more than anything in the world, which was why none of what Christy was saying made any sense at all.

"No." She shook her head sadly and walked over to the rack with some low-cut, body-hugging dresses. Cam watched as she picked one up and held it up to her body. It was a nice dress. A sexy dress. And a dress that Christy would never wear.

But that was before.

Before Christy had undergone this crazy transformation. First her hair, then her clothes and then…

"Oh shit."

Christy turned and looked at Cam, who stood with her mouth hanging open. "What?"

"Is this all part of…"

"What?"

"You know."

"No." Christy put her hands on her hips. "I don't know. Is this all part of what, Cam?"

She took a deep breath and exhaled slowly. "You know what I mean, Christy. Your hair, your clothes…is this like a mid-life crisis or—"

"Really? Are you serious right now?" Christy slammed the garment she was holding back onto the rack with so much force Cam thought it might tip over. "Are you seriously asking me if I'm having some sort of mental breakdown that would cause me to make such a drastic decision? Really?"

Cam thought about it for a minute. And ultimately decided on the truth. "Yes," she said. "That's what I'm asking." She held up a hand to stop her friend's rebuttal before it came. "And before you say anything else or get mad, I just want to say that the only reason I'm asking is because it just seems so crazy, Christy. It's a lot of change all at once."

Christy opened her mouth to say something but closed it again when Cam kept talking.

"First the hair—which I love, by the way. And then the new clothes. Also, nice. I like the new look, I really do. But then you started singing." She tilted her head to gain Christy's silence this time. She could tell her friend was chomping at the bit to say something, but Cam needed to finish what she had to say. "And I *love* that you're singing. I do. It was absolutely amazing to see you up on that stage, Christy. It really was. You are incredible. But that's not what worries me." She dropped her hand and her voice. "And I *am* worried, Christy." It was an unbelievable understatement, but Cam didn't know how to put into words what she was feeling for her friend.

"You don't need to be worried." Christy dropped her arms to her sides. "I loved Thursday night. It was probably the most fun I'd had in...I don't know...years, maybe. And isn't that something to think about, Cam? I can't actually remember the last time I had so much fun. I'm not even forty and I feel like I'm dried up, worn out, and all my life is gone."

"Christy, that's not true."

"Isn't it?" She shook her head and for a moment, Cam thought she might cry. Instead, Christy straightened her shoulders and stood up straight. "For my whole life, I wanted one thing. To be a mom. And now that it's not going to happen, I don't know who I'm supposed to be. And I really don't know who I am. I forgot how to have fun, Cam. I forgot how to be *me*. And that night, on that stage, it all came back. Hell, every time I pick up the microphone, it comes back."

Cam nodded. "I get that. It's probably a lot like how I feel when I pick up a camera." Christy nodded and she even got a glimmer of a small smile. "But I don't understand why you had to ask Mark to leave. Is it because he wasn't there last night? You said he was running."

Cam remembered hearing about the last time Mark trained for an ultra-marathon. It was before she'd moved back to Timber Creek, but Christy would send long text messages about how hard it was to be a *runner's widow* and lose her husband to the trails for days at a time. It had been hard on them and their marriage. She could absolutely understand being upset with Mark for choosing a run over her singing debut. Not for something so important. In fact, the more Cam thought about it, the more she thought that it didn't seem like something Mark would do.

He'd never miss something so important.

"He doesn't know," Cam said. It wasn't a question and Christy didn't deny it. She didn't say anything. After a moment of silence, Cam asked, "Why didn't you tell him, Christy?"

A tear slid down her cheek, and then another as Christy shook her head. "I don't know. I really don't. It just didn't feel right. I was so happy singing with Jamie, and it's not like I was doing anything wrong, but I guess I just felt like as soon as I told him, it wouldn't be fun anymore. It's like two totally separate lives, Cam. When I'm singing, I'm...free. Alive. I'm *me*. And when I'm with Mark, I'm...I'm so unhappy." She shook her head and refused to look at Cam. "Whenever I'm with him, I can't help feeling like I let him down, that even if he doesn't say so, he resents me. I know it doesn't make any sense."

"No. It doesn't." Cam crossed the distance between them

and pulled her friend in for a hug. "It doesn't make any sense at all. And he doesn't resent you." Cam didn't know whether that was true or not, but it felt like the right thing to say. Besides, she just couldn't imagine Mark thinking that about Christy.

"I love him, Cam."

"I know you do." She patted her back.

"I just don't know what I want anymore." Christy pulled back and sniffed loudly. "It's like a second chance at life and I don't know anymore how I want it to go."

"Do you want to sing?" What Cam really wanted to ask her friend was if Jamie, the man she'd mentioned, who was obviously the guitar player she'd noticed during the show, had anything to do with her decision. But it wasn't the right time.

Christy nodded so enthusiastically, her red hair flopped around her face. "I do. And the guys asked me if I'd play a few more gigs with them."

"Gigs?"

"It's what you call a show." She was so excited, just talking about singing and performing, that Cam could see how important it was to her. "Their usual lead singer is having some family issues and instead of cancelling the gigs, they asked if I could perform with them. It'll mean a few overnights to some of the towns around here, but nothing too major and since I don't have anything else going on…"

"Why not?"

"Right?" Christy's smile was full and genuine this time.

"Right." Cam nodded. "I think it'll be good for you. But…"

"No." Christy stopped her. "No buts. Please. Just let me have this."

There were a million things Cam wanted to say and a million more things she wanted to ask her. Instead, Cam forced a smile and tried to be happy for her friend, even though she couldn't even begin to understand what she was doing.

SHE NEVER SHOULD HAVE GONE out shopping with Cam. She was in no state to be around people, not even her best friends. Maybe especially not her best friends. Christy knew that Cam would never be able to understand what she was doing with Mark.

Tears pricked at her eyes at the thought of her husband and not for the first time in the last twenty-four hours, she wondered whether she'd done the right thing.

It had been hurtful and selfish to do what she'd done. She knew that. But she hadn't been lying when she'd told him that she felt like she was suffocating whenever she was with him.

She was.

And now, as she walked through her empty house, she could breathe again. She stopped in the hallway and inhaled a full breath. She let the oxygen fill her lungs completely before exhaling slowly.

She'd read on the online forums for infertility that she'd once been an active part of that many couples who'd been unsuccessful with their treatments drifted apart and marriages ended. Not because they didn't love each other, but because they simply couldn't navigate their lives and who they were supposed to be after going through something so all-consuming that resulted in a disappointment that was so incredibly devastating. At the time, she'd brushed over those personal stories, focusing instead on the tales of success and happiness. She'd been so sure that would be her.

For most of her treatments, she'd stayed optimistic, doing nothing but sending positive energy into the universe. It wasn't until the very end of the last treatment where she began to let herself believe that her story might not have a happy ending.

She glanced down the hall to the bedroom door that had been closed for the last few months. That was to have been the baby's room. She'd allowed herself to gather a few things over the years. A crib and change table. A few outfits. The walls were a pale yellow with framed pictures of cute baby zoo animals on them.

It was beautiful and perfect. And heartbreaking.

Christy turned away from the door and headed into the master. After her disastrous shopping trip with Cam, she'd gone off on her own and picked up a few things.

The room felt sad and stale, so she threw open the window and let the fresh summer air flow into the space. Then she plugged her phone into the portable speaker she'd just bought and cranked up some feel-good tunes.

She sang as she worked at stripping the bed sheets. She opened her packages and remade the bed in the bright orange and pink floral sheets she'd bought and threw on the new crisp white duvet. She finished it off with some matching orange and pink throw pillows and stood back.

It was perfect. Mark preferred grays and blacks in his bedding. She'd never cared before, not really. He rarely asked for anything when it came to how the house was decorated, so she'd complied and decorated the rest of the room with framed black-and-white floral images. It was crisp and clean.

But now it was bright and alive. And perfect.

She was just about to turn her attention to the ensuite bathroom and the new towels she'd bought when her phone rang. Because it was plugged into the speaker, the sound was amplified in the room and impossible to ignore.

When she saw the caller, a FaceTime call from Amber, she smiled and answered.

A moment later, Amber's face appeared on the screen.

"Hey there."

"Hey yourself," Christy said.

"Oh my God! Look at your hair!" Amber's mouth fell open and Christy laughed. She'd forgotten that Amber hadn't seen her since her mini transformation. "Holy shit, girl. It looks great. Turn around, let me see."

Christy did as she was told, hamming it up for her friend. "You like it?"

"I love it. You look great."

Amber was sitting too close to the screen for Christy to get a really good look at her, but Amber looked tired, which in and of itself wasn't unusual. She was always working too hard, getting too little sleep and not taking care of herself. But her eyes looked different. Big. And busy, darting all over the place.

"Thanks, sweetie," Christy said and added, "How are you doing? You look—"

"I'm fine. Working too much and keeping all the balls in the air. You know how it is."

She didn't.

"So tell me," Amber said. "What the hell is going on over there?"

Of course, Cam had probably called Amber and told her everything. "Cam called you?"

"You know she did." Amber blinked rapidly. "What's going on, hon? With Mark?"

"I really don't want to talk about it, Amber. Really." She propped the phone up and started unwrapping the new towels she'd bought in matching orange and pink colors. "I just need a little time and some breathing room to figure out what I'm going to do. I know it doesn't make sense to anyone else, but—"

"It makes sense to me."

"Pardon?" Christy looked back to the phone. "It does?"

"Hell yeah it does. You've been through a lot. Give yourself a little time."

"But…Mark?"

Amber nodded. "Mark is an amazing man. And he loves you. He'll give you anything you want, including space. You know that."

She did. "I just don't want to hurt him." Christy dropped her head and swiped at her eyes, determined not to cry again.

"Which is why you owe it to both of you to take a bit of time to sort yourself out. It's not fair to either of you to be unhappy."

Christy could hardly believe what she was hearing. "You get it."

Amber laughed. "Of course I do."

"But you've never been…"

"Married? In a relationship?" Amber finished the sentence for her. "Nope. I most definitely have not. But I pay attention. You don't get to be a successful lawyer if you don't pay attention to people, you know? For what it's worth, I do think you're doing the right thing."

"You do?"

"There's just one thing." Amber held up a finger. "Never forget how much he loves you and how much you love him. That type of love doesn't come along every day, and it's not something to be treated lightly. Or thrown away."

She nodded and was about to tell Amber how she agreed completely, when her phone buzzed with an incoming call.

It was Jamie.

"Are you getting another call?"

"Yes, but…" She hesitated, unsure of whether or not she should take it. Something had happened between them at the bar the other night, and she didn't know how she was supposed to feel about it. Or how she *wanted* to feel.

"Take it," Amber said. "I have to run anyway. My to-do list is insane. Talk to you later, hon. Love you."

She was gone before Christy could protest.

She stared at Jamie's name on her screen and, with a deep breath, answered the call. "Hey, Jamie."

"Hey. I just wanted to touch base with you after the other night."

The other night? Did he mean the moment they'd shared between them? Or was he talking about Mark moving out? Not moving out so much as…it didn't matter. Besides, he wouldn't know that. She shook her head to clear it. "The other night? What do you mean?"

"The gig? Performing…remember? It was your first time in front of a real audience." There was a lightness in his voice, and Christy couldn't help but laugh at herself.

"Oh yeah."

"Don't tell me you forgot already?"

"No." She shook her head and tossed her hair behind her head. "I most definitely didn't forget. It's just been a little… well, it's been a busy few days." That was a huge understatement. "But no," she said, refocusing on the conversation. "I didn't forget at all."

"Good. Because the guys wanted me to check with you if you were serious about coming on our tour with us."

"Tour?" That sounded like a whole lot more than just a few gigs in some neighboring towns.

Jamie laughed. "Okay, it's not a *tour* so much. But it sounds way cooler when we call it that, don't you think?"

She agreed with a laugh. "But it's just a few gigs?"

"Five, to be exact. We'd be gone about a week. You still up for it?"

She looked around her newly decorated space. A week wasn't really that long and it might be a good opportunity for her to get that distance she was looking for so she could figure out what it was she really wanted. "Yes." She nodded. "I'm totally up for it."

"Good. I'm glad to hear it." He paused for a minute. "I'll email you the details. We leave Thursday."

"Thursday? Like *this* Thursday?" That was only a few days away.

"That's okay?"

She bit her bottom lip. "It's fine."

They ended the call and Christy dropped her phone on the bed in front of her.

Things were moving so quickly. In less than seventy-two hours, she'd performed with the band for the first time, asked her husband to move out, and now was preparing to go on tour. Christy's mind spun.

She was filled with nerves and excitement. But there was something else, too. The underlying sadness that never seemed to leave her alone was still there. Being apart from Mark hadn't made her feel any better.

Only worse.

What good was being excited about something as amazing as her first real tour with a band when you couldn't even talk to your best friend about it? Her eyes drifted to the framed photograph on the nightstand.

It was taken on their wedding day. Mark insisted on keeping it on his side of the bed because he said it was his favorite shot of the night. The photographer had caught them in their first dance. They were staring so intently into each other's eyes that they hadn't noticed anything else going on around them. Christy remembered that moment as if it were yesterday. She remembered thinking that she was the luckiest woman in the world to be able to go through her life with this amazing man by her side, loving her and supporting her through it all.

Had things really changed so much?

She put the photo down and wiped a tear off her cheek.

She needed to talk to Mark.

Chapter Eleven

SOMEHOW MARK HAD MANAGED to make it through the weekend. True to his word, Aaron had gotten him drunk after their hard run. Not that it had helped. He should have known better. There was a reason why he didn't drink much.

Alcohol only made him feel worse. He wasn't even one of those people who could use drink to numb his feelings for a few hours. It just amplified everything.

After the one night of attempting to drown his feelings, he focused on running for the rest of the weekend. If he wasn't running, he was sleeping, only remembering to eat when Aaron put food in front of him.

The last thing he wanted to be doing that Monday was working, but he had patients who depended on him. And he knew better than to think that their illnesses and medical issues could be put on hold just because his world was falling apart.

After a morning seeing patients, he was almost thankful that Sarah had scheduled an in-house visit with Eric Ross. He'd just seen the man the previous week, but Sarah said there'd been a change over the weekend, and Drew had called and requested that Mark stop by to see him.

Mark had never been to the little house that Eric and Drew had rented. It was just down the street from where the Ross brothers grew up, their parents still living in their childhood home. Mark guessed they'd chosen the location to be close enough for them to help, but far enough away to have their privacy during Eric's last days.

He still couldn't believe that Eric was terminal. Despite his training, it never failed to shake him when a patient faced death. Particularly one so young. It just didn't seem fair. But if there was one thing Mark knew about disease, it was that nothing about it was fair.

He knocked on the door, not wanting to ring the bell in case Eric was resting. A moment later, a much older-looking version of Drew answered the door.

"Drew?"

"Thank you for coming, Mark." She backed away and gestured him inside. "It's been a rough weekend."

"What's going on?" He stopped short of asking her if she'd been taking care of herself throughout everything that was going on. She obviously didn't need that discussion at that moment, but he made a mental note to talk with her about self-care very soon.

"He was doing so well last week so we thought it wouldn't be a bad idea to sneak in a little date night."

"Sounds like it would be fine." Mark followed Drew into the house.

"I don't know if it was too much, or what, but when he woke up on Saturday morning, he just seemed weaker. More tired. Like…I don't know. Do you think it's…"

Mark put his hand on her shoulder and squeezed. "How about you go get yourself a cup of tea while I go examine him? Then we can all talk."

She nodded. "Austin is sitting with him." She managed a small smile at the mention of their young son. "He's *reading* to his dad." She made air quotes with her fingers. "Just send him out. Tell him I have cookies."

"Sounds like a plan." Mark chuckled. "And maybe later I can have one of those cookies, too?"

"Of course." She pointed down the hall. "It's the first door on the left. It should be open. Let me know if you need anything."

The house was small and it didn't take him long to find the bedroom. Mark stood in the door and watched the scene in front of him, hesitant to break it up.

Drew and Eric's son, Austin, sat cross-legged on the bed with a stack of picture books next to him. He faced his dad and very seriously was *reading* the stories to him. Eric was propped up with pillows next to his son and although his eyes were only half open, there was a smile on his face and he was clearly listening to Austin's every word.

Mark waited a moment until Austin finished and moved to pick up another book before he knocked lightly on the open door. "Excuse me, guys."

Eric's eyes flickered open and met his. "Doc? What are you doing here?"

Mark took that as permission to enter and approached the bed. "I was in the neighborhood and thought I'd say hi." They both knew it was a lie. "Austin, your mom told me to let you know that there were cookies in the kitchen."

The boy didn't need to be asked twice. He scrambled to his knees, pressed a kiss to his dad's cheek, and hopped down from the bed without a second glance.

"Cute kid. I don't think I've seen him since he was a baby and you guys came to visit."

"We should have done it more." Eric nodded. "He is a good kid. All of this is so hard, but he hasn't complained about any of it. Not leaving his little buddies to hang out with me in bed instead of the park—none of it." Eric's eyes took on a faraway look and Mark felt as though he were intruding on a private moment, but then it was over and Eric looked at him again. "Seriously. To what do I owe this visit?"

Mark pulled up a chair and sat next to the bed. "Drew called. She's worried. Said you had a rough weekend."

He nodded. "I think I just overdid it, is all. I'm feeling a bit better today, but…it's spreading." It wasn't a question, so Mark didn't answer. "I can feel it," Eric continued. "And I don't need any scans to prove it. I can't explain it, Doc. But I can actually feel the cancer growing in my body. I can feel it killing me."

Mark had had a few cancer patients in the past, and although everyone had different experiences, he had heard something similar before from a patient with breast cancer. It made no medical sense, but sometimes these things didn't.

"But I'm not going to stop doing things with my family," Eric said. "We had a good time on Thursday. And we missed you," he added almost as an afterthought. "Christy said you were running. Too bad. You should have been there, man. She was amazing."

It took Mark a minute to catch up with what he was saying. "I should have been where? Who was amazing?"

Eric blinked. "At the Log and Jam. Christy was amazing. She said you had a training run. Still, you shouldn't have missed it."

"Whoa." Mark held up a hand and shook his head. "The Log and Jam? I didn't know anything was going on. Sure, I had a run planned, but if there was something happening, I could have rescheduled. What did I miss?"

"Christy's performance. She sang with the band and she was great."

The other man's words reverberated in his brain. *Christy sang? With the band?*

"Drew said she's been rehearsing with them and might

even play a few gigs," Eric continued. He looked at Mark quizzically. "You knew about it, right?"

He could lie and make something up, but Mark didn't have the energy. *And what was the point in lying to a dying man?* He shook his head. "No," he admitted. "I actually didn't know anything about it." He ran his hands through his hair and stood. "To be honest with you, Christy and I are having a few problems right now, and maybe now I know why." He turned in a circle before he looked at Eric again. "Sorry, man. This isn't very professional. I just need to process for a minute."

"It's fine, Doc." Eric pushed himself up a little bit in the bed. "I didn't mean to say something I shouldn't have."

"You didn't. You're fine." Mark took a deep breath and forced himself not to think about the information he'd just gotten and focus instead on his patient. He exhaled slowly and forced a smile. "Don't worry. Now, let's talk about some ways to get you a bit more energy so you can keep enjoying all the things you want to for as long as possible." He sat down again and started going through the information he'd been researching for Eric. It wasn't a cure, but he'd read some studies of patients who'd started mega dosing fresh organic juices and other vitamins and were able to increase energy levels. It was promising enough to give it a try.

They talked for the next few minutes and Mark explained everything he could before taking his leave. He begged off the cookie Drew offered him and escaped to the heat of the day. It wasn't until he was in the fresh air that Mark allowed himself to think about what Eric had told him. He stood on their sidewalk and squeezed his eyes shut.

Christy was singing?

When they were young, she'd loved to sing and had even confessed to him that she'd dreamed of doing it professionally once upon a time.

The first question was followed by the next logical one.

Why hadn't she told him?

AFTER MARK'S receptionist told her that Mark had made a house call at Drew and Eric's, Christy contemplated waiting for him or sending him a text message, but ultimately, she got in her car and drove to Drew and Eric's.

Mark stood on the sidewalk in front of the house, his bag in one hand and his eyes shut. She left her car at the curb and stood in front of him.

"Mark?"

His eyes flew open and he stared at her as if he were seeing a ghost.

"Christy? What are you...why are..." He shook his head. "I was just leaving." He stepped aside as if to let her pass up the sidewalk to the house.

"No," she said. "I came to see you."

"Me?"

"Sarah told me you were here. I hope it's okay that I came."

He looked confused and disoriented. She wanted to reach out to him, brush his hair from his eyes. But she knew she couldn't. Not then.

"Why are you here, Christy?"

She took a deep breath. Everything she'd rehearsed saying in the car no longer sounded adequate. *How could she say that she missed him, wanted him, and needed him? How could she tell him she'd made a mistake and she was just confused and over-whelmed?*

She couldn't.

She had to.

"I wanted to tell you—"

"That you'd joined a band?" In a flash, his face twisted in

anger. His normally kind eyes blazed. "That you'd been spending your nights singing and I had absolutely no idea?"

"Mark, I…"

"I had to hear it from my patient, Christy." He shook his head and wouldn't look at her. "My *patient*, Christy."

She glanced up to the house. "You mean Eric?"

His head whipped around and he stared at her. "No, Christy. My patient. Eric is my patient."

"Right. I know that." She was flustered, and unsure as to how to talk to him. It had only been a few days that they'd been apart, but it felt like the distance was further than before. "I was just going to—"

"When were you going to tell me, Christy? Is this why you wanted the separation? Because of all of this? Is there something else? *Someone* else?"

"What? No!" She shook her head, her hair whipping back and forth around her face. *Separation*. The word sounded so terrible. So angry. So wrong. "That's not what I want. It's not."

He ran a hand through his hair. "Isn't it?"

"No." She didn't know what she wanted and she hated herself for it. But she knew that she didn't want this distance between them and she'd give anything to take it all back.

"I don't believe you." His eyes narrowed.

He'd never looked at her that way. He'd never looked at her with anything but love in his eyes.

"How could you say that?"

She took a step toward him, but faltered.

"How could you lie to me?"

His words pierced her. Each one a razor to her heart.

"I didn't. I…" Words failed her. Her heart beat so fast she couldn't make sense of anything. "It wasn't supposed to—" Mark started to walk away, past her to the car. Desperate, she turned and screamed, "Mark!"

He stopped walking and then very slowly turned around.

Exhaustion lined his face. "Do you know what it felt like to hear from Eric that my wife had joined a band? Do you know how terrible that made me feel? That I didn't know something like that? He said you were fantastic. He said you..." He looked to the ground and shook his head. "I should have known, Christy. You should have told me. You should have *wanted* to tell me."

"I know." She hated that she'd caused him any more pain. The last thing she wanted to do was disappoint him again. Maybe coming here had been a bad idea. Maybe all of it had been a bad idea. "I'm so sorry, Mark. I really am. I didn't tell you because..."

He waited for her to finish, but she couldn't because she still couldn't explain why she'd kept it from him. Confusion swirled through her head and she hated herself for it. The only thing she was sure of was that she loved him.

"But I want to tell you now." She ran to him as he once again turned to his car. "I want to tell you everything and—"

"No." He shook his head and pressed his palms to the car in front of him. "Maybe you were right about all of this."

"About what?" There was something in his tone. Something that scared the hell out of her. "What was I right about?"

Mark turned slowly and looked her in the eye. "Maybe we do need some time apart." He made a sound that might have been a laugh in a different circumstance. "I didn't want to see it, but maybe you're right. Maybe this is for the best."

"No." Panic filled her. White noise rushed through her ears and her legs threatened to give way. *What was he saying?* She'd come here to talk to him, to tell him everything and how she was feeling and that all she wanted to do was be with him and...

"Yes." The word was final and filled the space between them. "I know things have been hard, Christy. I know we've been through a lot together, but that was the thing—we were always together. Somewhere along the line, that must have stopped for you."

"It didn't," she pleaded with him, but there was a truth to his words that she couldn't deny.

"I should go."

She shook her head and tears streamed down her cheeks. This felt different. It felt wrong. It felt as if her entire world was fracturing and she and Mark were on opposite sides of the divide.

"Mark, don't do this."

"It's not me, Christy. I didn't want this. I didn't want any of this. *You* did."

She did. Or, she had. Or…she didn't know what she wanted anymore. She couldn't think. Her mind was going a mile a minute and the sidewalk was tilting. Somehow she managed to stay on her feet.

"Please," she whispered. "You mentioned counseling before. Maybe it's—"

"I just need some time, Christy." He shook his head. "I just need to process everything. I don't know if I even know you anymore."

"You do."

He looked at her again as though he were going to say something, but then, with a small shake of his head, he sat in the driver's seat and started the engine.

Numb, Christy took two fumbling steps backward and tears streamed down her face as she watched him drive away.

"Don't go," she said to the air. "I love you."

Chapter Twelve

CHRISTY SPENT most of the next few days getting ready to go on tour with the Lumber Kings. She was grateful for the distraction, because it kept her from replaying the last conversation she'd had with Mark over and over in her head.

Still, moments of sadness and disbelief crept in when she least expected it and she found herself crying as she stood in their walk-in closet, staring blindly at his clothes. Or when she tripped over a pair of his old running shoes in the garage and sat on the cold cement floor for twenty minutes holding the beat-up runner and sobbing.

She'd ignored calls from Cam, Amber, and even Drew. She knew why they were calling. Because no doubt they'd heard about what had happened, or in Drew's case, maybe even witnessed it considering her latest drama played out on Drew's front lawn. She didn't want to talk to any of them. Really, what could she say?

That she'd messed up? That she'd made one terrible decision after another until finally she'd ruined everything and Mark didn't want to see or talk to her anymore?

Christy had done such a good job of ignoring her friends

that she'd allowed herself to believe she might be able to escape on tour with the Lumber Kings without having to see them at all. But she should have known better.

The night before she was scheduled to leave, there was a knock on the door, followed by Cam and Drew walking into her living room.

"I should have locked the door," Christy muttered and turned her attention back to the television show she was watching. It was a rerun of some sort of dramatic medical program. Not that she was really paying any attention.

"Hello to you, too." Cam walked straight over to the TV and turned it off before sitting on the coffee table in front of Christy. Drew sank onto the couch next to her.

She was pinned in.

"You didn't think we were going to let you leave without talking to us, did you?"

Christy looked at Drew. "Word travels fast." She shrugged. Nothing was ever a secret in a small town.

"It certainly does," Drew said. "And you can't ignore us. We're your best friends."

"I wasn't ignoring you," Christy lied. "I was busy."

"Yeah." Cam laughed. "Busy ignoring us. But we're not letting you off that easy. Now spill it. What is going on with you and Mark?"

"We're taking some time apart, I guess." She shrugged, doing her best not to appear upset. She should have known better; her friends knew her too well. They saw right through her.

"Time apart like a little holiday?" Cam asked. "Or time apart as in…something more permanent?"

Christy shrugged again.

"Sweetie, what is going on with you?" Drew took her hand. "I know you've been through a lot with the whole—"

She raised her hand to stop Drew. "Please," she said. "I don't want to talk about that."

"Okay," Drew said. "We don't need to talk about it. Not right now. But what we do need to talk about is what is going on with you and Mark. I saw you guys the other day after Mark left. It looked…intense."

"And Evan said Mark is still living at the inn," Cam added.

"And Ben mentioned you're going on tour with the Lumber Kings, and…"

"Wow." Christy jumped up and squeezed past Cam on the coffee table. "You two have it pretty figured out, don't you?"

"Christy. We're just worried." Cam turned to look at her. "This isn't like you. You never would have asked Mark to leave. No matter what was going on."

"I know!" Christy cried. The emotion was too much. Everything she'd been feeling for the last few days had built up to the point where she thought she was going to explode. "I messed up." The tears started. "I've ruined everything."

Even through her tears, she could see the look her two friends exchanged before Drew stood and crossed the room to be closer to her. "What do you mean, sweetie? Cam told me it was you who asked Mark for the separation."

"No!" Christy's head shot up. "I never asked him for a separation. God…" She shook her head. "I hate that word."

"But that's what it is," Cam said. "If you're not together, you're…"

"I just needed some time," Christy said. "I needed some space to figure things out. To figure myself out. Everything is so different now. I don't know what to do, or what I should be doing, or who I should be, or anything." Her words were muffled through her tears, but once she started, she couldn't stop. "I thought I needed to be away from him to do that. And maybe I did, I don't know. But it just felt wrong without Mark.

I miss him." She brought her hands up to her face. "I just miss him so much."

Drew's arms were around her right away, and then Cam's, too. Together, they held her up and gave her the strength she no longer had on her own. They let her cry for a few minutes before gently leading her back to the couch. Drew held tight to her hand and Cam went into the kitchen to retrieve a bottle of wine and three glasses. "I think we could all use a glass."

She poured and after Christy managed to slow her tears, she had a sip. "I miss him, girls," she said softly. "I made a terrible mistake. I need him."

"Why don't you just tell him that?" Drew asked. "We all make mistakes. Hell, I've made plenty. Mark loves you. Why don't you just tell him you made a mistake and all this will be over."

A fresh round of tears started again as Christy remembered the look on her husband's face when she'd tried to do just that and in exchange it had been him who told her no. "I tried." Her voice was barely a whisper.

"He's just hurt right now, sweetie. He'll come around." Drew squeezed her hand tight. "When do you come back from your tour?"

"Next Friday."

"You'll talk then."

Drew sounded so sure of herself, but she hadn't seen Mark's face. She hadn't seen the hurt in his eyes because she'd kept her singing a secret. Maybe for some couples that wasn't a big deal, but for Christy and Mark it was huge. They didn't keep anything from each other.

So why didn't she tell him?

It was a question she'd asked herself a dozen times over the last week. She kept asking herself in the hopes that she might be able to give herself a different answer. But Christy knew the truth. She hadn't told her husband about her singing with the Lumber Kings because of the way it made her feel.

When she held the microphone she felt sexy, strong, and confident. Like a completely different person. And it scared the hell out of her. Because if she was a different person, where did that leave them?

———

"ARE you sure you don't want to do shots again?" Aaron teased as they pulled up a stool at the bar. After their run, Aaron had insisted on getting Mark out of the hotel and into society. And because the Log and Jam was the only pub in town besides the seedy strip bar, the End of the Road, on the edge of Timber Creek, they'd found themselves sitting at Ben Ross's bar.

"I'm good with a beer tonight," Mark said. "My days of shots are over."

"You know where to find me if you change your mind." Aaron laughed and raised his beer. "It's good to see you out, man. Seriously."

"I'm not out."

"You know what I mean."

Mark shook his head, but he did know what Aaron meant because for the last few days, all he'd done was go from the office, to the trails for a run, and then back to the hotel to crash. He'd barely stopped for food, let alone for any kind of socializing. The last thing Mark felt like doing was talking to anyone, not unless it was on a professional level. Even then, the days were getting harder and harder to get through.

"You look like shit, Mark. Have you talked to her yet?"

He shook his head and took a long drink of his beer. "She texted me that she was going on a tour with the band. I'll wait till she gets back. She wanted a break—she's getting it."

"Wow." Aaron shook his head. "I can honestly say I never

thought I'd see the day when I would hear you talk that way. This is Christy we're talking about."

"I know who we're talking about, Aaron. She wanted time apart." He didn't bother telling his friend that she'd come to find him, and had more or less begged him to forget about the whole stupid *break* thing. If he told Aaron that, he'd have to admit that it was him who'd pushed her away the second time.

He shook his head with the complexity of it all. *Was it Christy who wanted this? Or him?* He didn't know anymore. All he knew was that he was friggin' miserable, he missed his wife, his heart ached every moment that she was away from him, and he'd never been so goddamned unhappy in his whole life. But he was hurt. The woman he knew never would have kept such an important thing from him, like singing with a band. They told each other everything.

But there was more. She blamed herself for their infertility. *How had he missed that?* He never should have missed that. But he had. He'd let her go day after day feeling terrible, and he hadn't known.

Or had he?

There was one time, after their first failed round of IVF, where he'd seen her on the couch, crying. The way she was wrapped in the blanket, her arms around her knees, her head down—she'd needed him to go to her, to tell her it wasn't her fault. But he hadn't.

He'd backed away and pretended he hadn't seen her because on some level, in that exact moment, it did feel like it was her fault the treatments hadn't worked. Even if it was only for a flash of a second, he *had* blamed her for their infertility. Even though it didn't make any sense.

Mark felt terrible even remembering that moment. He'd tried to block it from his memories because it had been such a cowardly thing to do and he didn't really think it was her fault. He was just hurt and angry and feeling the loss himself in that moment. It had passed, and later he'd consoled her. But maybe the damage had already been done.

He cleared his throat and focused on the present. "I told her we'd talk when she got back from her *tour.*" Mark emphasized the last word. He didn't mean to sound like an asshole when he talked about her music. He really didn't. Christy had always liked to sing and he'd never forgotten the way she owned the stage in high school as Sandy in those tight black pants when she starred in *Grease.*

Damn.

Mark also hadn't forgotten all those conversations they'd had under the stars when he'd driven them out to the cliff, laid on a blanket and cuddled. Those were some of his favorite memories of them before life got in the way. When she'd just lie in his arms and they'd talk about their dreams, no matter how ridiculous or far-fetched they seemed. They'd dream together about their future and what it would look like. They were both so completely in love and neither of them would have been able to imagine in even their wildest nightmares that a day would ever come where they'd be separated.

It seemed like a lifetime ago. Time had a way of changing things. Adding bills, and mortgages, jobs, stress…infertility. They were different people now. But it didn't mean Mark had forgotten the way Christy had confided in him that she'd always dreamt of singing on a stage.

And now she'd lived that dream, and he hadn't been there.

Wasn't that the part that hurt the most?

She'd lived out her dream without him? Because that's the way she wanted it.

Frustrated that he couldn't put her out of his head for even five minutes, he drained his glass and put it on the counter with more force than he intended.

"Can I get you another, Doc?" Mark looked up to see Ben

Ross in front of him, a bar towel draped over his shoulder. "On the house."

"On the house?"

"Absolutely," Ben said. "It's the least I can do considering everything you're doing for my brother."

Right. Eric.

Sometimes it was easy to forget that Ben and Eric were brothers. They hadn't been close since they were kids and until Eric and Drew moved back to town, Ben rarely mentioned them at all.

"It's nothing," Mark said. "I'm just doing my job. It's the least I can do. He's a good man, your brother."

Something flashed in Ben's eyes but then it was gone. "That he is." He nodded. "He's a great father and a good husband. It's just not right."

"No," Aaron agreed. "It's not right. Cancer's an asshole."

They all nodded in agreement.

"I guess the blessing is that they came back to town, and you're able to spend some time together before…" Mark struggled to find the right word. "Well, it's good to be able to spend this time together."

"It is." Ben's lips pressed into a thin line. "And I should probably find more time, but it's…well…can I give you guys a bit of bartender advice?"

Mark nodded. "Go for it."

Ben looked at each of them in turn. "Don't let anything come between you and someone you love. And I mean anything. It's not worth it." He shook his head and stared past them into the bar.

Mark had heard a rumor that Ben had been in love with Drew when they were younger and after Eric married her, he couldn't stand being around them. He never put much stock in the rumor before. But then again, he'd never had much of a need to. Looking at Ben now, he wondered how much of it was true.

"Anyway," Ben said after a moment. "You never know what could happen, you know what I mean? One day you're upset about something that seems so important in the moment, and the next thing you know, there's a distance between you that you just can't cross and then...well, then shit happens. Cancer happens and all of a sudden, you're out of time."

Ben nodded and slapped his towel on the shiny counter. "So that's my advice," he said with a smile, the serious moment broken. "Now, how about that beer?"

Mark nodded and turned around on his stool to survey the room and think over what Ben had just said. Obviously he'd been talking about Eric, but it had made sense for him, too.

If he waited to talk to Christy, would it be too late? Would the distance be too great?

Movement in the corner of the room, by the stage setup, caught his attention. Two men worked to gather up the instruments, wires, and speakers.

The band.

"Hey," Mark said as he twisted around to accept the beer from Ben. "Who is that?"

"That's the band," Ben said. "Well, some of them anyway."

"*The* band? The Lumber Kings? The band Christy is singing with?"

"That's them," Ben said. "Looks like Jamie and Caleb. Josh must be out at the van. They're good guys."

"I'm sure," Mark muttered, but he wasn't listening to Ben anymore. He was staring at the men in an effort to size them up. He'd never been a jealous man, but his wife had never left him for another man before. Or *men*. Or in this case, an entire *band*.

He knew he was being dramatic, but he didn't give a shit.

"Don't even think about it." Aaron put a hand on his arm.

"Think about what?"

"Going over there."

Aaron knew him too well. He took another drink of his beer and put it on the bar behind him. "I don't think it'll hurt to introduce myself."

"Really?" Aaron stood and moved to block him. "It's not a good idea, man. Don't do it."

Aaron was probably right, but he didn't care. He pushed up from the stool and started across the bar. Aaron groaned, but Mark knew he was right behind him.

"Hey," Mark said when he got close. "You're the Lumber Kings."

"We are." The man, holding a cable in one hand, nodded a greeting. "You've heard us play?"

"No."

Both men, obviously sensing tension, now stood in front of Mark. He could feel Aaron on his right, but he didn't look to see. He didn't want any trouble, and he was definitely not the type of man who would throw a punch unprovoked. And as far as he knew, he was unprovoked. The thought that Christy could be intimately involved with either of these men wasn't an option he was willing to entertain. Christy would never do that to him. Besides, he knew on some level that he didn't have any right to be possessive or go all *caveman* on these guys. After all, it hadn't been all that long ago when he'd entertained, even for the briefest second, the idea of another woman. It had only lasted a moment, but the thought had been there with Alicia. It might be hypocritical of him, but it couldn't hurt to mark his territory a little bit. Especially considering Christy was going out of town with these guys. Mark widened his stance and crossed his arms over his chest.

"What can we help you with?" The other man crossed his arms, matching Mark.

Mark stared at each of them in turn and finally, knowing that singing with them was making Christy happy in some way, he extended a hand. "I'm Mark. Christy's husband." He thought he noticed one of the men's expression change, but he couldn't be sure, and he was likely only looking for trouble. "Thought I should say hi."

"Hey." The man with the cable took his hand. "I'm Caleb. I play the drums. Christy's great. And what a voice. Damn. We're lucky to have her along, helping us out this week. Thanks, man."

Mark didn't know what he was thanking him for. *Allowing* his wife to go on tour with a group of relative strangers? Maybe. Also, these men likely didn't know that Christy and Mark were having any kind of marital troubles.

Good. It was none of their business.

The other man still hadn't offered up an introduction, so Mark turned his attention to him. "And you are?"

"Jamie." He finally took Mark's hand and shook it. "I'm lead guitar."

Maybe Mark was supposed to be impressed. He wasn't.

"We're really happy to have Christy with us," Jamie said. "We would have had to cancel if I hadn't been able to convince her to come with us."

"You convinced her?" Mark stood up straighter. Something about the guy irritated him; he just couldn't figure out what it was. He was probably just being sensitive.

"Well, she wasn't too sure at first, but then something changed and she was in."

Mark knew exactly what had changed, but he didn't feel like talking to these strangers about it. Particularly when they were about to spend more time with his wife than he was.

"Well, we should probably get going." Aaron put a hand on his arm and tried to steer him away and back in the direction of the bar before he could say or do anything that would get him into trouble. "Come on, Mark."

But Mark wasn't quite ready to leave. Not yet. He shook Aaron off. "One more thing," he said to the guys. "You take care of her, understand?"

Jamie stared at him with something that resembled a smirk on his lips and Mark itched to wipe it off.

It was Caleb who spoke. "Absolutely," he said. "She'll be treated like a queen. You have my word."

Mark gave Jamie one last long look, turned to Caleb and nodded, and walked back to the bar, where he downed the rest of his beer.

Chapter Thirteen

"DOES IT EVER GET OLD?" Christy collapsed into a chair backstage and gratefully accepted a bottle of water from Josh. "Seriously?"

Jamie laughed as he took the seat across from her. Caleb and Josh each perched on barstools in the crowded change room that was actually an old storage room that had been cleared out just enough for the band. "Having fun then?" he asked.

"Oh my God." Christy sat up and chugged half the bottle of water before answering. "This is the most fun I can remember having in a long time. How are you guys not so excited all the time?"

It was Josh's turn to laugh. "I guess we're used to it."

"And it's not like we're playing in arenas or anything," Caleb added. "It's a small-town pub."

"It doesn't matter." Christy shook her head. "I think I'd feel this way if there was only one person in the audience. We get to perform for them. Do you understand how cool that is?"

She was practically bouncing out of her seat. It was only the second show of the week-long tour and Christy was pretty convinced that singing in a band was exactly what she wanted to do with the rest of her life.

The feeling of being on stage, with everyone's eyes on her while she sang, was completely indescribable. She couldn't believe how far she'd come in such a short time. She was no longer confused about what song was coming next, or when she was expected to speak to the crowd or just roll into the next song. She was still nervous before performing, that hadn't gone away yet and Christy didn't think that would ever go away. Which was fine by her. The nerves were part of it all, and they excited her.

"I think maybe we're all a little more used to it than you are, Christy." Josh laughed at her. "But it is pretty cool."

"It'd be even cooler if we could do it full-time," Jamie said. "It sucks to have to go back to the day jobs after all this."

Christy's smile dimmed a little. She hadn't thought about when it was over. She'd let herself get completely swept up in the fun of everything. But of course it couldn't last forever and they would have to go back to Timber Creek and their—well, the guys would go back to their jobs. *She'd go back to…*

"What do you guys even do for work? I just realized I have no idea." It was easier not to think about what she'd be going back to. "Isn't that crazy? We're spending so much time together, we should get to know each other better."

"Totally," Caleb agreed. "I'm an electrician in my other life. I'm working at the lumber mill right now." He shrugged. "Good benefits and enough time off for gigs."

Christy nodded and looked at Josh.

"I'm a songwriter. I have notebooks of originals that I'm trying to convince these guys to play." He shot the others a look. "But mostly I'm music teacher," he said. "I pretty much only have enough students to pay the bills. And when I need to gig…well…it's working out right now."

"It's barely working out." Jamie laughed and shook his head. "I think I lost count at how much you owe me."

"Hey." Josh shrugged. "That's what friends are for. Besides, when we do finally hit the big time, it'll be worth it."

"True." Jamie chugged back his bottle of water and threw it into the recycling bin on the other side of the room. "You'll never guess what I do in my real life."

She smiled and leaned back, pretending to examine him. "I bet you're an accountant."

Jamie burst out laughing. "No way. I'm not that boring, am I?"

"Well, hey, I know a few accountants and they're not all boring." She tried to be serious. "Okay, if you're not an accountant…"

"It's just as bad," Josh offered. "He's a computer geek."

"No way?" She spun to stare at him again. "You're a computer geek? But you look so…"

"Normal?" Jamie laughed. "What's a computer geek supposed to look like?"

"Glasses, pasty white skin, ripped t-shirts, lives in his parents' basement," Caleb offered with a chuckle.

"You guys are assholes."

They all laughed before Jamie turned the question to her. "What is it that you do, Christy?"

She shrugged and tried to look casual. "I'm between careers right now." It was mostly true anyway. "So it's a good time for us to get famous."

They laughed again and fell into easy conversation about how awesome it would be if they were in fact famous and not just playing gigs in small-town pubs for a few more minutes until it was time to clean up, pack up, and head to their motel for the night.

Even though it was almost two in the morning by the time they got back to their rooms, for the second night in a row,

Christy couldn't sleep. She was too wired from the show to stay in her room. Besides, whenever she was alone and quiet, she started thinking too much. So instead, she sat by the outdoor pool that the little motel boasted and dangled her feet in the cool water.

She raised her feet and let them swish through the water, casting shadows in the pool with the lights under the water. She tried to clear her mind and not allow her brain to settle on the thoughts she'd been trying to avoid. It didn't do any good to think of Mark, or home. It just made her sad. Because as much fun as she was having on tour with the band, it still felt wrong. Mark should have been there. Every night, when she stood on the stage and sang her heart out, she found herself subconsciously looking through the audience for her husband. She'd been wrong to keep it from him at all and more than anything, she wished she could take it back.

"Hey there."

Christy jumped at the voice. Her feet splashed in the water and she turned to see Jamie standing over her with a grin on his face.

"Sorry, I didn't mean to startle you."

"You can't sneak up on a person like that!"

"I'm sorry." He chuckled. "Can I sit?"

She nodded and looked back to her feet, focusing on the bubbles she was leaving in the water. She'd been a little worried about Jamie after their sort of-not really moment after the show at the Log and Jam. She didn't want to give him the wrong idea. Whatever that was. But after a few days with the band, she realized she needn't have been worried about anything. They were rarely not altogether. Between being piled into the van, setting up for the shows, and performing, there wasn't much time for anything else. Besides, the whole band was more like a big family than anything else.

She'd obviously been concerned about something that wasn't a problem at all, which just made her feel dumb.

"So," Jamie asked, "is touring everything you thought it would be?" There was a smile in his voice. "I know it's not all that glamorous, but it's a start."

"It's awesome," she said. "I really meant it when I said that earlier. This has been awesome. I never knew how much I loved singing. And never in a million years would I think that…"

"That you'd be part of a band?"

She nodded. "It's so silly. I'm too old for this."

"You are not old."

Even in the dim light, Christy could see the way he was looking at her and it made her stomach flip over. Maybe she had reason to be concerned over their connection, or whatever it was between them. She scooted over to the side, putting more space between them.

He noticed her move and held his hands up. "You don't have to be scared of me, Christy."

"I'm not scared." It was a lie, because mostly she was scared that she could have any thoughts at all about a man who wasn't her husband, especially when things were so confusing between her and Mark. "I just don't want you to get the wrong idea."

"Don't worry." He smiled. "We're friends."

"Friends." She repeated the word.

"But I'm not going to lie to you, Christy. You're incredibly attractive, and your energy is…well, let's just say that if things were different, I'd definitely be asking you out."

She breathed out a sigh of relief, but there was something else, too. "What do you mean, if things were different?"

"I met your husband the other day."

She wasn't sure what she'd been expecting him to say, but it wasn't that. She had no idea Mark and Jamie had met. "You did?"

Jamie nodded. "I didn't even know you were married until he introduced himself. So I guess that would have to be different."

He shrugged and Christy immediately felt bad. She hadn't meant to mislead anyone. She looked down to her left hand but she already knew there was no ring there. She'd taken it off ages ago when her fingers swelled during the fertility treatments. She must have forgotten to put it back on. She stared at her naked finger a moment longer, and couldn't help but wonder whether she'd ever have the opportunity to put the ring on again. The thought made her immeasurably sad, so she pushed it out of her head.

"He seems like a nice guy," Jamie said.

"He really is." There was so much she could have added. That she loved him. That he was her entire world. That she'd made a terrible mistake that she didn't know whether they'd ever be able to come back from. But it didn't feel like the right time. If Jamie noticed she was holding something back, he didn't push. A fact she was grateful for.

They sat in silence for a moment and it was finally Jamie who asked, "You don't really think you're too old for this, do you?"

She laughed. "For singing in a band or sitting on the side of a pool in the middle of the night?"

"Both." He chuckled. "I don't think you're ever too old to realize your dreams."

"You assume that singing is a dream of mine."

"Isn't it?"

She thought about that for a minute. *What were her dreams?* Once upon a time, she'd sort of randomly thought her dream might involve singing and maybe even being famous. But that was a long time ago and she'd never really been serious about it. *Had she?* After she married Mark, their dreams included raising a family and building a life together. It seemed kind of inadequate now, but that's only because the only thing she'd dreamt of as an adult would never come true.

"Maybe it once was," she answered after a moment. "But things change."

"They do." He nodded and focused on his feet in the water for a moment. "But I think it's important to have dreams and goals and things to look forward to. I don't know if I'd be able to get up every day if I didn't. Don't you think so?"

"Honestly, I don't know." All this talk about dreams was making her sad, and that was exactly what she'd been trying to avoid. "I mean, don't get me wrong, it's important to have dreams and goals and all of that."

"But?"

She shrugged and swirled her feet around again. "But I also think it's important to be real with yourself and manage your expectations."

"Wow."

"What?" She turned to look at him. "What's that mean?"

He shook his head. "I just think that's a terrible attitude. I mean, *manage your expectations?* How are you ever supposed to dream if you're constantly managing your expectations? You should be doing the exact opposite. Don't manage your expectations at all. Let them run free." He shook his head. "That's just terrible."

"You know what's worse?" She didn't wait for an answer. "Knowing that your dreams will never come true and having your whole life destroyed because it's all you ever wanted and you let yourself dream." She lifted her feet and dropped them with a splash.

Jamie was silent for a minute. Finally he asked, "Can I ask you a question, Christy?"

"Why not?"

He scissored his feet in the water and tilted his head to look at her. "Who are you?"

"What?" She had expected him to say all kinds of things, but that wasn't one of them. "What do you mean?" She laughed. "I'm Christy Thomas."

"But *who* are you?" He twisted his body so he faced her. "What is it that makes you *you*? What are your dreams, your hopes, the things you want out of life?"

She thought about it for a minute, and then another one. He didn't try to rush her or push her for an answer she couldn't give. Finally, she gave up. "I don't know."

"I don't think that's true."

Her head snapped up. "Excuse me?" *Who did he think he was, asking her such a question and then not accepting the answer?*

"I don't think that's true," he repeated. "And I think you're using that as an excuse not to find out." He held up a hand to stop her objection before it came. "I'm not going to pretend to know you, Christy. Although I would like to think that we're becoming friends. But I do know that if you really think about it, and you're honest with yourself, you're going to come up with the answer to that question." He hopped up and pulled his feet from the water. "And I think as soon as you figure that out, you're going to be able to fix whatever's going on between you and that husband of yours."

Christy scrambled to her feet and crossed her arms over her chest. "What makes you think there's something that needs to be fixed?"

"Because," he said kindly before he walked away and left her standing by the still pool, "if there wasn't, you wouldn't be here right now."

"HAS HE HEARD FROM HER?" Drew asked Cam the moment they were alone. Cam didn't need her friend to clarify who or what they were talking about because she'd just opened the door to Mark, who was making a house call to look in on Eric. They'd made a few minutes of polite conversation with him, purposely avoiding the topic on everyone's mind. *Christy.*

Cam shook her head and slid the sugar bowl closer. "I don't think so." She scooped a few spoonfuls into her drink and stirred. "But honestly, I haven't asked. You haven't heard from her, have you?"

Drew shook her head.

"I didn't think so." Cam took a sip of her coffee. "But I guess I was hoping that out of all people, if she wasn't going to touch base with her husband, she'd at least check in with you."

Drew shrugged. "I'm not worried. I know she's going through some stuff. She doesn't need to be worrying herself with my problems."

Cam was about to tell her friend that not only was it perfectly okay for all of them to be concerned about her *problems* as she put it, but that she also needed to stop worrying if she was stressing anyone out by talking about what was going on with her and Eric because she *should* be leaning on her friends.

But before she could say anything, Austin ran into the room and jumped up on his mom's lap. "Cookie, Mama."

"Austin." Drew pretended to be stern. "How do you ask?"

"Can I have a cookie, Mama?" He batted his long eyelashes and Cam was sure she would have given him one no matter how he'd asked, he was so damn cute, but Drew wasn't done.

"Try one more time, buddy."

"Can I *please* have a cookie?"

She laughed at his dramatic emphasis of the word *please,* as if he would most certainly combust on the spot if he didn't get a cookie right away. "Okay," Drew said. "Good manners."

Austin, still on his mom's lap, reached his chubby arm across the table and snatched one of the chocolate chip cookies that Cam had brought over. Morgan and her friend Jessica had recently discovered that they liked to bake. It wasn't a bad hobby for teenage girls, even if it did leave her kitchen in a constant state of disaster, but the girls were producing more baked goods than they could consume, so Cam had taken to bringing them to Drew on a regular basis.

He stuffed the cookie in his mouth and giggled when his mom raised her eyebrows. "Now what do you say?"

"Thank you." The words came out in a garbled mess because he still had cookie in his mouth, but Cam didn't care.

"You're welcome," she said to Austin. "I'll make sure to tell Morgan you liked them." She turned her attention to Drew. "You know, I was just thinking, if you ever wanted a night out and maybe wanted to give Eric's parents a night off, I'll happily volunteer Morgan to babysit. Free of charge, too."

"I'm sure Morgan wouldn't appreciate that offer." Drew laughed. "But I really do."

"Consider it a solid offer. Seriously."

"Thank you." Drew smiled so sweetly and Cam tried to pretend she didn't see the exhaustion lines under her friend's eyes. She couldn't even begin to imagine how hard it would be to keep a little boy entertained while taking care of his dying father. "But you know, it's not really babysitting I need. Austin here needs some playmates. Are you and Evan going to have any kids?"

Cam almost spit out her coffee but if her friend noticed, she didn't say. Instead, Drew stared intently at her as if just by looking into her eyes, she'd be able to see the truth Cam was trying to hide.

There was no way that Drew knew that she'd only a few

days earlier taken a pregnancy test and it had come back with two little pink lines on it. Cam hadn't told anyone. She hadn't even made an appointment to see Mark yet. It was so new that she and Evan were still trying to wrap their minds around the test result because it most certainly hadn't been planned.

They'd kind of vaguely talked about having kids at some point in the future, but that was as far as the conversation ever went. After all, they had Morgan and wasn't having a baby when your teenager was almost out of the house crazy?

Maybe.

But Evan didn't have any children of his own and as much as he loved Morgan, Cam knew he'd always wanted children of his own. Ultimately, they were excited about the idea that they were pregnant, but they certainly hadn't planned on telling anyone.

Not yet.

"Maybe," she answered Drew vaguely. "You never know." She fidgeted with her coffee cup to keep from looking at her friend.

"Okay, but don't wait too long, okay? This little guy needs someone to keep him busy." Drew stroked the top of his head and stood up, with him still in her arms. "How about you sit over here." She deposited him into a chair at the end of the table. "I'll let you play with your modeling clay." Austin cheered as Drew grabbed a bin full of tubs of different colored clay and various cookie cutters and other instruments before putting them in front of her son.

"That'll keep him busy for a little bit," she said to Cam as she sat down again. She took a long sip of her coffee. "I swear, this stuff is the only thing getting me through these days."

Cam looked at her own cup and felt a twinge of guilt for the caffeine. She pushed it away, mostly untouched.

"Not you?" Drew raised her eyebrows at the cup.

"I'm trying to cut back a little."

Drew nodded. "Can I get you something else? A glass of wine maybe…" She narrowed her eyes.

"It's the middle of the day."

"So? That's never stopped us before."

That was true.

Cam shook her head. "Not today. I have some work to do later and I—"

"You're pregnant!" Drew jumped out of her chair and pointed a finger at her.

"What?" Cam knew she might as well not even bother denying it. Drew would be able to see right through her; still, she tried. "I'm not pregnant."

"You are too. I can see it all over you."

"That's the stupidest thing I've ever heard. You can't *see* pregnancy when someone is only a few weeks along." She realized her mistake the moment it came out of her mouth.

"I knew it."

Cam knew when she'd lost. She gestured for Drew to sit down. "Okay," she admitted. "I'm pregnant." She held up a finger to silence her friend before she said anything else. "But it's still *super* early and we're not telling anyone. You can't say anything. Not even to Christy." She almost added, *especially* not Christy. With everything their friend had gone through with her fertility treatments, and now with her…whatever it was she was going through, the last thing she needed to hear was that Cam and Evan were expecting a baby they hadn't even tried for.

"I get it. And I won't say a word." Drew nodded in understanding. "So what does this mean for the wedding? Are you going to wait until after the baby is born?"

Cam flinched. She hadn't talked to Drew about the wedding yet. "We were actually thinking of putting it off for a little while anyway, so I'm not sure what we'll—"

"Why would you put it off? You and Evan have been

dreaming of your wedding since we were kids. It's about time to finally pull the trigger, don't you think?"

Cam got up from the table, unable to sit any longer. She poured herself a glass of water at the sink and drank slowly before answering. "It just didn't feel right to have a wedding right now, that's all."

Drew turned in her chair. "Because my husband's dying?"

It amazed Cam how her friend could say those words, but she could see the pain in Drew's eyes. It was always there lately, but whenever she spoke about Eric, the sadness seemed to radiate off her.

"Honestly?" Cam asked. "Yes. It doesn't feel right for me to be planning a wedding when you're planning a funeral." She shook her head. "I'm so sorry, Drew."

Drew's eyes clouded with tears. She glanced at Austin, who seemed oblivious of what the women were talking about, and nodded, almost to herself. "It's okay. I mean, it's obviously not okay, but we're going to be okay and life is going to go on. I know it will." She gazed at her son. "It has to."

"Sweetie." Cam wrapped her friend into a hug. "I wish I had something I could say that would make you feel better." She felt so useless around her friend's misery.

Drew returned her hug, and she sniffled against Cam's shoulder, but she didn't allow herself to fully let go. Cam knew it was because Austin was in the room, and as enthralled as he was with his clay, kids were perceptive and he most certainly would pick up on it if his mother had a breakdown in front of him. "Thank you," Drew said after a moment and pulled back from the hug. "I know it's the worst feeling in the world, wanting to do something and not knowing what to do. I feel exactly the same way."

Cam nodded. "It's totally not fair."

"No." Drew laughed a little. "It most certainly isn't fair. But you know what? Sometimes these things have hidden blessings.

I mean, obviously it would be a bigger blessing if you didn't need cancer to figure it out, but Eric and Ben have actually spent some time together lately and I know that means the world to Eric."

Cam sat across from her friend again. As far as she knew, Drew had no idea of Ben's feelings for her when they were kids. And even though Evan probably shouldn't have told Cam about them, she wasn't about to tell Drew now. It wouldn't serve any purpose, especially considering what she was already going through was so much deeper.

"I wish I knew what had happened between them all those years ago," Drew continued. "It just doesn't seem right for brothers to have so much distance."

"You're right." Cam nodded. "At least they're able to mend that bridge now. Before it's too late."

Drew's face fell again. She looked down at her coffee in silence. When she looked up again, her eyes were shining, but she had a smile on her face. "Enough talk about that," she said. "Let's focus on something happier, like this wedding that I absolutely insist is going to happen."

Chapter Fourteen

CHRISTY COULDN'T EVEN TRY to pretend that her poolside conversation with Jamie hadn't gotten to her. *Was she really so cynical that she didn't believe in dreams anymore? Or was it just that now with the dream of motherhood dashed, she was lost without something to focus on?*

How had she let herself become so completely focused on one aspect of the life she wanted that she'd forsaken all the other aspects of it?

Those were the questions that continued to swirl around in her head. In the van the next day, she sat in the back and put her earbuds in her ears, choosing to listen to music by herself rather than engage in the chatter and conversation with the guys for the first half of the ride.

Who is Christy Thomas?

She was Mark's wife. She was a friend. A community volunteer. She was…a singer.

Christy knew in her heart that now that she'd had a taste of the stage, she wouldn't be able to leave it behind. Not completely. But maybe not as a Lumber King either.

"Hey." She pulled one earbud from her ear and tapped

Josh, who was sitting next to her, on the arm. "Didn't you say the other day that you wrote music?"

"I do." He grinned and immediately pulled a notebook from his backpack. "Do you want to see?"

"Don't bore her with your songs," Caleb called from the front seat. "Poor woman puts up with enough."

Josh looked at her questioningly.

"Seriously," she reassured him. "I really do want to see them. I have a few ideas myself."

"Well, then." He handed the book over. "By all means."

Christy thanked him and put her earbuds back in as she flipped through the book. But she wasn't hearing the music coming from her playlist. Instead, she pored over every song Josh had written. There were a handful that she really liked. She made note of the ones that sparked something with her, and then grabbed a notebook of her own, where she started scribbling down ideas. By the time they got to the pub to start setting up for the show, Christy was amped up, but for a completely different reason.

"These are really good, Josh." She gave him his notebook back and they gathered their things. "I started working on a few things, too, and if it's okay with you, I think we might make a good team."

"Like song writing team? I'm game. Let's take a look when we're done with the setup."

The setup and sound check went quickly, and Christy was so excited to sit down with Josh that she would have happily skipped dinner, just so they could have more time.

"Eat," Jamie ordered as he put a bowl of soup in front of her. "You can't perform on an empty stomach." She looked at him, but he shook his head. "It's not optional."

"Whatever, Dad." But she pushed her notebook to the side and picked up a spoon.

"It's cute that you're indulging Josh with this song stuff."

Jamie nodded toward the notebook. "He's been trying to get us to play one of his songs for ages."

"Why haven't you?"

"Seriously?"

"Yes, they're not bad." Christy washed down a spoonful with a gulp of water. "I think with a few tweaks that I have in mind, we might actually have something worth performing. I mean, I'm no expert and I'm still *so* new at this, but I really think it's worth a try, don't you? I mean, wasn't it you guys saying that you couldn't make the big time just playing covers of other artists' songs?"

Jamie nodded and looked genuinely surprised. "They're really good enough?"

"Not yet." Christy grinned. "But they will be."

After she ate and was able to escape the food police, Christy went in search of Josh and they spent the few hours before the first set working through some of the suggestions Christy had and nailing down a melody. The song wasn't done, but it was close and she was confident that it would be ready to rehearse very soon.

The show, like the others, was great. Christy was riding high not only from the exhilaration of performing, but also from the additional energy of working on the song with Josh.

"I really think we have something here," she said to the guys after the show. They'd barely had a chance to grab a bottle of water before she started telling them about Josh's song.

"It's our song, really," Josh said. "Christy's put so much of her touch on it. It's good."

"You've said that before." Jamie looked skeptical.

"Really," Josh said. "It's way different now. Trust me."

"You'll like it." Christy smiled as brightly as she could. She was so enthusiastic about the song that the guys would have to give it a chance. "Just let us play it for you."

"I don't see why not." Caleb settled into his chair and crossed one leg over the other.

Christy and Josh didn't bother waiting for Jamie's agreement. Josh grabbed his guitar and immediately played the intro. After the second bar, Christy started singing.

She kept her eyes on Josh and focused on the lyrics until they were done. It wasn't until Josh smiled at her that she looked up to see Jamie and Caleb's faces.

"Well?" she asked when they still hadn't said anything. "What do you think?"

Jamie and Caleb exchanged glances before finally looking at Christy and smiling. "I liked it." Caleb nodded. "I mean, it's great."

"Really?" She looked to Jamie next.

He laughed. "I can't even believe I'm saying this, but it really is great, guys. Who knew you had it in you, Josh?"

"Hey." Josh shook his head. "It wasn't just me. It was Christy who brought this to life."

"Do you think we could play it?" Christy asked the question she was really dying to have the answer to. It was one thing to write songs; it was another thing to be able to perform them. "I mean, you said we needed to get some original material and—"

"We?" Jamie grinned at her and she blushed at her forwardness.

"Well…I mean, I'm just supposed to be filling in while your friend is gone, but I was hoping…" She took a deep breath and asked for what she knew she wanted. "I was hoping I could maybe be a permanent member of the Lumber Kings."

"No way." Caleb shook his head.

"What?" She stared at him and willed the tears that she felt welling up in her eyes to stop. She could not cry in front of these guys. Not if she wanted to be taken seriously.

"Not the Lumber Kings." He stood and nodded at Jamie, who stood as well and looked to Josh.

"I agree," Jamie said.

Christy looked between the men and then to Josh. Surely, he'd advocate for her. *But even so, did she want to be part of a group who didn't want her?* The sad answer was, yes, she did want to be part of their group. Badly.

Josh met her eyes and then looked back to Jamie. A grin slid across his face. "I don't think you should be part of the Lumber Kings, Christy."

"I can't believe that you'd…" Despite her best efforts to stop them, a tear slid down her cheek. She swiped at it and was just about to plead her case when Jamie squeezed her arm.

"Hey," he said. There was a smile on his face. "We said we don't think you should be part of the Lumber Kings, but not that we didn't want you to be part of our band."

She blinked hard and wiped her face again. "What?"

"What we're trying to say is," Caleb took over the explanation, "maybe it's time for us to disband the Lumber Kings and start a new band. After all, if we're going to be playing original music, we should have an original name, too. Don't you think?"

She looked between them all, trying to put together what they were saying. "Wait. What about Grant?" If she was being honest, she had selfishly not given much thought to the missing band member, but if they were really saying what she thought they were…she needed to know. "What if he comes back? I can't just…"

"Grant's not coming back," Josh said. "He's decided to move back to Arizona to be with his family. The band was always more of a hobby than anything serious for him. So you're not stepping on any toes. Don't worry about that."

"So?" Jamie asked. "You didn't answer us."

Christy's head spun with everything they were saying. She

needed to clarify. "To be clear, are you asking me to be part of a band with you?"

"Yes." Josh laughed. "Will you?"

"Absolutely!" She didn't bother to hesitate, because even though she still had a lot of work to do in figuring out exactly who she was, one thing she knew for sure was that singing and performing was definitely part of that.

———

AFTER HIS VISIT WITH ERIC, which was more to sit and chat rather than talk about anything medical, Mark drove straight to the Riverside Park parking lot, used the public bathroom to change into his running gear, and hit the trails.

Aaron couldn't join him for their training run that afternoon. Something about too much work to do, or something, but Mark was pretty sure he'd exhausted his buddy's energy sources over the last few days. Ever since Christy left for her tour, Mark had been running harder, faster, and farther than before. The doctor in him knew it wasn't a good idea to push his muscles so hard, but he didn't care. It made him feel better to burn off the stress.

Besides that, it gave him time to think clearly, which was better than the alternative of sitting around his hotel room, watching some stupid television show. He knew he could have stayed in the house while Christy was gone, but it didn't feel right to be there when she wasn't.

Nothing felt right.

He dumped his clothes in the backseat of his car, did a few jumping jacks to warm up and was just about to head out for the trails when he heard a familiar voice.

"Hey there."

He turned to see Alicia. He hadn't noticed her Jeep, but then again he hadn't noticed much of anything lately.

"You just heading out?" she asked him.

He nodded. "You?"

"I was. Mind if I join you?"

He should probably just tell her no. He'd only seen her once or twice on the trails after their awkward misunderstanding when she thought he'd been flirting with her. And now with everything going on with Christy, it just didn't feel right to be spending time with another woman in any capacity. But then again, it might not be a bad idea to have a little company. After a moment, he nodded.

"Sure. But just know, I'm running hard these days."

"Oh?" She pulled a leg up into a stretch. "Part of your training plan?"

"Part of my mental coping plan," he said with a wry smile.

Alicia shot him a look. "Anything you want to talk about?"

"Not yet." Mark jumped up and down, eager to get going. "We'll see how I feel after a few miles."

"Fair enough." Alicia took off down the trail, and Mark quickly fell into step beside her. "You go ahead and set the pace," she said.

"You think you can handle it?"

She laughed.

"I meant your ankle," he clarified. "How is it, anyway? Healed up okay?"

"It's great." She did a little hop step. "I had a good doctor."

"Well, I don't know about that. But I'm glad it's not bothering you." He fell into silence, and thankfully Alicia didn't push any attempt at conversation.

He put one foot in front of the other, dropped his head and pushed to go faster. His arms pumped at his sides, and soon the familiar burning filled his lungs as he ran harder. Mark expected that Alicia would drop away as soon as he started picking up the pace, but he was surprised to see her right there next to him.

He ran faster.

She was still there.

It wasn't that he was trying to lose her, not really. After all, he had said she could run with him. But with someone else there, even if they weren't talking, he couldn't concentrate on his thoughts of Christy. He couldn't properly imagine what she might be doing right at that moment. He couldn't pretend he was going to watch her perform instead of being hundreds of miles away, torturing himself on the trails of Timber Creek.

Mark turned down a path that lead to a steep incline and increased his speed. Still, Alicia was there by his side. In fact, she sprinted up the hill and made it to the top before he did.

When he crested the top, he was finally ready to give himself a break. He slowed his pace into a walk and gulped down the water he always carried with him.

"That's quite the coping plan you have there," Alicia said after they'd both caught their breath.

"Pardon me?"

"You said you were running hard as part of a mental coping plan," she explained. "By what I just witnessed, I'd say you're working through some heavy shit. Am I wrong?"

He shrugged. "It's all relative, I guess." It wasn't heavy compared to what Eric was going through, but everyone's problems were their own.

"Ready to talk? Sometimes going over things with someone who isn't involved is a good thing. Maybe I can offer a different perspective on whatever it is that's going on."

He glanced over at her. *Maybe she was right.* He'd already gone over it all with Aaron. More than once. He'd run every conversation he'd had with Christy through his head more times than he could count, and still he was no closer to figuring out what he should do to put his marriage back together. Alicia didn't know them. He shrugged. "It can't hurt."

"I'm all ears," she said. "But if you want me to focus, maybe we can keep the pace to something a bit less intense?"

He agreed with a smile. "Deal."

They jogged at a much slower pace for a few more miles while Mark told Alicia everything that had happened with Christy in the last few weeks, including how she'd asked him to leave, and then how it had been him who had turned her away. He gave her a quick summary of their failed fertility treatments, and finally finished with how Christy had been singing with a local band and had left for a tour with them. And how he'd missed her so much it was almost a physical ache that nothing was able to dull.

"Wow," she said when he was done talking. "I was right. You have a lot going on. Based on what you just told me, and the way I just saw you run, I can probably guess that you haven't spoken to her since she left."

Mark shook his head.

"Why not?"

It was a good question. He'd been dying to hear her voice and to hear about how the shows were going and well…just anything. But he hadn't so much as texted her. That wasn't entirely true. He'd texted her dozens of times, only he'd deleted all the messages before he could actually send any of them.

He shrugged. "I guess I thought she just wanted her space to do her own thing."

"Why would you think that?"

Why did *he think that?*

"Did she tell you to leave her alone while she was away?"

Mark shook his head. "No, but I—"

"I'm just going to stop you right there." Alicia grabbed his arm and he spun around. "I don't really know you that well, so

I hope you don't take it the wrong way when I tell you that you're being an idiot."

"Excuse me?"

"You heard me."

Mark jerked his arm away and started walking again. "I'm not being an idiot."

"A stubborn asshole then?" She caught up to him and kept walking. "It's one of the two. Because I don't understand how you are here and she is there."

He spun on her. "Because we're on a break."

"This isn't a nineties sitcom, Mark. This is your life. And you're obviously not okay with the way things are going."

"No," he agreed. "I'm not. Not at all. But I don't know what else to do."

Alicia took his arm again and gestured to a park bench. Mark nodded and she led him over to sit under a tree in the shade. "I think you do know what to do," she said when they were seated. "Don't you?"

Did he? He wasn't sure. Part of him wanted to track her down, pull her into his arms and tell her in no uncertain terms that no matter what had happened between them, he never wanted to be apart from her again. He wanted to kiss her until she was breathless and felt his love for her deep in her bones so there was no mistaking how he felt for her.

But. That wasn't him. He didn't do things like that. He didn't go all *alpha male*. Ever.

It was more his style to sit back and let Christy decide what she wanted and what would make her happy. She knew he loved her. *Didn't she?* She had to. *How could she not?* He'd spent almost his whole life loving her.

"What's going on in there?" Alicia asked. "You look like you're having some sort of inner battle."

"I think I am." He dropped his head in his hands.

"Well, as far as I'm concerned, there's nothing to battle

about." He looked up to see his new friend leaning back with her arms crossed over her chest, staring at him pointedly. "If you love her and want her, you *show* her. Period. You do whatever it takes because you know that if you don't, you'll regret it for the rest of your life and you'll always wonder *what if.*"

Mark watched as Alicia's eyes changed while she spoke. There was something more behind what she was saying, maybe a story of her own. Maybe he'd ask her about it one day, but for now, he needed to focus on the woman he loved.

"You're right." He stood. A renewed energy filled him. But this time, it wasn't the energy to run until he was breathless and his muscles ached. It was the energy to run to his wife and do exactly what he needed to do. What he should have done months ago.

Chapter Fifteen

IT HAD BEEN two days since the band had made the decision to play some of their original pieces and Christy had barely slept. As soon as she picked up a pen and started writing, the words poured out of her. Josh rose to the challenge and picked out melodies for her lyrics and then with the rest of the guys, they polished the tunes until they weren't only happy with them, they were all equally as excited as Christy.

They'd had a break between shows, and the band spent an entire day practicing the new pieces and rehearsing them until they were all convinced that two of the songs were ready to be performed at their next show.

It was the biggest show they'd play on their tour, as well as the last one. It would be the perfect timing to debut their new songs.

And their new band name.

"Are you nervous?" Jamie took a seat next to her at the table in the back of the pub, where she'd been quietly sipping at a glass of ice water.

She shook her head. "Not really."

He examined her for a minute. "You don't seem to have

your usual excitement," he observed with a chuckle. "Normally you're bouncing off the walls before a show."

It was true. Over the course of the week, the guys had started to tease her for how excited she got before she performed. And then again after a show. Christy didn't mind— it was all in fun, and besides that, it was completely true. She'd always had a bubbly personality, but performing brought out a completely different side in her.

But even the high of performing couldn't compare to what she felt when she was writing a song. It was hard to believe that she'd only been doing it for a few days, and even harder to believe that she hadn't discovered this outlet before.

"I think I'm even more excited," she said to Jamie and laughed. "If that's possible. I mean, we're going to play *our* songs tonight, Jamie. That's huge." She shook her head. "Bigger than huge."

"It really is. And that's the problem, isn't it?"

Her head shot up and she stared, open-mouthed, at the man. They hadn't known each other very long and in that short time, their relationship had undergone a lot of changes, although Christy was pretty sure it would settle into a deep friendship. "Why would you say that?"

Jamie smiled and reached for her hand. He stilled the pen she'd been bouncing against the table top and looked into her eyes. "That's why you're not your normal excited self," he said. "It's a huge deal what you're about to do and I have a feeling that there's someone you'd rather be sharing the moment with besides us guys."

She dipped her head and battled against the tears that sprang out of nowhere. He'd nailed it. She'd done her best to try not to dwell on the way she'd left things with Mark before she'd left. She'd tried to focus on the band, her songs, and performing. After all, when she got home, that particular situation would still be there waiting for her.

And wasn't that the problem?

It would still be at *home*. And Jamie was right: she wished more than anything that Mark was there to see her debut the original songs. Hell, she would have liked him to be there to watch her sing, period. She'd been so wrong not to tell him about her playing with the band.

"Don't cry." Jamie squeezed her hand once before he let go and handed her a napkin. "I didn't mean to make you sad, Christy. Really."

"I know." She wiped at her tears and took a deep breath. "And you didn't make me sad. That's not your fault. There's a lot of things…well, it's fine. You don't want to hear about it, I'm sure." She looked away and straightened her shoulders.

"Hey. We're friends, remember?"

Her lips twitched up in a smile as she remembered their poolside conversation. Things could have been much more awkward between them considering she hadn't been very upfront about things. Thankfully, Jamie was a good guy and she was grateful for their friendship. And his honesty. If it hadn't been for their frank conversation only a few nights ago, she wouldn't have allowed herself to open up and write the lyrics she had and she would not be preparing at that moment to get up on stage and sing her very own song.

"I remember." She smiled broadly. "Thank you for that."

"Forget it." He waved his hand away, brushing her off. "Now come on. What do you say we go introduce the world to Timber Heart?"

Her smile only got bigger at the sound of their new band name and she knew she was ready. "I think that sounds like the best idea I've heard all day." Christy took his outstretched hand and let him lead her through the now crowded bar to the stage where the other guys were waiting to get started.

AFTER HIS CONVERSATION with Alicia and a subsequent chat with Aaron, who completely agreed with a woman he'd never met, Mark had quickly showered and thrown a few things in a bag. He was just about to hop in the car and make the long drive to Crescent City in Northern California, where a quick internet search had revealed the Lumber Kings would be playing, when his phone vibrated with a call from his emergency clinic after-hours number.

His first reaction was to ignore it, but he knew he couldn't do that. It was his duty to answer emergencies.

"Doctor Thomas." He threw the bag in the backseat of his car as he took the call.

"I'm sorry to bother you, Doctor Thomas," the woman from the answering service said. "But we just received a notice that your patient Becky Potter has gone into labor."

Dammit.

"Is Doctor Young on call tonight?" He already knew the answer to the question, but more than that, he also knew that no matter what doctor was on call at the hospital, Becky Olsen was going to need him to deliver her baby. She was a very young, unmarried mother with no support system to speak of. She hadn't had a very easy pregnancy with some high blood pressure issues and was extremely nervous about the birth of her first child. He'd promised her that he'd be there for her and he couldn't in good conscience release her to a doctor who didn't know her or her history. "Never mind," he said before the woman could answer. "I'll be right there."

Mark disconnected the call and took a deep breath before jumping in the driver's seat. On his way to the hospital, he did the mental calculations on how far way Christy was and how long it would take him to get there. The only unknown was how long it would take for Becky's new baby to make his or her appearance in the world.

There was no help for it. Besides, he still had time to get to Christy's show. He'd make it.

He had to.

Eleven hours later, Mark was exhausted but happy he'd made the decision not to send an on-call doctor to take care of his patient. Becky had been nervous and scared when he'd arrived at the hospital. Almost hysterical and with no one there to support her, she'd calmed down dramatically when he'd arrived. Although the labor did turn out to be difficult, he'd been able to avoid the caesarean section she so desperately didn't want and deliver the child naturally without incident. It was the type of moment that had led him to become a doctor.

After filling out his paperwork, and checking on the baby girl in the nursery, Mark returned to Becky's room to make sure the girl was doing okay. She was only eighteen and the last time he'd asked, her father had kicked her out of the house and she was living with her boyfriend and his parents. The boyfriend was suspiciously absent from the birth, which didn't surprise him too much considering he'd also missed all of her previous doctor appointments.

Still, Mark's heart ached for the young mother.

"Knock knock." He gently shook the privacy curtain that surrounded her bed.

She looked up and gave him a weak smile when she saw it was him. "Doctor Thomas. Hi."

"Hi yourself." He pulled up the empty chair and sat at her bedside. "How are you feeling?"

"Tired. Wow."

"Wow indeed." He smiled. "You did great. You worked hard for that little girl. Did you decide on a name yet?"

"Mya."

"Mya," Mark repeated. "That's a beautiful name and she looks great, too. I just peeked in on her at the nursery."

"Yeah." Becky's smile faded. "I was just so tired. The

nurses thought I should send her to the nursery for a bit so I could rest. Is that okay?"

"That's fine. You're not going to get much rest once you get the little one home."

Becky's lower lip started to tremble and tears sprung into her eyes.

"Hey," Mark said quickly. "I wasn't trying to make you cry." He'd dealt with plenty of postpartum women, and he knew very well that their emotions often bounced wildly for the first little bit of motherhood. He also knew this was different. "Is everything okay, Becky? I couldn't help but notice that your boyfriend wasn't here today. Have you called him?"

She nodded.

"And is he coming?" Mark knew the answer before she shook her head. "Is anyone coming, Becky? Where are you staying right now?"

The tears slipped down her cheek. "Troy broke up with me." Her voice was soft. "He said he was too young to be a father."

"Well, he doesn't have much of a choice in that now."

She shook her head. "But my dad said I could come home for a bit until I can figure things out. I can go back to work in a few weeks and I have a bit saved up for an apartment so…"

"I'm going to have the nurses give you a list of organiza-tions that can help you out, okay? The important thing is that both you and your little girl are healthy."

"I know." She nodded and swiped at her face. "I just wish I didn't…it doesn't matter."

"Are you having second thoughts, Becky?" When Becky had first come to Mark's office to confirm her pregnancy, they'd had a number of long conversations about her options. She'd said from the beginning that she wanted to keep her baby, so Mark hadn't pushed the issue either way. It wasn't his job. Becky was a good kid and not involved with drugs of any kind. Her baby wasn't in danger. And beyond the fact that they both faced a struggle in the coming years, there was nothing Mark could do but support and respect his patient's decision.

Becky was silent for a few minutes but finally shook her head. "No. I love her. We'll be okay."

He patted her hand and stood. "You'll be great. And remember, if you need anything at all, if you have any questions or concerns, don't be afraid to reach out, okay?"

She finally smiled again. "Thank you, Doctor Thomas. For everything."

***

THE SUN WAS STARTING to come up when Mark finally left the hospital. He was exhausted but he couldn't go home to shower and sleep the way he needed to before a day of seeing patients. He had something much more important to do. He called and left a message at the office for Sarah to clear his day and reschedule his patients. Never before had Mark cancelled an entire day of patients. Of course, never before had Mark been facing the biggest crisis of his personal life.

He glanced at the time on his phone. He might be a little late, but he'd make it to Christy's show.

After making a quick stop at Daisy's Diner, where Mark ordered four cups of strong, black coffee and with the tray of drinks on his passenger seat, he started the ten-hour drive to his wife.

***

THE FIRST SET WENT SMOOTHLY. From the moment Christy grabbed the microphone and introduced them as Timber Heart, the new and upgraded version of the Lumber

Kings, the audience was with her. They played all their usual cover songs and then it was finally time to sing an original.

"Hey," Christy said into the microphone. "We have such an awesome crowd here tonight." Cheers went up throughout the audience. "And because you're all so awesome, I thought maybe we could try a little something new tonight." There were a few hollers of encouragement. "The guys and I have been working on a few original songs, and you're the lucky audience we're going to debut them on." She looked to Jamie, who smiled and played a riff on his guitar. "So," she continued. "Without further build-up, here's our very first original song, 'Let's Be Us.' I hope you like it."

She took the microphone from its stand, looked at her feet and took a deep breath as the guys started to play behind her. When she looked up again, she stared out into the crowd and started singing.

"Once upon a time, it was just you. It was just me.
We had love and dreams and little more.
Together we had everything."

CHRISTY LET herself fall into the music and the lyrics she'd written to her husband. She knew he wasn't out there, but if she closed her eyes, she could picture him standing next to the bar, leaning on the post, a beer in his hands, his eyes on hers, seeing right into her heart.

"Days turn into years.
Dreams die and love fades.
But I don't want it to ever be the end."

SHE OPENED her eyes to sing the chorus and she blinked hard, almost missing her cue when her gaze landed on Mark.

Her heart did a little flutter in her chest and she sang the words she'd written, directly to the man she'd written them for.

"LET'S BE US. The way we were.
The way our hearts know how.
Close our eyes…Open our hearts.
It's time to be us again."

WHEN SHE FINISHED THE CHORUS, tears blurred her vision so she had to look away from Mark. Instead, she focused on a point through the crowd on the back of the wall and continued to sing. It wasn't until the song was over that she looked back to where Mark stood. She couldn't quite see his face from where she was, but it didn't matter, because he was there. He was standing there, watching her perform and he'd heard her sing the song she written just for him.

That's all that mattered.

"Wasn't that amazing?" Jamie had taken the microphone and addressed the crowd, who cheered in response to his question. "Timber Heart's first original song, ladies and gentlemen, written by our very own Christy Thomas. I hope you liked it because there's plenty more where that came from."

Christy looked from Jamie, to the other guys, and back to Mark. She couldn't take her eyes off him. She knew she was supposed to talk to the crowd and tell them they were going to take a quick break but would be back in ten minutes. But she couldn't.

Fortunately, Jamie took over and signed off, signaling they got their break. It wasn't until he switched off the microphone and touched her lightly on the shoulder that she became aware of what was happening.

"Go talk to him," Jamie said to her. "We're back on in ten, but if you need more time…"

"Thanks, Jamie." Christy smiled gratefully at her friend and slipped off the stage.

It took her a bit longer to make her way through the crowd to her husband as she was stopped by a number of people congratulating her and commenting on how much they were enjoying the show. Christy, of course, stopped to talk to each of them. She smiled and thanked them before politely excusing herself. Finally, she found herself in front of Mark.

"Hi."

"Hi." He smiled a little but she could see the hesitance.

"You're here."

"I am."

Her chest was tight and it was hard to breathe. She wanted to reach up and touch his face. He looked so tired, as if he hadn't slept. But he was there.

"I didn't think you'd—"

"You were—"

They spoke at the same time. Christy bit her lip and tilted her head. "You go ahead."

"You were amazing," Mark said. "I mean it. Absolutely incredible." He shook his head slightly and kept talking. "And you look…" He reached out to take her hand but stopped himself and tucked it into his pocket. "You're gorgeous, Christy. I'm totally at a loss for words. I had no idea."

Of course he had no idea. She hadn't told him. Sadness flared within her. So much of what had happened between them was her fault. But so much of it wasn't anyone's fault.

"I only have a few minutes," she said in response. "Do you want to go outside maybe? It might be quieter."

"More than anything."

She led him through the crowd out into the fresh summer night.

Christy took him to a bench she'd spotted earlier, far enough from the front door that they could have a little bit of privacy. They sat in silence for a moment, neither knowing what to say.

How could it be that this man she knew better than anyone, this man she'd loved almost her entire life, made her inexplicably nervous all of a sudden? She giggled a little at her own ridiculousness.

"What's so funny?"

She shook her head. "I was just thinking about how crazy all this is."

"What specifically?" he asked. "You singing in a band? Me driving all day after being up for the last I don't even know how many hours? Or the fact that I feel like I need permission to touch you?"

The smile fell from her face as she remembered how much distance was actually between them. "Mark, you don't need permission to touch me."

"Don't I?"

She reached across the space that suddenly felt cavernous and took his hand. "No." She squeezed it in hers. "You don't."

BY THE TIME Mark had arrived in Crescent City after driving all day, he'd been exhausted. The only thing keeping him going was the thought that he needed to get to his wife. And once he'd arrived at the pub and seen her standing on the stage with a microphone in her hand, all thoughts of needing to sleep were gone.

Watching her sing gave him a completely renewed energy. She was amazing—the way she moved, the way she held the microphone and sang to the audience directly. She hadn't even noticed he was there, at least not until she started singing *that* song. It was the original song and Mark knew without a doubt she'd written it just for him.

Now, sitting there on the bench with Christy, his hand in hers, there was so much he wanted to say. To ask. But all he could do was sit and stare.

Finally, he managed to form words. "You are incredible. I had no idea. I mean...I knew. Of course I knew you could sing, but this..." It didn't seem adequate. Nothing he could think of to say could possibly be enough to tell her what she meant to him and what it had felt like to be apart from her. He shook his head and tried again. "Christy, I..."

"It's okay." She squeezed his hand and smiled. "We both have a lot to say and there's so much we need to talk about, but...I still have another set to do and I know if I start talking to you, I'm never going to stop."

Right. She had another set.

"I can't wait to see you on stage again."

The lights illuminated her face, and Mark could see the blush creep over her cheeks.

"What?" He reached out to touch her cheek, stopped himself momentarily and then remembering what she'd said earlier about not needing permission to touch her, gently traced a finger over her heated cheek. "You're not nervous because I'm here, are you? Is that why you didn't want to tell me you were singing?"

Her face changed and her eyes dipped down and Mark knew it had nothing to do with her being nervous. "It's okay," he said quickly. "We don't have to talk about it right now. I just want you to focus on the show."

"Okay." She nodded and glanced behind her as the door of the pub opened. "I should probably get back in there."

"Of course." Mark didn't want to let go of her. Now that he was touching her again, the idea of not feeling her skin on his caused a physical ache in his chest. When she released his hand, he clenched his fingers into a fist to hold onto the feel of her as long as he could.

Christy got up and smoothed the skirt of a dress he'd never seen her wear before and he was struck once more how there could be so many changes in such a short amount of time.

"Are you coming?"

"I wouldn't miss it."

Chapter Sixteen

HE WAS THERE. *Mark was there.*

And he didn't take his eyes off her for the rest of the night.

Christy felt his gaze on her the entire time she was on the stage and it gave her power. She sang and performed with more heart than she ever had and the audience responded to every beat.

She still couldn't believe he'd driven all day to see her. She couldn't get over it. There was still so much between them that they needed to talk about and figure out, but just the fact that he was there with her, watching her and supporting her, meant that he hadn't given up on them.

It meant everything. Absolutely everything.

It was late by the time she finished her last song, and the band played an encore. Something they'd never done before. She was exhilarated and exhausted all at the same time, but when she saw Mark, still sitting at the bar, his eyes still fixed on her as if they'd never left all night, which she was pretty sure they hadn't, she was renewed.

"Just go," Jamie said as Christy wrapped up a cord. Over the course of their mini tour, she'd found a few clean-up jobs that had become her responsibility. She liked doing them and contributing to the group, but she couldn't help but be keenly aware of Mark, still at the bar, looking more and more exhausted with each minute that passed.

"Are you sure?" She looked at Jamie expectantly, already knowing the answer.

"Get out of here." He smiled and took the cord from her hands. "You have more important things to take care of right now."

She gave him one last look of gratitude and went to her husband. "Are you ready to go?"

"Are you sure you don't have anything else you need to do? I can help with—"

"Let's go." She took his hand gently and led him out to the parking lot that by now was nearly empty. She gave him directions as Mark drove them back to her motel and then they were finally alone. It occurred to Christy too late that maybe Mark might have his own hotel room, or maybe he should get one. After all, they'd been living apart for a few weeks already. *Was it strange to assume that he would stay over? And even so, what did that mean if he did?*

"You must be exhausted," she said the moment the door closed. "Can I get you something?" She gestured to the coffeepot and the mini fridge where she'd stashed some bottles of water, but beyond that, there wasn't really much to offer him at all.

"I'm fine." He looked around awkwardly, finally choosing to sit on one of the double beds. He perched on the edge and gestured for her to sit as well.

"This is strange, isn't it?" She laughed nervously. "It's crazy that this should feel so weird. I mean, you're Mark."

"And you're Christy."

She nodded and tears sprang to her eyes. "Mark, I'm so sorry for—"

"No." He stopped her. "Don't be sorry. You have nothing to be sorry for."

"I do," she protested. "I asked you to leave. I ruined this."

"You didn't ruin anything."

Tears flowed freely down her cheeks now. She shook her head because she didn't believe him. She *had* ruined everything. She'd taken their marriage, their love and she'd thrown it away by asking him to leave her. She'd lied to him, snuck around, and taken him and everything they had together for granted.

"I did," she finally said. "And I'm so sorry."

Mark shifted and came to sit next to her. He turned to her and reached for her hands. It felt so good to touch him, to have him hold her, even if the touch was small. "Listen to me," Mark said. "Christy, please. Look at me." She lifted her eyes and met his. They weren't angry or upset the way they should have been and she wouldn't have blamed him if they were. "You didn't ruin anything."

Christy shook her head, still unwilling to believe him.

"You know what you did do, though?"

She freed one hand and used it to wipe at her face. "No. What?"

Mark's lips twitched up in a small smile. "You gave me a chance."

Confused, she shook her head. "A chance?"

He laughed a little. "I know it doesn't make any sense, but the last few weeks have been so hard without you, but at the same time the distance was good because it gave me the chance to finally realize something I should have realized a long time ago." He looked down at his hands before looking up again into her eyes. "Our life together isn't defined by the family we may or may not have, because we *are* the family. You and I. All I ever need is right here with you. We put so much pressure on having a baby that somewhere along the line, whether we meant to or not, we lost sight of the fact that we already had everything we would ever need as long as we had each other."

Her heart swelled listening to the words come from his mouth because they were spot-on and everything he said was exactly what she was feeling and so much more.

"I lost sight of that," he continued. "I think we both did. I've been on autopilot for too long and I need to apologize to you because I had no idea how much you blamed yourself for our inability to conceive. I should have seen it. I should have—"

"No." She stopped him. "You couldn't have seen it. I didn't want you to. And that wasn't right. I blamed myself for all of it. Maybe I still do. But that wasn't fair to you either because by taking all the blame I could convince myself that it wasn't hard on you, too."

Mark shook his head. "Oh, hell yeah, it was hard. It's all been so hard. But nothing has been more difficult than thinking even for one minute that I might lose you. I can handle anything life throws at me, Christy. But not that. Never again."

She opened her mouth to tell him he never had to worry about it again, that the last thing she wanted was to lose him, but instead of the words, a sob rose from her throat. She clamped a hand over her mouth.

"When you asked me to leave, my entire world came down on me."

A flash of guilt sliced through her.

"And then when I found out you'd been singing and hadn't told me, I was so hurt." He shook his head and she looked away.

She couldn't bear to see the pain on his face.

"I felt so betrayed."

Another flash flared in her gut and she flinched. She'd been absolutely terrible. "Mark. I'm so, so—"

"Please don't apologize." He lifted her chin with two fingers until she looked in his eyes again. "I mean it, Christy. We both own a part in this. It's not all on you. You know that, right?"

She shook her head. *How could she possibly know that? This was all on her.* She'd been confused and hurt and just so unsure about everything that she'd reacted irrationally.

"I don't know that," she finally said. "I know that in a relationship there are two people, Mark. I mean, obviously. But I'm not sure if you understand. I was just feeling so lost and confused. After that last appointment, when the doctor confirmed everything, I just didn't know what to do. I'd let you down. The only thing we'd ever wanted was a family and I couldn't give you that. And if I couldn't be a mom, who was I? I just didn't know and I didn't know how to handle any of it."

"And now?"

She dipped her head and thought for a moment. "And now…I think I'm starting to figure it out," she answered honestly. "It's taken me a little while, but I think it's coming."

He smiled and wiped a tear from her cheek. "Good. It's important."

"It is."

They were silent for a few moments. "Christy?"

She nodded.

"You need to know that you didn't let me down."

She shook her head as a reflex.

"No." He stopped her. "You didn't. Not at all. And I need you to understand it. *Really* understand it. In your heart. I should have done a better job telling you this all along." He squeezed his eyes shut for a moment before he continued. "That's my fault. I should have told you this more. Infertility… that's not just on you. It's a terrible thing, and it's hard. So, so hard. But it's not your fault. None of it is. And it's not something that defines you or us. I mean, we're not the *infertile* couple. We don't have to be."

"But it's all we ever wanted, Mark. Ever since we were kids, we talked about having our own family one day and—"

"It's not *all* we ever wanted."

She stopped and looked at him. There were tears shining in his eyes now. Christy couldn't remember the last time she'd seen Mark cry.

"Having a family has been a dream, yes," he said. "I'm not going to lie to you and tell you it wasn't important. But it absolutely is *not* the only thing I've ever wanted or that we've ever wanted."

Confused, she tilted her head in question.

"Christy, all I ever wanted was you. From the moment you gave our frog specimen a memorial service in science class, I fell in love with you, and I knew without a shadow of a doubt that the only thing I would ever want or need was you. Would a family of our own be a blessing on top of our love? Yes. Absolutely. But if we never have a child of our own, or a family of any kind, I will still have every single thing that I'll ever need as long as you are by my side. You, Christy." He held her face between his hands and looked straight into her eyes. "It's always been you. You're all I need, sweetheart. As long as you're healthy and happy and next to me to walk this life together, I don't need anything else. I have it all."

She let his words sink in and while she sat and absorbed everything he'd just said to her, he never once looked away from her. She could see it in his eyes, the love he had for her. And after a moment, everything he'd just said made perfect sense, as if she'd heard him for the very first time. But she still needed just a little bit of clarification.

"You mean, if we never have a child, you could still be happy?"

"Christy, I *am* happy." He shook his head and laughed. "I

mean, I *was* until all of this. But I meant it when I said it earlier —maybe we needed a little shake-up, you and I. We've been through a lot, and it's important that we remember that and that we also remember that we can survive anything. Even if we need to make a few changes to get through it. You reminded me of that."

IT WAS TRUE. She *had* reminded him that they needed to refocus on each other and what their lives would look like now that they knew they weren't going to be having any children of their own. Their marriage had taken a hit, but it was strong. And now that he'd finally had a chance to look into his wife's eyes and see the love there, he knew they'd be okay.

"I think sometimes we get so caught up in the drama of what we're going through that we can forget about the other person, and somewhere along the line, I think we even forgot that we're doing this together. Maybe we could have come to that conclusion even if you hadn't asked me to leave, but maybe not. And it doesn't matter because that's what happened and this is where we are right now."

She nodded. "We still have a lot to talk about."

"Oh, baby." He laughed. "We sure do. But the one thing I need to make sure you hear right now is this." He took her face in his hands again because he needed to see it in her eyes that she understood exactly what he was feeling. "I love you more than anything else in the whole world and that will never change. You are the only thing I need to feel complete and no matter what, I will always be by your side because you, my love, are my everything."

Her eyes flashed and even through the sheen of tears, Mark could see that the message was delivered. Christy reached up and put her own hands on his face before gently pulling him into her. Her lips pressed to his. Softly at first, hesitant. But all he needed was the slightest taste of her to know he wanted more.

Forget that he'd been up for forty-eight hours or that he hadn't eaten since breakfast. Nothing mattered except kissing his wife and holding her in his arms. And that's exactly what he did.

His lips moved on hers, increasing the intensity until he heard a soft moan escape her throat. His hands slid down her body, needing to touch her, and never let go. Her hands traveled as well, one resting on his back, the other cupping the back of his head, pulling him into her, as desperate for his kiss as he was for hers.

"Christy, I need to feel you." The clothes between them were too much. He needed to see her, to touch her.

Reluctantly, Christy broke the kiss to stand in front of him. She untied the knot at the side of her dress and unwrapped it from her body in a sensuous striptease. As the fabric fell to the ground and revealed the black lacy bra and panties beneath, Mark's heartbeat quickened, his need for her growing.

He stood in front of her and let his hands softly travel the length of his wife's body before once again pressing his lips to hers. He moved his mouth down her neck, licking and tasting her sweetness, and to the swell of her breasts before he stopped himself long enough to scoop her up in his arms and deposit her gently on the bed, where he could make love to his wife properly.

THEY DIDN'T GET much sleep, not that Christy cared. Even with only a few hours, she felt amazing and rejuvenated. There was still a lot they had to talk about, but they were back. They were *them* again. Christy and Mark. And it felt so good.

In fact, it felt better than it ever had, if that was even possible.

Maybe Mark had been right—maybe they'd needed the shake-up in their lives in order to have the opportunity to wake up and remember that even through all the stress of infertility treatments and all of the uncertainty that they'd gone through, that as long as they had each other, they could get through anything that life threw at them.

Christy giggled at her new, fairy-tale attitude the next morning as she pressed a kiss to Mark's cheek. He was still sleeping, and he needed it. She'd let him get a few more hours before they had to check out of the hotel and go home. She was too charged up to sleep, so she might as well meet the rest of the guys for breakfast. Besides, she wanted to talk to them about writing and performing some more original music.

"Well," Caleb said when she walked into the motel restaurant. "I didn't think we'd be seeing you this morning."

"Where's the mister?" Josh made a show of looking behind her before adding, "Is everything…"

"It's fine," she said quickly, just so they wouldn't think there was even more drama than there already had been. Thankfully, the guys had been mostly unaware of everything that had been going on with Mark. She didn't want to bring chaos into a situation where she was still trying to find her place. "He's sleeping."

"I bet he is." Caleb winked and then immediately caught himself. "Sorry, Christy. I'm used to hanging out with the guys. I shouldn't have—"

"No," she interrupted him. "It's okay." It was better than okay. She loved that Caleb felt comfortable enough with her to tease her. They were good guys and they'd been so welcoming of her and she really did feel as though she belonged. "Besides, you were right." She winked back at Caleb and the guys laughed.

"We were just about to order," Jamie said. "Have a seat. You hungry?"

"Totally."

Over coffee and pancakes, the group discussed the success of the show the night before, including the debut of the new songs and their brand-new group name. And it had been a success, too. The crowd had been awesome and everyone reported that they'd been stopped and congratulated on the new sound.

"The manager wants to rebook us already," Jamie reported. "For next month. It's a long way to go for one gig, so I'm happy to organize another little tour. What do you think, Christy?"

What did she think? She was in. Without a doubt or second thought.

But…

That was before. Before Mark had heard her sing. Before he'd come to find her, to talk to her. Before they'd…what? *Fixed things?*

"Christy?"

"It's okay if it's not a good time, Christy." Jamie picked up on her hesitancy. "We'll understand if you need to—"

"No." She held up her hand and then laughed at herself. "It's not that it's not a good time. It's just…what if we waited? Just a little bit," she said quickly, seeing the way the guys reacted. "Just long enough to get a few more songs. You heard the way the crowd reacted to our original stuff." She sat up in her chair, getting excited just talking about it. "Wouldn't it be great if we have more new stuff for them next time? I'm not saying that we shouldn't go on tour again. I'm saying that we should, but we should be ready. Really ready before we go. Maybe we can even line up a few talent agents to come watch us?"

Josh stared at her as though she were speaking a different

language and Caleb laughed. It was Jamie who finally smiled and explained their reaction. "You've sure come a long way in a short time, haven't you?"

"What do you mean?"

"Christy, it wasn't that long ago that I could barely convince you to come up and try singing with us at the Log and Jam. Remember?"

She nodded, but it seemed like a lifetime ago. She could hardly remember that woman who'd been nervous to stand up and hold the microphone in her hand. Who'd tentatively sung the notes of the first few bars. Things *had* changed a lot. *She'd* changed a lot.

She wasn't the same woman as she'd been then. Not really.

"Well," she said after a moment. "Things have changed."

"They certainly have." Jamie smiled and sipped his coffee. "I do hope they haven't changed too much though."

"What do you mean?"

"I hope life on the road hasn't hardened you."

It was her turn to laugh. She shook her head. "Not yet. But I do want to thank you guys. This has been the most incredible experience and…" She let her thoughts trail off because she didn't want to get emotional. Christy swallowed hard and chuckled. "And…I'm tired so I probably should stop talking before I make a complete fool of myself."

"I don't think that's possible." Caleb blew her a kiss across the table and they all laughed again.

While the group finished their breakfast, they agreed that they should wait a bit longer before going back on the road, get a few more new songs on the set list and line up some talent agents to watch them perform. They all agreed that Timber Heart was going to be something special.

As they left the restaurant, Christy pulled Jamie aside. "Hey, I just wanted to thank you."

Jamie's smile was easy. "For what?"

"For all this." She waved her hands around the motel's cement parking lot. "Okay." She laughed. "Maybe not all this. But you know what I mean. Honestly..." She turned serious. "I really mean it. Thank you."

"You don't have to thank me, Christy."

"I do." She grabbed his hand and his eyes met hers. Things could have been different with him and in that instant, she realized, maybe for the first time, just how different they could have been. But that wasn't what she wanted. She might have thought she wanted it for a brief moment in time, but she knew better now, and thank goodness Jamie had been a gentleman. A friend. "I know things could have gotten awkward with us after...well...you know."

He smiled. "I do know. And things will never be awkward, Christy. You're great. You know that, right?" She looked away for a moment, but he gave her hand a shake and she looked back into his kind eyes. "You really are, Christy. You're beautiful and talented and you have such a huge heart. If things were different..." He laughed. "But they're not and Mark is a very lucky man."

"No," she corrected him. "I'm a very lucky woman to have such an amazing husband."

"I don't doubt that for a moment."

They looked at each other for a moment before Christy spoke again. "I'm going to ride home with Mark."

"You better."

He opened his arms for a hug and Christy let him squeeze her tight. "I'm really glad that whatever was going on with you two seems to be on the mend."

She nodded against his shoulder.

"Love like that doesn't come along every day."

Tears sprang to her eyes again and she pulled back to wipe her face.

"It looks like Sleeping Beauty might be ready to go." Jamie

gestured behind her and she turned to see Mark standing in the door of their room, watching.

She waved and turned back to Jamie to say good-bye but he stopped her before she could say anything.

"Give us a call when you're ready to rehearse again, okay?"

Christy nodded.

"But take your time. Really. There's no rush."

She nodded again and blew him a kiss before running across the parking lot. To her husband.

Chapter Seventeen

IT HAD BEEN two weeks since Mark had gone to Crescent City to rediscover his wife, but it may have been the best two weeks of their relationship. On the drive home, Mark did something he'd never done before and called Sarah, cancelling all his patients for the rest of the week, rescheduling any emergencies to his colleagues who more than owed him a few favors, and instead of driving straight home, they decided to take the long way.

Mark drove them up the coast, spending a night in Portland and then a night in Seattle, where they ate fish and chips on the wharf and spent the day wandering around Pike Place Market. It had been years since the two of them had spent time together that way, just relaxing and laughing with no pressures of any kind.

They held hands like teenagers and talked in a way they hadn't for years. And when they were finally done being tourists, they went home and spent another few days locked up in their house, wrapped up in each other's arms. They took turns between making love, watching movies, and doing even more talking.

They'd been so immersed in the details of fertility treatments, Mark realized, that somewhere along the lines they had lost sight of the other dreams they had together. Sure, they'd wanted a family but there was more to it than that. They'd wanted to build a life together and there was more than one way to do that.

On the last night of their self-imposed reconnection staycation, Mark wanted to do something special, so instead of ordering in food or finding something in the freezer to defrost the way they had been doing, he slipped out to the store to pick up a few things. The plan was to get in, buy what he needed, and get out before anyone saw him. They'd done a good job of shutting out the world, and although it couldn't last forever, he wanted just a few more hours before he had to share her again.

He kept his head down as he loaded the groceries onto the conveyer at the front of the store and went over the recipe in his head, doing one last mental check to be sure he had everything to make Christy her favorite stuffed chicken with béarnaise sauce. *Lemon...check...asparagus...check...butter...*

"Doctor Thomas?"

His head shot up at the sound of his patient's voice. "Becky?" He blinked hard. *How was this young girl standing behind the till ringing in his groceries? She'd only just given birth.* "What are you...are you feeling okay? How's little Mya?"

Myriad emotions played across the young girl's face. "I'm fine," she said after a moment. "And the baby...she's fine too."

Becky didn't look fine. She looked pale, exhausted, and impossibly thin for someone who was only a few weeks postpartum. "You're back to work already?" He glanced around as he realized that he didn't know Becky worked at the grocery store.

"I just started here," she said. "The timing isn't perfect but I was lucky to get the job." She rang up the package of chicken and wrapped it neatly in plastic before putting it in the bag. "I still waitress at Riverside, too. But that's nights and weekends mostly."

Mark blinked. "You're working *two* jobs? What about the baby?"

She smiled sadly. "I have friends watching her while I'm at work. It's not…well, it's working for now. But I need the money. Rent is expensive, and my dad decided that living with a newborn wasn't really…well, anyway, it's fine."

It didn't sound fine. Not even a little bit. Mark's heart ached for his patient.

"I was actually hoping I could make an appointment to see you," Becky said as she scanned the package of eggs. "Your receptionist said you were on vacation and I didn't want to bother you."

"No. It's no bother, of course." He knew without even checking with Sarah that when he went into the office the next day, his schedule would be jam-packed after taking time off. "Why don't you come in first thing tomorrow? I'll be in early. Eight o'clock? Would that work around your schedule?"

She nodded, and looked away, obviously trying not to cry. "Thank you, Doctor Thomas."

"Of course."

"That'll be $20.45."

He handed her two twenties. "I'll see you tomorrow then." He offered her a big smile, picked up his bags and walked away, pretending he didn't hear her when she called after him that he'd forgotten his change.

CHRISTY HAD IGNORED her phone for almost an entire week. It was an amazingly freeing feeling to be so disconnected from the world. Especially while she and Mark were reconnecting. She didn't think it was possible to have so much fun just hanging out in the house, having sex, cuddling, watching movies and…having more sex. It had been so long since they'd had a no-pressure, just-for-fun sex life, and Christy had forgotten just how awesome that was.

The mini vacation had been nice, but it was almost over. In the morning, Mark would get up and go to the office, and she would have to figure out her next move. She'd been doing a lot of thinking and talking it over with Mark, and she was excited to talk to the rest of the band about some of the ideas she'd been tossing around for them and how they could proceed.

She'd enjoyed their time off, but she was ready to get moving on things and rejoin life again. Which meant she should probably return Cam's calls. Her friend had left a number of voice mails for her, prefacing each one with things like, "Everything is okay." Or "It's not an emergency, but…"

She knew she was breaking the rule they'd decided on to pick up her phone, but one little call to Cam to set up a coffee date couldn't possibly hurt too badly.

Her friend picked up on the second ring. "Where've you been? Never mind, I know where you've been. In the bedroom with your husband, no doubt."

Christy laughed. She could almost see Cam wiggling her eyebrows on the other end of the line. "That's exactly what I've been doing, and I don't regret one minute of it."

"And nor should you." Cam laughed for a moment, before she asked, "Are you guys okay then? I mean, you've talked about everything?"

Christy nodded. "We've talked a lot. But we still have more to do. There's still a lot of things we need to figure out."

"But you're going to be okay?"

Christy smiled when she heard the front door open as her husband returned from the store. "We're going to be fine," she said because she knew it in her heart. They still needed to talk about a few major things, including the fact that Christy had decided that she'd like to put all conversations about starting a family on hold. Obviously a child of their own was out of the question, but years ago, they had discussed the idea of adoption. Although Christy wasn't against it then, and she certainly wasn't now, it wasn't the right time to talk about any of it.

"Will you have time for a coffee in the morning?" Cam asked. "There are a few things I want to talk to you about and I want to hear all about your tour. Do you think you have time for me? I know Mark's going back to work, so I assume your holiday is over."

Christy laughed. "Sadly, it is over and of course I have time for you. How's nine?" She waved at Mark and tried to take a bag from his arms as he joined her in the kitchen, loaded down with groceries.

He side-stepped her and started putting groceries away.

"Nine's great. And Christy?"

Distracted by her husband, who'd started dancing as he put the groceries away, Christy almost didn't notice the way her friend's voice changed. Almost. "What's up? Is everything okay, Cam?" She turned away from Mark to focus on the last of the conversation.

"Everything is fine. I just wanted to let you know that I'm really glad you're doing better and that you and Mark are working through everything. You know I love you, right?"

"Of course. I love you, too, silly."

"Okay, I'll see you tomorrow."

"Was that Cam?" Mark moved across the kitchen and gave her a kiss on the cheek.

"Yes. I'm sorry I broke our no-contact rule, but I figured I should probably return her call before she started to think there was something wrong. And you did go out to the store, so..."

"It's fine." Mark laughed and kissed her again. "I guess we can't hide from the world forever, can we?"

"No." She cuddled up into his arms and put her head on his chest. "But it sure has been nice."

He murmured into her hair and bent to kiss her neck.

The touch of his lips on her skin sent shivers through her to her core. "I could get used to these cuddles."

"I hope you do," he said. "There'll be lots more cuddles, that's a promise. I've missed this. I've missed you."

She pulled away enough to look into his eyes. "I've been right here."

"I know, but you know what I mean. Everything has just been…well, we got kind of lost for a while, didn't we?"

She nodded. They'd already talked for hours about how hard the last few years had been and she didn't feel they needed to go over it again. But there was one thing she did need to say. Christy took Mark's hand and led him through to the living room, where they sat on the couch side by side. "I think we should talk about the elephant in the room, Mark."

He tried to joke by making a show of looking around for the elephant, but Christy wasn't smiling and soon he grew serious too. "What's going on, sweetie?"

She took a deep breath and grabbed his hands in hers. "We need to talk about the baby." He sat up, startled, and his mouth fell open. She held up a hand to stop him before he could let his imagination run away with him. "The baby that we're not going to have," she said in clarification. "We haven't really talked about that and isn't that kind of a big deal?"

He nodded. "It's a huge deal. The quest to start a family, well…it's been…" He drifted off because there was no point saying what they both knew. It had been beyond difficult. The very thing that they thought would pull them together had broken them apart.

"That's exactly what I'm saying." Christy took a deep breath and sat up straighter. She'd been thinking about it for days, and it wouldn't be easy to say it, but for the sake of her marriage and her own sanity, it needed to be said. "I think now that IVF is off the table, we should maybe take a break from all of it for a bit."

"From all of what?" He sat back, but Christy wouldn't let him let go of her hands. "We kind of are taking a break, aren't we? I mean, Dr. Duncan said we're out of embryos and the cost is…well, it's not really an option right now."

She shook her head in agreement. "We'd talked about other options once and we'd agreed to revisit them if and when the time came." She remembered that conversation. Neither of them had actually thought that time would come. They were so sure that IVF would work. "And while I'm not saying no for forever," Christy continued, "I'm saying no to right now."

"No to…"

"No to thinking about adoption, or fostering, or…anything else with starting a family."

Mark let out a whoosh of air and pulled his hands free from hers. The loss of his touch was immediate, and she had to stop herself from lunging forward to grab him again. "Wow."

Christy clasped her hands together. "I know it's not really what we talked about and maybe that's not fair, but I just think that considering everything that's been going on and how I've been feeling and how you've been feeling, maybe this is the right time to focus on us again. I'm going to work on my music and try to make some progress with that. I don't know if it's really fair if we—"

"Christy." He held up a hand to stop her wild rambling. "It's okay." Mark's lips turned up into a soft smile.

"It's okay?"

He smiled and finally took her hand again. "It's okay. If you need time, I completely understand. At the end of the day, it's you and I who are the family and whatever we decide to do, we decide together. It doesn't have to be right now. It doesn't have to be tomorrow."

"I'm not saying no forever, Mark." It was important he understood that.

"I know, sweetie."

She searched his face for a sign that he was upset. "And you're okay with it? You're not disappointed?"

He laughed, giving her the answer she needed. "Upset? Sweetie, as long as you and I are together, I couldn't possibly ever be disappointed. You are my everything. You're all I need and everything else that may or may not come, will only add to this. But together, we are enough." He squeezed her hands and repeated himself. "We are enough."

"You're sure?"

He smiled and she could see in his eyes that he meant it. "I'm sure." Mark leaned forward and kissed her squarely on the lips. "And if you're ready to talk about it again—"

"*When* I'm ready to talk about it," she corrected him.

"Right. *When* you're ready."

He smiled again, and Christy couldn't remember the last time she'd been so happy. The last few months, even longer, had been a whirlwind and a crazy ride of ups and downs. Never did Christy imagine she'd be living the life she was. It was not at all the life she'd imagined, that was for sure.

But things had a way of working out. She was confident that when the time was right to start thinking about how they intended to expand their family, it would present itself. Until then, she was looking forward to having things slow down a little bit so they could just focus on each other.

Chapter Eighteen

CAM WAS both nervous and excited as she walked through the front door of Daisy's Diner. Daisy's had always been a spot to meet up with friends, have a small bite to eat or just a cup of coffee. It was perfect for almost every situation, and it was definitely the right choice for the conversation she was about to have with Christy.

For the last few weeks, while Christy had first been on tour and then holed up with Mark on their little reconnection stay-cation, Cam had been stressing and fretting about how she was going to tell Christy that she was pregnant. And she had to tell her, too, because it was time for a prenatal appointment. It was actually *past* time. But there was no way she could see Mark without talking to Christy first.

She almost contemplated going to a different doctor, but that felt wrong, too.

Small-town problems to be sure, but problems nonetheless. That would change today. She'd called and booked an appointment to see Mark later that afternoon, but first she was meeting Christy for a coffee.

Cam ordered herself a mint tea from Daisy at the counter

and looked around the space. Christy wasn't there yet, so she put in an order for a latte for her friend as well and went to grab a table in the corner. It had been a strategic move to meet Christy in a public place, and also a bit of a chicken-shit move. But more than anything, Cam didn't want her best friend to be upset or hurt that she was expecting a baby at a time when they'd only vaguely discussed having children together, when Christy and Mark had gone through so much heartache in their own quest.

It didn't seem fair and although deep down, Cam knew that Christy would be happy for her—of course she would—she just wasn't quite sure how she would react. And the last thing she wanted was to hurt her.

Cam found a quiet table and fidgeted with the glass vase in the middle of the table that held a single fresh daisy for a few minutes before Daisy herself brought over her drink orders. "You sure you don't want coffee?" Daisy asked. "I know how teenage girls can be." Cam couldn't help but laugh when the older lady winked at her. Despite having children of her own, who had long since been grown, Daisy also had to deal with high school students who had been using her diner as a hangout spot since before Cam's time, never mind her teenage employees.

"I hope Morgan hasn't been giving you any trouble." Cam already knew the answer. Morgan loved her job at Daisy's. Or maybe it was the paycheck that came with it. Either way, Cam didn't expect to hear anything she didn't know.

"Morgan's great." Daisy waved her hand, dismissing Cam's potential concern. "You know what they say—kids are always better behaved for someone else. It's their mamas they save all the good stuff for."

Cam laughed and her thoughts went instinctively to her new unborn baby and all the *good stuff* he or she would reserve just for her. "That's the truth," she said after a moment. "Thanks, Daisy."

"You let me know if you change your mind about that coffee."

"Of course."

With a nod and a wink, the older woman turned away and returned to her post at the counter. A moment later, Christy, looking refreshed and happy in her blue tank top and cut-off shorts, walked in.

She smiled as soon as she saw Cam, who pulled her into a hug when she reached her. "You look amazing, Christy."

"I guess that's what a little bit of reconnection with your husband will do." She laughed and sat down. "Is this mine? Thank you."

Cam nodded. "Tell me all about your tour and playing with the band. I heard there was a name change?"

"You heard?"

"Ben." Cam shrugged. "Evan was playing pool with him last week and the guys came in," she explained. "Timber Heart? I love it. So I guess this means you'll be playing with them some more."

"Not only playing but writing too." Christy leaned across the table with excitement as she told Cam all about the songs she'd written and how well they'd been received. The conversation slid naturally into how things had progressed between her and Mark, and Cam couldn't have been happier for her friend and her rediscovered happiness.

"You're absolutely glowing, Christy. You're like a totally different person. I know it's been so hard for the last little while."

Christy's smile faded, but only for a second. "It has," she said. "But you know what? I wouldn't have traded anything that Mark and I went through because if none of that had happened, none of this would be happening."

"Everything happens for a reason?"

Christy nodded. "I believe that. I really do."

"I'm really glad you feel that way." Cam took a deep breath.

Her friend stiffened and tilted her head in question. "Why do you say that?"

"I have something to tell you and I know it might be hard to hear, but I hope you'll be happy and—"

"You're pregnant."

"I'm—wait." Cam shook her head and sat back in her seat. She stared at her friend. "How did you know?"

Christy laughed. "I didn't. But when anyone starts a conversation like that, Cam...there are only a few possibilities. Congratulations. You guys must be so excited."

Cam ignored the congratulations, concerned instead for her friend. "Are you okay? I mean, I know...I don't mean for..."

"Cam, I'm fine. Really." Her smile looked genuine, and Christy wasn't one to lie to her, but still...Cam was concerned. It was a sensitive topic. "I really am happy for you and Evan. Really."

"Really?"

"Really!" Christy laughed for a moment and then got serious again. "I'll be honest with you, it does sting a little."

Cam felt a twinge in her gut.

"But," she continued quickly, "I really am happy for you. I know that just because it isn't going to happen for Mark and me doesn't mean that the rest of the world is going to stop having babies. And I meant what I said earlier. I really do think that everything happens the way it's supposed to happen. Your baby is the same and I can't wait to spoil him crazy."

"Him?"

Christy shrugged. "It's just a hunch. Based on nothing." She laughed. "But still. Now tell me, how excited is Evan? Are you guys going to get married before or after the little guy is born?"

Together, they laughed and talked, and Cam felt ridiculous for ever thinking that Christy would be upset with her for being pregnant. She should have given her friend more credit because Christy was strong and even though her heart must be hurting, at least a little bit, she was every bit the best friend she'd always been.

CAM WAS GOING *to have a baby.*

She'd be lying if she said it hadn't stung a little.

Christy's hands floated to her belly as she walked down Main Street away from Daisy's Diner after finishing her coffee catch-up with Cam. She let her hands rest on her stomach, for a minute. *There would never be a baby in there. She'd never feel the swell of her belly with a baby growing inside her.*

It was the first time she'd really allowed herself to acknowledge that particular fact since that last appointment. She would never carry a child. But that didn't mean that she wouldn't be a mother.

Christy had meant it when she told Cam that everything happened the way it was supposed to. She'd always believed that to be true, and after the summer they'd had, she believed it more than ever. She also believed that somehow, at some time in the future, she'd be a mother. She just had no idea what that looked like yet.

And more than that, she was perfectly okay with not knowing. If she'd learned one thing in the last few months, she'd learned that she didn't necessarily need to know how everything was going to play out, because life always threw a curveball and it probably wouldn't work out that way anyway.

It was a beautiful day and not too hot for the middle of

August, so she took the path that led down to Riverside Park and walked through the naturalized areas next to the river. It was beautiful and peaceful and gave Christy a chance to process the fact that Cam was pregnant.

She was happy for them. She really was, but she still allowed herself the moment of pain, too. Honoring herself and her feelings was important. She found a park bench that looked out to the river and sat in the shade, enjoying the sound of the water rippling over the rocks in this quieter part of the river.

It was still new, but the best way Christy knew to honor her feelings was to write about them. She reached into her purse and pulled out the notebook she'd started carrying around with her. Opened to a blank page and started writing.

The tears flowed as she let the words spill out of her and onto the page.

THERE ONCE WAS *a time I dreamed a dream of you.*
I wished, I hurt. I tried, I cried.
But you're not here, and my heart breaks.
Dreams are wishes that the heart makes,
And baby you're mine.
I won't give up.
I'll keep dreaming.
I'll keep wishing.
My baby one day you'll be.

SHE DIDN'T KNOW how long she sat there writing, working and crying, but when she was done, Christy sat up and stared at the notebook on her lap. She'd written pages and not only did she have a new song, she felt better. A lot better.

She'd been holding on to a lot of feelings and even though

she knew on some level that she'd been ignoring them, she hadn't realized the depth of what she was really feeling or how those feelings had affected everything.

Just getting it out on paper made her feel better. So much better than she could have imagined. She tucked the notebook away and stretched her arms over her head, laughing at herself as she did so for being so blind to her own emotions.

"Excuse me?"

Christy's laughter cut off as she spun to see a woman standing next to her. She was tall, blonde, and dressed in running clothes.

"Are you okay?" the woman asked. "I don't mean to be pushy, but as I was coming down the path you looked like you were crying and then—"

"I started laughing," Christy finished for her and almost started laughing again but she stopped herself so the woman didn't think she was a total lunatic. "I'm fine," Christy said. "I was just feeling a little emotional is all. But thank you," she added. It was nice to have people in town who still cared about the well-being of a stranger, and she told the woman so.

The blonde smiled. "I totally agree with you," she said. "Honestly, if it hadn't have been for the kindness of stranger a few months ago, I wouldn't be training for my big run right now."

"Oh yeah?" Christy turned, genuinely interested in hearing the story. "What happened?"

"I twisted my ankle on a run and was prepared to pretty much ignore it and hurt myself more, but another runner who happens to be a doctor stopped and looked at it, gave me some instructions, which I actually listened to, and now I'm back to full power."

A running doctor? Christy smiled. "Did your running doctor savior happen to give you his name?"

The woman nodded and smiled. "He did. His name is Mark, and I'm guessing you know him?"

"I do. Very well."

"You must be Christy."

"I am." Christy sat up straight. She was used to meeting Mark's patients and other people whose lives her kind husband had touched in some way, but she wasn't used to them knowing who she was. "Who are you?"

"Sorry." The woman stuck her hand out. "My name is Alicia. I'm training for the same race as Mark and after my ankle healed, I've run into him a few times and we've trained together."

Maybe at one point, not too long ago, Christy would have felt jealous or threatened in some way by this beautiful and fit woman in front of her. There were a lot of things Christy wasn't sure of in life, but her husband's love for her wasn't one of them. What she was feeling was guilt for the fact that Mark hadn't been training lately for his big run. She'd forgotten all about it during their stay-cation and he hadn't once mentioned that he needed to go for a training run.

"It's nice to meet you," Christy said distractedly. "I'm glad your ankle is feeling better. You're running the Polar Peeks Ultra too?"

"I am. But you know, I haven't seen Mark lately. Is he injured or just…well, he mentioned that…"

Christy laughed to put the woman at ease. "Look, I'm not a runner but I've lived with one long enough to know that some-times on those long runs you guys get chatting about stuff." She was more than used to Aaron knowing all kinds of things about their lives, just the same way Mark knew all kinds of details about Aaron. "I'm not surprised if he shared a few things with you."

Alicia looked relieved. "It was nothing too personal," she said quickly. "Mostly I told him to stop being such a *guy!*"

"So I have you to thank for my husband's appearance at my gig?" Christy laughed. She could hardly believe she was having this conversation with a complete stranger, yet she liked Alicia instantly and it didn't feel as weird as it probably should have.

"Not at all," Alicia said seriously. "That was all him. He loves you so much."

Christy's heart swelled in her chest because she knew that was true. "Don't I know it."

"Well, I'm just glad it's all worked out," Alicia said after a moment. "And that he's not injured."

"Definitely not. We had a bit of a vacation, but he should be out training soon. I'll make sure of it." And she would. It was important that even when their lives got busy and other things started to take priority, that they still made a point of doing the things that were important to them. "You'll see him out here soon."

"Good," Alicia said. "And maybe he can bring that friend of his, too?" She blushed a little and looked away.

"Friend?"

Alicia nodded. "Mark mentioned his usual running partner and I've seen him on the trails a few times. I was just—"

"Aaron?" She nodded again and Christy laughed. "Oh, I think we can definitely make that happen. Aaron's a great guy."

They chatted for a few more minutes before Alicia resumed her run. Christy pulled out her cell phone and tapped out a quick message to her husband.

Just thinking of you. I hope your day isn't too crazy.

A few moments later, he texted back.

Totally crazy! Are you having a good day?

She smiled because he must be swamped, but he still took a moment to respond to her.

I met your running friend, Alicia. She mentioned something about wanting to meet Aaron. Maybe it's time for some match making? ;)

Maybe on your run tonight?

She snuck that last part in because she wanted Mark to know it was totally cool with her if he wanted to finish the training for this run. In fact, it was more than cool with her. If it was important to him, it was important to her.

Sounds good. But not tonight. Something came up. I was actually about to call you. We need to talk.

Chapter Nineteen

MARK HAD ARRIVED at the office early to meet with Becky, just the way he'd said he would. The girl looked even more tired than she had the day before.

"She's not sleeping," Becky said. "At all. I can't get her to close her eyes even for a minute. And everything she eats, she spits it right back up again. Did you know that a baby could throw up so much?"

Mark chuckled. "I have heard about it, yes."

"It's not right, Doctor Thomas." Tears swelled in Becky's eyes. "There's something wrong with her."

"I'm sure that's not the case. Let's take a look."

Becky handed him the car carry seat, not bothering to unclip the infant from her seat. Mark didn't mind. The girl obviously needed a bit of a break. He took his time undoing the little girl's snaps.

"Well, hello there, Mya," Mark cooed as he lifted her out of the seat. "How are you today?"

In response, the little girl scrunched up her face and started to scream.

"See? She's miserable," Becky moaned. "I literally don't know what to do to make her stop crying. She hates me."

"That's not true," Mark said. "Is it, Mya?" He turned his attention back to the baby, who did look miserable. But Mark knew better, and he knew that Becky did too. She was just an overworked, exhausted new mother who didn't have any support system at all. He couldn't even begin to imagine how hard it would be for her.

Mark spent a moment bouncing the baby and settling her down before beginning his examination. By the time he was finished, Mya was contentedly sleeping on the exam table. "That wasn't so bad now, was it?" Mark scooped her up and wrapped her in a soft pink blanket covered in yellow ducks that Becky had brought with her.

"I don't know how you did that." Becky shook her head. "You must have had a lot of practice with your own kids."

Mark felt the familiar pang of hurt in his chest, but he pushed it away and shook his head. "Unfortunately, no. My wife and I haven't been able to have any children of our own. Not yet," he added, remembering the conversation they'd had just the night before. It wasn't the right time to discuss other options right now, but it would be one day.

"Oh," Becky said. "Well, you're really good with her. How do I make her stop puking?"

"It's probably just a bit of reflux. Are you nursing her?"

The girl shook her head. "Between working two jobs and trying to find babysitters, it's just not practical."

"That's okay," Mark reassured her. "There's nothing wrong with formula at all and there are so many different options. Maybe we'll try you on a different brand." He couldn't help but notice Becky's face when he mentioned the brand of formula he usually recommended. He knew it was expensive. "You know what," he said. "I think we have some sample cans in the back and Sarah can rustle you up some coupons as well to help out."

"Thank you." Becky finally reached out for her baby and Mark handed her over. He watched carefully while she took her time buckling the infant into the seat and covering her lightly with the blanket.

"You're doing a great job, Becky." He patted her shoulder. "If you need anything, anything at all, you let me know, okay? Don't hesitate."

The girl bit her bottom lip and nodded. "I should get to work. Thank you, Doctor Thomas."

He didn't have any time to think any more of his meeting with Becky and little Mya because right after they left, his day took off in a whirlwind of patients and treatments and paperwork while he played catch-up from his little holiday. He was exhausted and exhilarated all at the same time because he loved his job and as much as it was absolutely perfect to spend so much time with Christy, he was also glad to be back doing what he loved.

Despite being rushed off his feet, everything had been pretty normal for most of the day. It wasn't until he was trying to sneak a few minutes in his office to eat his sandwich before getting back to paperwork that things took a turn.

"Doctor Thomas?"

He swallowed down the bread and pressed the button to activate the speaker on his desk phone. "Yes, Sarah?"

"I'm sorry to bother you on your lunch break, but I think you should...well...maybe I'll come...umm..."

"Get to the point, Sarah." He was too busy to try to play a guessing game or decipher what she was saying.

"Something was delivered for you. I'll bring it...I'll be right there."

She disconnected and Mark rolled his eyes. Whatever it was

that was delivered could likely wait. Sarah must be having an off day. She didn't usually bother him with such minor details.

A moment later, there was a knock on the office door, followed by his receptionist carrying a...baby carry seat.

"What is that?"

"*Who,*" Sarah corrected him. "It's your delivery."

She turned the seat around and Mark could clearly see the pink blanket with yellow ducks he'd seen earlier that day. "Mya? Where's Becky?"

Sarah nodded. "She was just here. She left the baby and said something about giving her to you. She wasn't making any sense and then she said something about having to get to work and she didn't have a babysitter and she left. She said you'd be a better parent than she would and she couldn't do it anymore."

Mark's head spun. *Becky had left the baby?* For *him?* It didn't make any sense.

"Where did she go?"

Sarah shrugged. "I assume to work. What would you like me to do? Should I call the police? Surely she can't just abandon her baby?"

The police?

Mark didn't want Becky to get in trouble. That was the last thing the poor girl needed. But she clearly did need some help. He'd seen that earlier. She was overwhelmed and exhausted and at the end of her rope. He should have seen it earlier. If he hadn't been so busy himself, maybe he would have noticed some warning signs.

"I'll call Evan Anderson," Mark said. "He'll be able to put us in touch with the proper authorities without getting her into too much trouble. In the meantime..." He looked between the baby and Sarah in search of an answer to a question that he didn't even know how to ask.

"I'll watch her," Sarah said. "Until we can figure out what to do."

"Good." He nodded, relieved that she'd suggested it. "How long until my next patient?"

"Cam Riley is waiting in room one. But you have a short break after that."

Mark worked quickly to put his thoughts together. "Okay. I'll go see Cam, make the call to Evan and then…"

"You'll call your wife."

His eyes snapped to Sarah's in question.

"Doctor Thomas, if I may say something?"

His shoulders sagged. "Please."

"Sometimes things work out just the way they're supposed to." *That was what Christy had said the night before.* "Becky Olsen is a young girl, but she's also a smart girl. If she's making the decision to give up her baby for adoption, particularly if she's made the choice to give her baby to you, well…I don't have much experience with this type of thing, but I'd say that's a pretty big sign that this is maybe how things are supposed to work out, don't you?"

IF HAVING an infant abandoned into his care at his office was a sign, then meeting with Cam Riley, his wife's best friend, to confirm her pregnancy was only a bigger one. Mark did his best to stay focused on his patient while they discussed dates, and ultrasound appointments and prenatal vitamins. Mark was thrilled for them both and he told Evan so when he called the officer twenty minutes later. Right before he asked him to come to the office to discuss a very sensitive issue involving an infant.

Mark dropped his head into his hands and tried to rub some of the tension out of his temple before he did exactly what Sarah had suggested—call his wife. Maybe she was right.

Maybe Becky Olsen and her baby were a sign? Maybe they were meant to adopt little Mya? Maybe…he should call Christy?

But before he could do that, his phone vibrated with a text from her.

"I DON'T UNDERSTAND." Christy paced in Mark's tiny office. She'd arrived quickly and Mark had filled her in on Becky and the baby. Her mind was spinning and she was having trouble processing what was going on. *Mark's patient* gave *him a baby? How did that make any sense?*

Christy shook her head and looked again to the baby carrier in the corner, where the infant was sleeping. She'd wanted to go to her immediately and pick her up, but she knew better than to wake a sleeping baby.

Mark and Evan were seated at Mark's desk as he tried to explain everything to Evan, who was taking a statement.

"She's just a young girl," Mark said. "I don't want her charged with anything. I don't think that's the right way to handle this at all."

Evan nodded and scribbled something in his notepad. "I agree. And I don't think there's any need for that. But I will need to go talk to her and we'll need to establish if adoption is something she seriously wants to consider or if she was just reacting to stress. But if adoption is what she wants…" His gaze traveled to Christy and then back to Mark.

"Then what?" Christy asked.

"Well," Evan turned in his seat, "if she does want to follow through with adoption and she's selected the two of you, you'll need to make a decision."

"A decision?" Christy stared at Mark and then at the sleeping child. "About her?"

"About *adopting* her," Evan clarified. "There's still due

228

process of course, and I'll admit I don't know everything about it, but open adoptions where the birth mother selects the parents are often much easier to facilitate."

"Adoption?" Christy was vaguely aware that she sounded like a broken record but she couldn't process what was happening fast enough. "Like us adopting her?"

"Yes."

"Becky did say she thought we'd be better parents."

"She doesn't even know me." Christy spun to face Mark. "How could she just—"

"She's young, overwhelmed, and has no support." Mark put his hands on her shoulders. His presence helped ground her. He seemed so much more in control, so calm, so...*okay* with everything. "I've been there for her."

"You're her doctor."

"I don't understand it either." He tipped her chin up so she was looking at him. "But it is the situation right now and—"

They were interrupted by a high-pitched cry from the corner. Without hesitation, Christy moved to the baby carrier and attended to the infant. She unsnapped her from her seat and gently scooped her up.

"Ssh, sweetie. It's okay." She snuggled her to her chest and rubbed her back gently. "Do you think she's hungry?" Christy peered down into the baby's scrunched-up face. "Are you hungry, sweetheart?"

"Sarah said there was a diaper bag up at reception," Mark said. "There should be something there."

Christy hardly took her eyes off the baby. "I'll figure it out. Come on, Mya. Let's go see what we can find."

After locating the diaper bag, which was remarkably empty, Christy prepared a bottle. After Mya drank her fill, she changed her diaper and rocked her back to sleep in one of the empty exam rooms.

She couldn't stop staring at the perfect little pink face. She was so tiny, so perfect and...*not her baby*. She needed to remember that and not forget it. Becky may have dropped her off but like Mark said, she was a scared and unsupported young woman. Almost a child herself. She could change her mind. She could be back any moment. After all, from what Mark had told her about Becky, she was a good kid, a hard worker, and she'd wanted and loved her baby from the beginning. The chances that she'd be back for Mya were good.

And that was the right thing.

But what if she didn't come back?

What if adopting the baby was *the right thing?*

She ran a finger down the baby's chubby cheek. *A decision,* Evan had said. If Becky was serious about going through with an adoption, they would have to decide what to do.

But she'd just made a decision. She'd just settled on the idea of waiting and focusing on their relationship and themselves before they considered moving forward with an adoption or other options.

And now...

"KNOCK KNOCK." Mark opened the door of the exam room slowly. "Everything okay in here?" He asked the question, but he could see it was. It took his breath away to see Christy holding the newborn, her body curled protectively around the baby, the care and concern in her eyes as she gazed at the tiny face.

"She's just perfect."

Christy was born to be a mother. It just looked so right on her.

But he needed to remember the circumstances they were in. This was not a normal situation, to be sure, and nothing was definite. Nothing at all. Because not only was there all the legal issues to go through, they still needed to talk to Becky and then…they would have a lot to discuss. They'd been through so much. *Was it the right time to think about adopting a baby?* Christy had just said she didn't think it was.

So many questions swirled through his head as he stood there watching his wife that he hardly noticed when Evan came in behind him and spoke. "Turns out that Becky is working her shift at the store right now."

Mark turned and nodded. "We should head over there and talk to her."

"Exactly. I told the manager that we'd need a few minutes with her. Everything is to be handled as discreetly as possible."

"What's going on?"

"It turns out that Becky is working her shift at the store right now," Evan said. "I spoke with the manager, and Mark and I are headed over there to talk to her."

It had meant cancelling more patients, something that Mark really hadn't wanted to do. But this was not a normal circumstance, and it had to be dealt with sooner rather than later.

"Christy…" He wanted to ask her what she was feeling, what she was thinking. But Evan was there and it wasn't the right time. Not that there would ever be a right time. But he also wanted to let her know that no matter what happened—if Becky decided not to give the baby up, if Christy wasn't ready, if…no matter what—they'd do it together. Instead of saying any of those things, when she looked up from the baby, all that came out of his mouth was, "I love you."

He hoped it would be enough.

"Okay," Evan said a little awkwardly. "Are you ready to—"

"Excuse me, Doctor Thomas?" They all turned to the door to see Sarah, looking very apologetic and wringing her hands. "I know you're busy but I just got a call from Drew Ross. It's Eric. She needs you to come."

Behind him, Mark heard Christy make a sound between a gasp and a cry. Instantly, he reached for her hand.

"Should I tell her…" Sarah looked between everyone in the room. Her eyes landed on the baby in Christy's arms. "What should I tell her?"

"Tell her I'll be right there." Mark gave Christy's hand a squeeze. "Evan, you'll have to go on your own to talk to Becky. I'm sorry."

"I'll go."

Mark stared at his wife. "You don't know her. She's just a—"

"I think I should talk to her. Woman to woman." Christy nodded and looked down at the baby again. She couldn't seem to look away for long. "Besides, if she is serious about giving up her baby for adoption, especially if she's serious about us, I need to meet her."

He couldn't argue with that. Not really. "Evan?"

His friend shrugged. "It's not a bad idea and I'll be there. It'll be okay."

"I'll watch the baby," Sarah offered. "Just go do what you need to do. I'll manage things around here."

Mark knew if Drew was calling the office, it was an emergency. She wouldn't ask him to come in the middle of the afternoon if it wasn't. "I should get going," he said to Christy. "Are you sure you want to—"

"Go. Drew and Eric need you. I've got this." She glanced between the baby and him, and Mark's heart swelled. No matter how things turned out with Mya and Becky, he had Christy and together they would be fine.

He leaned over and kissed her hard and fast.

Chapter Twenty

THE ALMOST IMMEDIATE emptiness of her arms after she handed the sleeping baby to Sarah surprised Christy. She'd only known Mya for a few hours and already she was attached.

That probably wasn't a good thing. There were so many variables. So many things to think about. They weren't even considering adoption right now; it wasn't the right time with her music and the band and…*one thing at a time.*

She kept repeating those words to herself.

One thing at a time.

And the first thing was to talk to Becky. Evan needed to take a statement and get some information from the girl, but Christy's goal was to get a feel for the girl and what it was she really wanted. Was she just scared and she'd made an irrational decision? Was it an impulse she wanted to take back? Did she really want to keep her baby with the proper support? If that was the case, Christy would help her find the resources she needed. Or did she really want Mark and Christy to adopt her baby?

And what if she did?

Christy forced herself to take a deep breath.

"Are you okay?" Evan asked her as they approached the grocery store. "Do you need a minute?" They'd driven the short distance to the store from the office, which was nice because Evan's police car felt like a safe respite—no matter how false—from the craziness that was swirling around them. For a Monday, it had definitely been a doozy.

"I'm fine." She nodded and smiled. "It's just a lot, you know?"

"It is a lot." Evan smiled. "And it would be good if Mark were here. If you want to—"

"No," she interrupted him. "I can do this. No. I *need* to do this. And Mark needs to be with Eric and Drew." She squeezed her eyes shut for a moment. "God, I hope everything is okay there."

Evan put his hand on hers and squeezed. "We can't think of that right now, okay? I texted Cam and gave her a heads-up in case Drew needs support. But right now, it's you and me and we're going to go and talk to Becky. Okay?"

Christy nodded. "I'm ready."

The second they walked into the store, Christy identified Becky Olsen. She was petite, with brown hair pulled back into a ponytail that revealed very sad and tired eyes. She looked as if she hadn't slept in weeks—maybe she hadn't—she almost slouched over the till and looked as if at any minute she might break down in tears.

Christy's heart instantly went out to her. She'd always wanted a baby of her own, but that was always as a married woman with a husband and family to support her. She'd never once imagined what it would be like to be young and broke with no one to help her with late-night feedings, diaper changes, or just to help rock a cranky baby to sleep. Never mind to pay for the formula, the never-ending supply of diapers, the clothes, and everything else that went along with having a baby. The poor girl. No wonder she looked like she was about to break.

The manager of the store met them as soon as they walked in the door, and she and Evan exchanged a few words before she left to talk to Becky. Christy watched as the manager said something to the girl. Instantly, Becky's head shot up and she looked much more awake. Her eyes were wide and full of fear as she looked at the police officer and strange woman, staring at them. Her boss put her hand on Becky's shoulder and led her over where Christy and Evan were waiting. "You can use the staff room if you like, Officer?"

"Thank you." Evan looked to the girl. "Or would you rather get some fresh air? You're not in trouble, Becky. We just want to talk to you for a few minutes, okay?"

Becky nodded numbly. "Okay."

Evan took that to mean that they should go outside. He kept a hand on her shoulder as he guided them out to the parking lot and to a picnic table on a grassy area next to the store. As soon as they were seated, Evan started the conversation. "My name is Officer Anderson, Becky. And this is Christy. Doctor Thomas's wife."

Becky's eyes got wider, if that was possible, and she stared at Christy.

"It's okay, Becky." Christy did her best to smile despite the fact that she was no doubt as equally scared and unsure of what was going to happen.

"We need to ask you a few questions."

She nodded.

"Do you have a daughter named Mya, who is approximately two weeks old?"

As a tear slipped down the girl's cheek, Christy's heart broke a little.

"Yes." Her voice shook with the first word she'd actually spoken since they'd arrived. "She's seventeen days old."

Christy did the quick calculation. Mya was born the day before Mark arrived in Crescent City. *That's why he was so tired.* She offered Becky a small smile.

"And did you see Doctor Thomas at his office today?"

"Yes," Becky said. "He came into the store last night and told me to come in for an appointment this morning before office hours started. He was trying to be nice because I had to work later and I didn't have much…" She trailed off, no doubt realizing how much she was rambling. "I took her in for a check-up. She's been spitting up a lot and…I wanted to make sure she was okay. Is she okay?" She addressed the question to Christy.

"She's fine. Spat up a little for me, too, after I fed her." Christy kept the smile on her face, even when fresh tears spilled from Becky's eyes.

Evan made some notes in his book before he continued. "And did you then drop your child off at Doctor Thomas's office later this afternoon? Approximately two hours ago?"

Her hands came up to her face and she crumpled over her knees as sobs racked her body.

Evan looked over to Christy.

"Hey." Christy stood and went to the girl. She rubbed Becky's back slowly. "It's okay." She let Becky cry for a minute before she asked the question that Evan was no doubt leading up to. He probably had some sort of protocol to follow, but at that moment they were talking about the welfare of not only a newborn but a young girl who was clearly distraught, and Christy needed to step in. "Becky." She said the girl's name softly. "Did you leave your baby for Mark and me to adopt?"

Becky didn't look up from her hands, but she nodded and Christy's breath hitched in her throat.

"And is that really what you want to do?" She held her breath as she asked the question because all of a sudden, it seemed that the whole world rested on her answer. "It's okay if you changed your mind."

It seemed like an eternity, but Becky nodded again and looked up into Christy's eyes. "Yes," she said.

Christy's heart leapt and in a second, she had her answer about what decision she'd make when it came down to making the decision of adopting baby Mya or not. But there was still a big *if* in the equation. She couldn't get her hopes up. She couldn't afford to be disappointed again.

"Becky?" Christy took a deep breath and asked another question. "If there were some resources we could help set you up with, maybe an agency who could help you figure things out…would you still want Doctor Thomas and me to adopt your baby?"

Christy had to force herself to breathe while she waited for Becky's answer.

In.

Out.

If Becky said no, she'd do whatever she could to help the girl make a good life for her and her baby. *But if she said yes…*

It felt like minutes passed and still Becky hadn't answered.

Finally, Evan spoke. "Becky, I'm sure you know that you can't just leave a child in a doctor's office, right?"

She nodded in answer.

"If you really are prepared to surrender your child, there are proper steps to take. We will have to contact social services, who will counsel you regarding your choices, and depending on what kind of adoption you—"

"No." Becky sat up straight. "I know what I want. I made my decision and I don't need to be counseled. I want Doctor Thomas and his wife to adopt my baby."

Christy didn't even realize that she'd gasped until Becky looked at her.

"If you want her, of course."

"I do!" Christy clapped a hand over her mouth. "I mean… we need to follow…"

"There's a lot to discuss still." Evan took over the talking, a fact Christy was thankful for considering she couldn't trust herself to speak. "But you're sure of your decision?"

Becky's bottom lip quivered but she looked Christy directly in the eye when she said, "Yes. I love her so much." Her voice shook, but she swallowed hard and continued. "But…I'm too young to give her the life she deserves. I have no money. I'm working all the time and I have no one to take care of her while I'm at work. And…she needs a father." Tears spilled down her face. "She needs so much more than I can give and I'm just a kid. My dad was right. She'll have the life she deserves, with the parents she deserves if Doctor Thomas and…" She looked to Christy. "And his wife would be willing to take her."

"But you don't even know me."

"I know you'll love her. I know you're a good person." She tried and failed for a little smile. "Doctor Thomas has been so kind to me. He cares. He really cares and that's more than I can say for her father." She looked at her feet. "Or her grandfather, or really anyone in her life."

Christy put her hand on Becky's arm and squeezed. "Except for you. *You* care."

"But I'm not enough," Becky said. "I know that now. She deserves more." She looked to Evan. "Officer Anderson, I want the Thomases to adopt my baby. If they'll have her," she added quickly.

Christy nodded. Although she still hadn't had a chance to talk it over with Mark, she was confident that this baby was meant to be theirs. Her entire attitude had done a complete turnaround in the last twenty-four hours but that was before. And just as she'd said to Cam earlier, everything happened for a reason. She believed it.

"What do I need to do to make sure the Thomases can adopt her?" Becky asked Evan, with more self-assurance than she'd expressed since they'd gotten there. "If I can't be the mother she needs to be, I want her to be raised by Doctor Thomas and Christy."

"I'll make a few calls. I'm sure we can get Judge Stewart to rule the Thomases as temporary guardians until we sort it all out legally. Okay?"

Becky nodded and when Evan excused himself to start making the necessary arrangements, the girl crumpled with a mixture of exhaustion and possibly relief.

Because she didn't know what else to do, Christy slid over on the picnic table bench and wrapped her arm around the girl. Almost at once, Becky spun into her embrace and rested her head against Christy's shoulder, where she cried until there weren't any tears left to cry.

Chapter Twenty-One

IN HIS CAREER, Mark had lost patients before. It was part of his profession. Doctors healed, but there were times when, despite their best efforts, there was no more healing to be had. When he walked out of Eric's room for the last time, he knew it was one of those times. There was no longer anything he could do.

"I'm sorry, Drew." Mark fought tears as he spoke to his friend. "He doesn't have long."

Drew nodded and swallowed hard. "I know," she said. "Is there anything…"

"The pain seems to have subsided now," Mark finished her thought. Often when terminal patients neared the end, the pain they'd lived with for so long inexplicably vanished. "Just go be with him. I'll stay in case there's anything else you need."

"Thank you."

Mark watched as Drew made a few quick phone calls before she took little Austin down the hall to say good-bye to his father. Numb and feeling helpless, he rummaged around the kitchen. He found a box of cookies that he put on a plate, made a pot of strong coffee, and washed a bowl of grapes that he set out on the counter as the front door opened.

He knew Eric's parents and Ben would be coming by to say their good-byes, and it was his job to stay as unobtrusive as possible. When they arrived, he handed out coffee, snacks, and tissue and did his best not to think about the man he'd grown up with and called a friend in the other room who was prepared to die and leave his young family behind.

He'd spoken to Christy only briefly to hear that they'd met with Becky, and Evan was looking into the legalities of what came next. They had a lot to discuss before they made any decision final, but they'd agreed to wait until he came home and his place right then was with Eric and Drew.

It would be almost impossible to put it out of his mind, but when Drew emerged from the back bedroom, her eyes red rimmed and crying, he knew that was exactly what he had to do.

"Is he…is everything…"

"He's in with his family. I wanted to give them some space."

Mark led Drew to the table and put a cup of coffee in front of her without asking.

"And Austin?"

"I tucked him into bed." She shook her head a little. "I don't think he really understands, you know? He said good-bye, but it's like he thinks he'll see his dad in the morning. I don't know how to tell him…" A sob escaped her. Mark hadn't seen her cry much; she'd been so strong throughout everything, but everyone had their limit. "I don't know how to tell him that his daddy will be gone in the morning." She looked to Mark in question but there was no doubt for either of them that Eric wouldn't make it through the night.

"He'll be okay," Mark said. "He has you and his grandparents and Ben, and all of us." He pushed the box of tissues across the table. "Whatever you need, Drew. You know we're all here for you."

She nodded and attempted a smile. "I know. Thank you."

They sat in silence while Drew sipped at her coffee. Eric's parents came out and then finally Ben. "He's asking for you," Ben said to Drew.

She nodded and went to her husband.

At some point, Cam arrived and started making sandwiches and plates full of food.

It was just before eight when Drew emerged from the bedroom and went straight into Cam's arms for a hug.

TWO HOURS LATER, Mark, after taking care of the arrangements, finally arrived home. He'd left Drew in the capable hands of Cam and Evan, who'd arrived after his shift. It wasn't going to be easy, but she'd be okay.

He was completely wrung out when he arrived home, but the moment he stepped in the front door, the new and unexpected energy hit him. The house felt different. *There was a baby there.*

Mark moved straight to the bedroom across the hall from theirs and peeked in the door that was open a crack. Christy had spent so many hours picking out the furniture for that room over the years, insisting that it wasn't bad luck to prepare it just in case. She'd spent hours folding little clothes and finding just the right prints for the walls. At some point during the last treatment, she'd stopped going into the nursery. It filled Mark's heart with love to see her in there now, sitting in the rocking chair, the swaddled baby in her arms.

"Knock knock," he whispered.

Christy turned and smiled.

It was the most beautiful sight he'd ever seen, but he knew

in his heart he had to manage his expectations. Mya wasn't theirs. Not yet. She might never be. They had a lot to talk about.

"Is she sleeping?" He mouthed the words, not wanting to wake the baby.

"She is." Christy stood, but made no move to put down the sleeping child. "But she'll sleep through anything. Once she gets to sleep, that is. Do you want to hold her?"

He did. More than anything. But first he needed to know what had happened.

"How did it go?" he asked instead. "With Becky?"

"It was hard," Christy said. "She's hurting and confused."

He thought back to the girl in the hospital, determined to raise her baby even without the father. And then to the girl he'd seen at the grocery store—tired, wrung out. And then finally his thoughts went to the Becky he'd seen in his office earlier that morning. *Was it really only just that morning?* That Becky had been overwhelmed, defeated and broken.

"But?" he asked, sure there was a *but*.

"But she's sure about giving her up for adoption."

Hope leapt in his chest. "And…"

"She wants *us* to adopt her."

"Really?" Still, Mark wouldn't let himself get his hopes up. Even when Christy nodded in confirmation, he still had one more very important question. "And you, Christy? What do *you* want?"

She didn't answer right away, but Mark was sure he saw the answer on her face as he gazed at the sleeping child. Still, he needed to hear it.

"Yes." She sniffled when she looked up and even in the dim light, Mark saw the tears in her eyes. "Yes," she said again. "If this is what Becky wants, I want us to be her parents, Mark. We can give her a good home, we can love her, we can…"

"We can." He nodded. "But you said it wasn't the right

time right now. Just yesterday you said you wanted to wait and focus on—"

"Things change." She grinned and he laughed.

"Yes, they do." He shook his head and took another step into the room. "Can I hold her now?"

"Of course." She handed him the baby and even though he'd held her before as a patient, this was different. So very different. The moment he felt her gentle weight in his arms, his heart swelled to the point where he thought it might burst.

His body started to naturally sway and he stared down at her perfectly tiny face. "We can do this." He spoke almost to himself, but Christy slid her arm around him and rested her head on his shoulder.

"Yes, we can."

IT HAD BEEN a long night but instead of being exhausted, Christy was exhilarated. Mya needed to be fed every few hours, and then Christy and Mark would take turns rocking her back to sleep. Aware that the child had been through a lot in her short life, they spent extra time and care cuddling her and soothing her. They also spent that time talking. Mostly about Mya and Becky and what an adoption would look like and what their next steps should be, but also about Drew and Eric.

She'd known it was coming, but when Mark told her that Eric had passed away, it hit her fresh. It had never felt fair that her friend should lose her husband and father of her child so young, but somehow it seemed extra cruel that Drew had experienced such an intense loss on the same day that Christy and Mark had gained so much.

Christy was rocking Mya in the living room when the sun finally came up. She'd barely put her down all night, needing to hold her, smell her, and watch her every movement to actually believe that it was really happening. *She was finally going to become a mother.*

It still felt so surreal that her entire life could change so dramatically in such a short span of time. If she hadn't been so tired, she would have laughed at the irony of it all. She should know better than to think she could control her own fate when destiny had different plans.

Yesterday she'd been ready to wait when it came to motherhood, and now…nothing felt so right.

Her feelings bubbled over and her fingers itched to hold a pen and record them. Finally, reluctantly, she put Mya down in the bassinet they'd brought out of the nursery and she settled into the chair next to her with her journal as she began writing.

"Good morning."

Christy looked up and smiled at her husband. "Morning."

"How is she?" Mark kissed Christy on the cheek before peeking in at the sleeping infant. "Did you get any sleep after that last feeding?"

"A little." She shrugged. There'd be time for sleep later.

"Are you writing?"

"I am! I have so many feelings, so many thoughts and…I just needed to get them down. I think it'll be a beautiful song."

Mark smiled. "I have no doubt. I'll go put some coffee on. Let me know if she wakes up and I'll watch her this morning so you can get some writing done."

She didn't think she could love him any more than she did. "Mark?" She caught him before he disappeared into the kitchen. "I love you." She smiled. "We're going to do this."

"We absolutely are." He blew her a kiss. "As soon as I get the coffee on, I'll call the lawyer's office and see what our next steps are, okay?"

She nodded. "I'm going to go see Drew this morning, too.

She's going to need a hug and some support. I need to be there."

"Of course you do. Did you want me to take the morning off? I can watch Mya while you—"

"No," she stopped him. "I'll take her. You have enough to worry about this morning. And really…this is our life now. We just didn't have as much time to adjust to the idea as others do."

"Or any time at all."

She laughed, but when she looked down at the sleeping baby again, the laughter died and was replaced by emotion so thick she could barely swallow. Time or not, she didn't care. Everything about Mya was perfect.

IT DIDN'T FEEL RIGHT that it should be a warm, sunny day with the birds chirping outside of Drew's kitchen windows. Cam had slept on the couch the night before, not because she thought she'd be needed during the night, but more because she knew Drew would appreciate her presence and if her friend did feel like talking or crying or…sitting and staring into space with a friend by her side, that's what she'd be there for.

The night before, Drew hadn't wanted to talk at all. Instead, she'd gone to bed, choosing to cuddle in with Austin instead of her own bed across the hall from the room where Eric had passed away. Not that Cam could blame her. There would have to be a lot of adjustments in the coming days and months.

But first, breakfast. She felt so helpless, but there was one thing Cam *could* do and that was cook breakfast for Drew and her son so that even though they were waking up to a world where everything was different, at least they'd have pancakes. It seemed silly, but when Drew finally made her appearance in the kitchen, she took one look at what Cam was doing—the bacon in the skillet, the pancakes on the griddle, and the coffee in the cup that was handed to her—and smiled.

"Thank you," she said. "Austin will be thrilled. He's been begging me for pancakes and bacon for days."

"It's not much," Cam said. "But maybe it will…"

"It is a lot." Drew's smile faded into sadness. "Especially for a little boy who doesn't really understand. It means a lot, Cam. Really."

Cam made herself a tea and they sat together at the table for a few minutes. "What now?" she asked after Drew had a chance to have a few sips. "I mean, what's going to happen? What do you need me to do? Anything at all, you know that, right?"

"I do." She nodded. "Thank you. But it's all taken care of. I'll make some calls to the funeral home and we'll pick a date. Probably not for a few weeks, just so we can make sure family has a chance to come in."

"Makes sense."

"But other than that, it's all taken care of. Eric made all the arrangements. He didn't want me to have to worry about anything." A tear slipped down her cheek. "Anything except learning to live without him, I guess." Drew dropped her head as sobs racked her body. "I'm sorry," she managed. "It's just finally real, you know."

Cam nodded, although she certainly didn't know.

"I feel like I've had forever to prepare for this, but it wasn't long enough. Forever could never be long enough."

"No," she agreed. "Forever would never be long enough. But I know you'll be okay. You and Austin, you'll both be okay. I know it."

Drew nodded. "We will. Eric made me promise not to stop living just because he did, and I won't. That's not fair to Austin. Life goes on, I guess."

Cam shrugged, once again amazed at the strength of her friend. She knew Drew would need her, need all of them, in the coming months, but she'd meant it when she said that she knew Drew would be okay. She would.

"You know we're here for you. No matter what you need." She'd said it before, but she'd keep saying it. "Christy's on her way over," Cam said. "She wanted to be here earlier, but…well I'm going to let her tell you."

Drew gave her a look. "Is everything okay?"

"Everything's fine." Cam smiled. "More than fine. She was a little unsure if she should come by today, but…"

Drew looked confused, but too tired to ask any more questions, which was fine because a moment later there was a soft knock on the door, followed by Christy walking into the kitchen.

"Drew?"

The other woman stood and Christy immediately pulled her into a fierce hug. They held each other for a few moments before Cam got up and joined them. Together, Christy and Cam surrounded their friend in love. They would be the strength to hold her up.

"Thank you for coming," Drew said when the girls finally released her. "Cam said you had something—"

They were interrupted by the sound of a shrill baby cry and Drew's mouth fell open. Christy, who looked just as tired as the rest of them, smiled and held up her finger. "I'll be right back."

She was gone a moment to the front foyer, returning with a baby carrier in her hand.

"What the hell is that?"

Christy laughed. "A baby."

"Okay." Drew watched intently as Christy unbuckled the infant and expertly cradled her, soothing the baby's cries at once. "Better question," she continued. "Whose baby is it?"

Christy's eyes filled with tears. "She's mine and Mark's. We're going to adopt her."

Cam already knew the story from Evan, who'd filled her in when he stopped by the house the night before but hearing it from Christy's mouth gave her chills. This baby was meant to be theirs and her heart swelled with happiness for one friend at the same time that it ached for her other friend.

"I know the timing isn't great," Christy apologized. "And I know you're going through…well, I can't imagine what you're going through, Drew. But I needed to see you and…"

"Don't apologize for anything." Drew smiled through her tears. "A baby? It's so great, Christy. I know how badly you've wanted this and don't give the timing another thought. Everything happens the way it should, don't you think?"

They all nodded.

"I believe that," Drew said. "I have to, otherwise I—"

There was a movement in the kitchen doorway that drew the women's attention. Austin stood in his pajamas, a ratty stuffed frog hanging from one hand, the other rubbing his eye, still full of sleep. "Mama?"

Drew's hand flew to her mouth at the sight of her son and the realization of what she'd have to tell him.

"I agree." Cam stood, breaking the silence of the moment. She moved to the stove to finish off the breakfast she'd put on hold. "And right now, I think it's time for some breakfast. How do you feel about bacon and pancakes, Austin?"

Chapter Twenty-Two

ERIC'S memorial service had been a beautiful celebration of life. And that's exactly what it was. A celebration. He'd requested everyone to wear bright colors, and ordered no tears, although that wasn't an order Christy could follow. She'd cried throughout the speeches and recounted memories and then it was over and everyone spilled out of the banquet room at the Creekside Inn that was the only place big enough to host the celebration, and into the warm September day.

It was hard to believe it had been two weeks already since Eric passed away and Mya came into their lives. So much had happened in such a short time, that it hardly seemed real.

Christy looked at her husband, who held their baby girl in his arms, and smiled. Her heart was completely full. After the chaos of the first day, Mark had contacted a lawyer and together with social services, they'd put together an adoption agreement, which Becky had signed. They'd decided on an open adoption that allowed Becky to continue to be part of their lives, and despite being completely sleep-deprived and exhausted, Christy had never been happier.

She looked around the grassy lawn that sloped gently

down to the river and watched her friends. Despite the sadness of the day, everyone was trying to honor Eric's wishes and not be too sad. An almost impossible task for almost everyone.

Her eyes landed on Amber and Cam, and she went over to join them. Amber had arrived in town from San Francisco only a few days ago. She looked sleek and perfectly put together, the way she always did in her tailored suit, with her shiny dark hair hanging down her back. Christy had always thought Amber could have been a model with her striking good looks, but the only things she'd been interested in was school, getting good grades, and becoming a lawyer.

A mission she'd accomplished with ease. It was remarkable to all the others how Amber could be so intensely focused at the expense of all distractions, including the men who constantly threw themselves at her. But if she ever noticed, she didn't say so. In fact, to Christy's knowledge, Amber had never even been in a serious relationship.

"Hey, girls." Christy wrapped her arm around each of them as she joined them next to the river. "It was a nice service, wasn't it?"

"We were just saying that," Cam agreed. "I think Eric would have liked it."

Amber nodded. "How do you think Drew is doing?"

Their eyes traveled across the lawn to where Drew was standing, her hand in Austin's, chatting with a group of Eric's relatives. Ben stood nearby, as if keeping watch on his widowed sister-in-law. He'd been a very steady presence in the weeks following Eric's passing. Always close, but he kept his distance at the same time. It was good. Drew was going to need all the support she could get.

"I think she's doing as well as can be expected," Christy said. "I bet she's glad you're here."

Amber nodded, but she didn't smile. "I would have liked to

been here earlier, but I just..." Her eyes drifted away and wouldn't meet Christy's. "I couldn't get away."

"Big case?" Cam asked.

"Not really." Her eyes darkened.

There was something going on with her and it wasn't the first time Christy thought so. When she'd spoken with her on the phone earlier in the summer, she'd seemed *off* somehow. Even at the reunion in the spring, Amber had been distracted and not herself. And it was definitely not normal for her not to be there for her friends unless there was something very important keeping her away. Even when Amber was at her busiest, she always found time for her best friends. Always. Christy wasn't even going to pretend that it wasn't weird that Amber didn't come right away when she heard that Eric had passed away.

It was beyond weird.

"Is everything okay with you, Amber?" She might as well ask her straight out. "You just seem a little..."

"Not yourself," Cam finished for her.

Good, she wasn't the only one who'd noticed Amber's strange behavior.

"In fact, you just don't really seem—"

"I'm fine." Amber smiled broadly and stared at each of them in turn. She'd always been an impeccable liar and had a poker face like nobody else. It was definitely one of the traits that made her such a successful lawyer, but as her friend, it was annoying as hell when you were trying to get to the bottom of something. "And even if I wasn't," she added, "I don't think this is the time or place to discuss it."

So there was *something going on.*

"I agree," Cam said. "I think we should go rescue Drew from making small talk with Eric's extended family and get her out of here, don't you think?"

"Absolutely." The girls agreed readily, and after making sure that Austin was well taken care of between both sets of grandparents, they whisked Drew away for a little much-needed girl time.

They didn't go far, just to the riverbank, far enough away for a little privacy but close enough for Mark to bring her the baby when it was time for him to go with the guys for a special tribute to Eric at the Log and Jam.

"This is nice." Drew lay back on the cool grass, letting her purple dress float around her bare legs. "I needed this," she said to the girls, who'd joined her, lying down. "Thank you for being here."

"Of course." Christy reached for her hand and squeezed.

"I'm not even going to ask you how you're doing," Amber said.

"Oh please don't!" Drew beat her feet against the ground before laughing. "If one more person asks me how I'm doing, I'm going to scream."

"No doubt," Cam agreed. "I mean, I get why people ask, but really, what kind of answer do they expect?"

"Right?" Drew sat up and looked at each of them. "You know what's going to be the hardest?"

Christy shook her head although in her head, she could think of a laundry list of events and dates that were going to be challenging for her friend.

"Just being alone." Drew dropped her head and focused on picking blades of grass from the lawn. "I've never been alone. I'm not sure I know how."

"You don't have to be."

Cam and Christy both sat up at the same time and stared at Amber, who'd spoken. She was always the one out of the four of them who had all the answers, but she couldn't possibly have the answers to this particular problem.

"I mean it," Amber said, addressing their unasked questions. "You don't have to be alone, Drew, because I'm not going to let you."

"Pardon?" Drew let the picked pieces of grass slip from her fingers. "What do you mean, you're not going to let me be alone?"

"I'm moving in," Amber said with authority. She jumped up easily and dusted off her pencil skirt. "I'm moving back to Timber Creek," she clarified. "And in with you."

The girls all looked at one another. Amber was known for her strong opinions and once she made her mind up about something, she followed through. But even for Amber, this was a bit much.

"What do you mean?" It was Christy who finally asked. "You're moving back to Timber Creek? What about San Francisco?"

Something flashed across her face, but Amber still didn't give anything away. She waved her hand, dismissing Christy's question. "I'm done with San Francisco."

There was *definitely* something going on. Christy had always had a good sense for these things, and she knew something was up. She also knew it wasn't the right time to push for answers because Drew was crying tears of happiness and had jumped up to hug Amber.

"Really?" Drew asked. "You're really going to move in with me?"

Amber still hadn't asked for permission, but she wouldn't and Drew didn't seem to mind.

"Absolutely. I won't even go back to pack. I'll just have my things sent." As Amber spoke, Cam looked just as confused as Christy felt, but obviously, Drew was too wrapped up in everything else to notice. "I told you that you wouldn't have to be alone, Drew. And I meant it. I've got you."

There were so many questions swirling around Christy's head, but they could wait. And at the end of the day, what did they really matter? Amber was moving back and they'd all be together again, just like when they were in high school. And there couldn't be anything bad about that.

"TO MY BIG BROTHER." Ben raised a pint of beer from the end of the table, and the other men joined them in the toast. "A loving son, an amazing father, and a fiercely loved husband," Ben said. "I missed out on a lot with my brother." He paused. "And I'll regret that every day. But he was a good man and he will be terribly missed. He touched many lives, had many friends and…" He swallowed hard before looking up again and raising his glass higher. "To Eric."

"To Eric!" the group chorused and drank deeply.

Mark put his glass down and looked around. Sitting around the table was a mixture of people, all of whom had been important to Eric in some way. Not for the first time, Mark was struck by the rippling impact death had on a community. No one was untouched.

"I just want to say one more thing," Ben said and Mark returned his attention to the head of the table. "My brother made a special request for today."

Mark thought of the envelope Eric had given to him to hold on to for Drew. He'd locked it into his safe at the office and that's where it would stay until next summer when he was to give it to Drew.

"Beyond asking you all to be here, he requested that after I toasted him, in whatever form that took," Ben shook his head with a laugh, "that we stop mourning him and celebrate everyone else's life." A few of the men at the table muttered and looked around, confused, but Ben continued. "What Eric didn't want was for everyone to sit around sad and dwelling on death when there was so much life to live. He made it very clear to me in his final days that life was for living and if I wasn't living it to my fullest potential, then I was doing a disservice not only to myself, but to everyone I cared about.

"Eric didn't get a chance to do a lot of the things he wanted to do," Ben continued. "But that doesn't mean that we can't. In fact, according to my big brother, not only *can* we live our best life, we *better*." There were a few cheers from the guys and chuckles of laughter. "So, further to my brother's wishes, let's celebrate the living. Who has something to celebrate?"

Finished, Ben looked around the table, his eyes finally landing on his best friend. "Evan?"

It took Evan a moment to collect himself, but then he stood, raised his glass and toasted. "I'm celebrating because I'm going to be a father. Cam and I are expecting our first baby in March."

The group cheered and toasted. More beer was poured and Evan pointed at Mark, who didn't hesitate. He knew exactly why he was celebrating.

Mark stood and raised his glass. "I'm celebrating because I never thought it would be possible, but I *am* a father! And Christy and I couldn't be happier."

More cheers and toasts. Aaron patted him on the back when he returned to his seat.

There were more toasts of celebrations, more drinking and more cheering when a man Mark only vaguely recognized stood at the far end of the table. "I'm celebrating," the man said. "Because I'm two years clean." It was only then that Mark noticed the man toasted with a glass of water. Everyone cheered and the man sat to give others a turn.

Mark nudged Aaron. "Who is that? I don't know him."

"Sure you do." Aaron grinned. "That's Logan Myers."

"*Little* Logan?" He certainly wasn't little anymore. The man was over six feet and had muscles that rivaled a professional athlete.

Aaron nodded. "The one and only. He works out on Blackstrap ranch out of town, and volunteers at the fire department."

"Are you talking about Logan?" Evan leaned into their conversation. "Amber didn't recognize him either at the anniversary dance this spring. Although, I can't blame you guys. He's grown up."

"And clean? Was he—"

"Alcohol mostly," Evan finished. "Some recreational drugs too. But he's a good guy. I've worked with him a few times. Accident scenes, mostly. Nice guy, for sure. If I remember correctly, he said that he'd always looked up to Eric growing up. I guess Eric used to babysit him and his little sister."

"Small world." Mark nodded and then laughed. "Or just a small town."

"Definitely a small town," Aaron agreed. "Another beer?"

"Better not." Mark waved him away. "We have a training run in the morning. Don't tell me you forgot?"

Mark hadn't been able to get out as much as he would have liked, what with the new baby and the complete and total upheaval that had brought to their lives—in the best way, of course. He'd tried to back out of the race altogether, but Christy wouldn't hear of it.

"I meant it when I said it's important for us to keep ourselves even now that we're parents," she'd said. "I'm still going to sing; you're still going to run. It's just going to look different than it did, that's all."

And it did look different, but his wife was right. It was important for them to retain the parts of themselves that made them the people they were and outside interests were important, too. Even if things had to be modified, they'd make it work. So together they'd sat down and made a schedule so he could still compete his training for the ultra-marathon. When it was finished in a few weeks, they'd agreed that he would scale down his events so they didn't require such intense training.

"I certainly didn't forget." Aaron winked. "Especially since you promised to finally introduce me to your friend."

Mark laughed. With everything that had been going on, he'd almost forgotten about Christy's promise to Alicia to introduce her to Aaron. Once he'd been reminded, Aaron was one hundred percent behind the idea and hadn't let up about it until they'd finally organized a long training run. Mark was pretty sure that once the introduction was made, he'd be running by himself a whole lot more, especially if the two of them got along even half as well as he thought they might.

Chapter Twenty-Three

THE NIGHT before her first rehearsal back with Timber Heart at the end of September, Christy was worried that she might have forgotten all the words to their songs, or how to hold the mic, or how to properly count the guys in. She was terrified that her singing career, such as it was, would be over before it began.

Jamie and the guys had been more than understanding when she explained everything that was going on. She needed some time alone with Mya to get established and let the realities of motherhood sink in. But she was also determined not to give up on the band and singing. Not now that she'd found such an outlet and maybe even for the first time in her life found something that she loved almost as much as her family.

"Welcome back." Jamie gave her a hug as soon as she walked into the garage where the band was already tuning up their instruments.

"Hey there, little mama." Caleb hugged her next, followed by Josh, who handed her a box wrapped in pink paper.

"This is from all of us," Josh said. "Open it."

She laughed at the pink paper that upon closer inspection had little musical notes imprinted on it. "Perfect paper."

"If you think that's perfect—"

"Shut up." Caleb smacked Josh and looked at Christy seriously. "Open it."

She did as instructed and pulled out an impossibly tiny black leather jacket. As tiny as the jacket was, it would still be too big for Mya for quite some time. "It's so cute." She lifted it from the tissue paper to examine it and when she turned it around, she squealed.

"Do you like it?" Jamie asked.

Christy's eyes filled with tears and she started laughing and crying all at the same time.

"Aw, damn," Caleb said. "I knew it. New mothers are always so hormonal."

That made Christy laugh even harder. She couldn't be hormonal; she hadn't given birth. Although she could be exhausted. Which she was. "I love it," she finally managed to say. "It's absolutely perfect." And it was, because on the back of the jacket, the guys had "Timber Heart #1 Fan" embroidered in bright yellow. "I can't wait until she's big enough to wear it. Thank you." And then she was crying for real because it really was amazing that she'd found such a great group of guys who were not only her band mates, but also friends.

"Okay, okay." Josh moved away to pick up his guitar. "That's enough tears for one afternoon. We have work to do. If we only get Christy for limited time, let's make the most of it."

She couldn't argue with that. They'd been really understanding about everything, even when she emailed them all the new lyrics for some songs she'd been working on in the middle of the night when she was rocking Mya back to sleep. It turned out that all of her recent life events had been a huge well of inspiration for her.

"Have you guys had a chance to look at any of the new

songs?" Christy tucked the jacket away and moved to the microphone. She lifted it in her hand and felt the weight of it. It felt right. Very right.

"Not only have we had a chance," Jamie said with a strum of his guitar. "We've been practicing."

"One, two, three." Behind her, Josh counted them in with his drumsticks and they started playing.

It took her a minute to realize which one it was since she mostly only worked on lyrics while Josh and the others put the melody together, but then Jamie started singing and she almost started crying again.

"One Day." She almost whispered the name of the song, she was so moved.

Jamie nodded, but she didn't need confirmation to know it was the song she wrote only hours before Mya was put in her arms. It was perfect.

Somehow she managed to pull herself together long enough to join in and for the very first time, she sang the song of her heart with her new band.

The rest of the rehearsal went smoothly. They spent more time trying out the new songs and finished off with some of their old favorites just to have fun.

"That was great," she said as the last note faded away. "It felt so good."

"It sounded great," Josh said. "Motherhood suits you."

She laughed. "Well, it's certainly been a change."

"For all of us." Jamie handed her a bottle of water. "We were just getting used to our new group and then..." He shrugged.

"I'm sorry."

"Don't be." He laughed. "I'm kidding. Really. And Josh is right, motherhood suits you. These songs are dynamite, Christy. They really are."

"But we were wondering." Christy turned to Caleb. "How do you feel about touring again and playing gigs?"

It was a good question. One she knew was coming and she was ready for it. She'd talked it over with Mark a few times. "Well, if you're okay with it, I'd like to play some local gigs for a while. Maybe try out our new material and stay close to home. Timber Creek and maybe some towns in driving distance. We can use that time to make sure our new stuff is solid, and maybe even get a few talent agents out. I know it's kind of out of the way, but we can offer them a stay at the hotel and maybe turn it into a little holiday?" That was a reach, but Aaron had offered a discounted rate on some rooms if they wanted to try to lure a few agents to town to hear them. "And then, in a few months, when Mya is a bit older and more settled, we can try some shorter tours again. But hopefully by that time we've sorted out the details for a demo record."

"A demo?" Jamie raised his eyebrows. "Really?"

"Really." She'd been doing some research during all those late-night feedings and she had a few ideas on how they might be able to secure some studio time. "We can talk more about it, but I have some ideas. And I'm serious about it, guys. I am."

"We believe you." Josh whistled. "And I have to say, I'm impressed."

Christy beamed. She wasn't delusional; she knew it wasn't going to be so easy all the time, but so far she was juggling the balls of motherhood and her budding music career as well as doing her best to make sure she and Mark stayed connected throughout it all.

At the thought of Mark, she checked her phone and the time. "I've gotta go, guys." She drank down the rest of her water and moved to grab her purse. "I have to get home so we can get ready for tomorrow. Mark is running the Polar Peeks Ultra-marathon tomorrow and Mya and I will be there to cheer him on." She grinned, thinking of the matching t-shirts she'd made for herself and her daughter to wear at the race the next day.

"Same time next week, Christy?"

"I wouldn't miss it."

She walked down the street, carrying the box with the baby leather jacket in it and singing her brand-new song, "One Day," as she made her way back to her little family and the life she loved more and more with every day that passed.

HE WAS OUT OF BREATH, his legs burned, and every muscle in his body ached. Yet, Mark never felt more alive as he crossed the finish line of the Polar Peek Ultra-marathon. He'd just run over fifty kilometres in less than twenty-four hours and was ready to drop, but he laid eyes on his gorgeous wife and beautiful new daughter. Christy's shirt read "Run Honey Run" and even though Mya's matching shirt was covered up with a blanket to protect her from the cool mountain air, he knew it read "Run Daddy Run." Just seeing them gave Mark a burst of energy that could have kept him going for another fifty kilometers.

Of course, the moment he collapsed on the ground at Christy's feet, that idea went out the window. He was done. And he'd never been happier to be done, because the time he'd just spent away from his new little family was far too long.

"I'm so proud of you." Christy dropped to her knees next to him and wrapped her arms around his stinky, sweaty body before pressing a bottle into his hands. "Drink."

He nodded, unable to form the words he needed. He was unable to do anything but lay back and breathe.

"Come on, buddy." Evan stood over him and offered him a hand. "Let's get you out of the way and into a proper chair."

All of their friends had come out to support them. Evan

and Cam were there, Amber had come out, and Ben of course. Even Drew and Austin had come along to join in the celebration. Mark let Ben lead him over to a camping chair, where he sat gratefully while someone took his shoes off and Ben handed him a cold can of beer.

"You're my favorite person right now," he said and then laughed as he met Christy's eyes. She was holding Mya again, and his heart swelled. "I lied," he said to Ben.

"Don't I know it." Ben laughed as he looked to see where Mark was looking, as if he even needed the confirmation. "You're a lucky man."

"A fact I'm thankful for every single day."

He winked at Christy, who blew him a kiss.

"Did Aaron and Alicia come across the line already?" Mark had lost sight of his training mates early on and he'd encouraged them to go ahead. Ever since Mya had come home, he'd managed to maintain his training runs, but they definitely weren't as intense as they should have been and he was much slower for it. But Mark didn't care. He was happy to have finished the race because it would be his last one for a while.

"Don't you know it." Aaron slapped him on the shoulder, and Mark turned in his chair to see his best friend and his new training partner looking rested and refreshed enough that they'd definitely crossed the finish line before him. "Good job, buddy. You did good."

"Not as good as you did."

"I had a good partner." Aaron nudged Alicia with his elbow, and Mark couldn't help but notice that they didn't look nearly as cozy as he assumed they would by now. After the first introduction, Aaron had more or less replaced him as his main training partner in favor of the beautiful tall blonde. Not that Mark minded; it's just that he assumed maybe something had happened between the two of them.

He watched them while they exchanged race details and race notes.

Soon, Mark was swept up in the festivities and celebrations and despite the total body exhaustion that pulsed through him, he'd never felt better. How could he not? When he looked around, he was surrounded by friends and family and the two most important people.

"How are you doing, babe?" Christy handed him his little girl, and Mark pressed a kiss to Mya's forehead before wrapping his other arm around his wife.

"Perfect." He kissed her softly. "Absolutely perfect."

"I love you." She touched the baby's cheek, but Mark knew she was talking to both of them. "And," she looked up into his eyes, "I love that we are *us*."

"Me too." He pulled her as close as he could without disturbing the baby. "More than anything."

Together, they looked down at Mya, who was sleeping soundly, wrapped in her blanket. Every single time he looked at her, Mark loved her even more than he had the moment before, if it was possible. He could hardly remember what it was like before she came into their lives. The pain and heartache they'd gone through before she came along was a distant memory. But not a forgotten one.

Never completely forgotten.

Everything they'd gone through that summer had led them to the very moment they were in right then and as Christy was so fond of saying, *everything happened for a reason.*

And his reason was right there in his arms. And he was never letting go.

Thank you for reading When We Were Us! I hope you enjoyed Christy and Mark's love story!

The love continues in When We Began because Amber is back in town, and you'll never guess what she's been hiding from her friends. A strong, independent woman... can she get past her secrets long enough to let love in?
You can read a sneak peak right after this...

For more love and happily ever afters, I have an exclusive sweet novella that's not for sale anywhere. You can read it HERE!

When We Began

_____

Please enjoy this excerpt from Amber's Story—When We Began .

It had been a long time since Amber Monroe had stood in front of the doors of Timber Creek Elementary. It had been decades since she'd accepted her _graduation_ certificate from the principal and marched out the door toward bigger and better things.

Like eighth grade. And Timber Creek High School.

But that was just the beginning for Amber. She'd been ambitious from the start. Her mom used to say she was born with an agenda.

And maybe she had been.

Amber had been nonstop as long as she could remember. Always looking ahead to the next thing instead of stopping to enjoy the moment she was in. Driven, her mother had called it. Before she'd died, when Amber was barely thirteen, she'd made Amber promise never to lose her drive and she hadn't.

In elementary, she'd organized a bracelet club in grade two, appointed herself leader and had run meetings at recess where they made friendship bracelets and sold them for charity to the other kids. It lasted two weeks before everyone quit because Amber wouldn't allow them a day off to play four square.

Once she was in high school, it was a lot easier to find roles she could excel in. Student body president in the eleventh grade, a role she gave up her senior year to concentrate on college admissions; editor of the newspaper; co-chair of the graduation committee; and countless other committees. Amber was in her element when she was in charge of something. When she had a plan. When she had control.

Which was why she didn't hesitate to take control when her best friend Drew Ross put off her son Austin's first day of pre-kindergarten...again.

Austin was already two weeks late starting the year. It was understandable, considering he'd just lost his dad to cancer. But the boy needed normalcy. He needed routine. He needed to get on with his life. What he didn't need was his mother holding him close while she cried into his hair every night instead of reading him a bedtime story.

Which was exactly why Amber was back in Timber Creek. Her best friend needed her. And that's also why she was once again standing outside of Timber Creek Elementary school with Austin's tiny hand clenched tightly in hers. Once upon a time, she'd promised that she would never set foot inside that school again until there was such a time she was asked back to speak to the students about women's rights in business. Or equal wages, or whatever it was that she was passionate about at the time.

She'd never been asked back. Despite the fact that she was a successful lawyer at a huge law firm in San Francisco. So successful she'd made partner.

Correction. *Almost* made partner.

She shook her head and straightened her shoulders. It wasn't the right time to think about what *almost* was.

"Auntie Amber?"

Amber blinked hard and looked down at Austin, who was staring up at her, wide-eyed.

"Are we going in?"

Amber forced herself to be present in the moment. She didn't need to think about the past or home or anything at all. She just needed to get through today. And then tomorrow. And then—

Focus.

She squeezed the boy's hand, forcing herself to be in the moment. There was nothing else.

Just Austin.

She smiled and hoped the boy believed it was genuine.

"Absolutely," she said. "Are you ready for your first day of school?"

Austin nodded readily. "Yes. Mommy said I didn't have to go. But I want to go."

"That's good." Amber squeezed his hand. "You'll have fun." She took another step forward toward the school, but Austin tugged on her hand.

"Auntie?"

Amber looked back into his troubled face. He was only a little boy. He should be smiling and laughing. But he'd lost so much for someone so young, it broke her heart. "What's up, kiddo?"

"Do you think I should stay home? Mommy wanted me to stay home. Will I have friends? What if the kids don't like me? What if the teacher is mean?"

He fired the questions at her like popcorn in a hot pan, but Amber grabbed each kernel as it popped.

"I don't think you should stay home. Your mommy is just sad right now, but she wants you to go to school. Of course you'll have friends. The kids will love you and I happen to have it on good authority that your teacher is super-duper nice."

Austin grabbed onto the last detail. "She is? What's her name?"

Amber bent to give him a kiss on the cheek. "Why don't we go find out?" Before he could answer, she started to walk again and this time he followed along.

Walking through the heavy doors was a blast from the past for Amber. Not much had changed since she'd been a student there but there were a few new touches. Including the young female principal who greeted her the moment they stepped inside.

"Mrs. Ross, it's nice to—"

"Monroe," Amber corrected. "I'm Amber Monroe. Mrs. Ross couldn't be here." She gave the woman a look that she hoped was understood. The school had been briefed on Austin's situation and Amber had called and spoken with the principal personally when Drew only stared at Amber blankly upon the suggestion of Austin starting school.

The woman's face changed, and her face split into a smile. "It's nice to meet you, Amber." She turned her attention and extended her hand. "And you must be Austin."

The little boy, suddenly way too old for his age, took the principal's hand and shook it seriously. "Nice to meet you."

"Well, aren't you the sweetest thing?" The principal straightened up and grinned at Amber. "He's very sweet."

Amber nodded in agreement.

"I'm Principal Foster. Maggie Foster. It's nice to meet you both. Did you want to go with Austin to his class and see him settled in?"

Amber looked to the boy. She knew he was nervous but she also knew he was trying to be brave. He'd never admit that he wanted her to go with him. "You know what." Amber looked back to Maggie Foster while she gave Austin's hand that was still wrapped up in hers another reassuring squeeze. "I think his mom would prefer it if I went with him."

"I think that sounds perfect," Maggie said. "Are you ready, Austin? Your teacher is excited to meet you. I think you're going to really like Mrs. Brewster."

"Is she nice?" Without him even realizing it, Austin released Amber's hand and started to follow his principal.

"She's *very* nice and there are a lot of little boys your age in your class that I think you're going to be very good friends with."

Amber trailed along behind them and listened as Austin peppered the principal with a new list of questions, his nervousness fading as his excitement grew.

She smiled to herself. Bringing him to school had been the right choice. She hadn't meant to steamroll Drew's wishes to have him at home. In fact, Amber felt badly about it. But it was easy to see that the real reason Drew hadn't wanted Austin to start school had nothing to do with the child himself and everything to do with her.

And that's why Amber was there, to help Drew get through these difficult few weeks, maybe months, and then she'd go back to—what?

"Ms. Monroe?"

Amber blinked hard as Maggie Foster came into view in front of her. She'd been daydreaming and not only had she not realized they'd arrived at the class, she also hadn't noticed as Austin had bravely gone inside. Without so much as a look backward.

"I don't think you need to worry about Austin at all," Maggie said. "He looks like he's settling in already." She gestured to the door and Amber peeked in. Sure enough, Austin looked fine. He sat in a circle on the floor with a group of children, a wide smile on his face.

Careful he didn't notice her, Amber whipped out her cell phone and took a picture of the scene to show Drew when she got home.

Satisfied, Amber left the boy in the capable hands of Mrs. Brewster and the class, and walked back to her car, where she sat behind the wheel and took a deep breath as she stared at the cell phone still in her hand. Not that she actually expected it to ring. There likely weren't any voicemails waiting for her either. And her email inbox would be just as empty.

The anxiety started to creep in around the edges again. She could feel the fingers of it wrapping slowly around her chest, squeezing until she struggled to take a breath. Amber closed her eyes and did the breathing exercises she'd learned. After a moment, the panic was gone again, but the emptiness wasn't.

Would she ever get used to it? The quiet? No one needing her or waiting for her to make a decision?

She didn't think so.

Amber pulled her shoulders back and took one more deep breath.

There may not be anything work-wise she needed to do, and the law firm might no longer need her, but there was plenty she could fill her day with. She started the car and pulled out of the parking lot, headed back to Drew's. Her best friend needed her, and she was the biggest project of all.

By eleven o'clock, Amber had already done everything on her list for the day, which mostly included throwing in some laundry and running the vacuum in the living room. She was just putting the finishing touches on a salad for her and Drew to share for lunch when her friend finally appeared from her bedroom.

"Well, good morning." Amber tried to keep her voice light, but she was getting dangerously close to offering Drew some tough love, best friend style.

"Whatever," Drew mumbled before she slumped into a chair at the table and dropped her head into a hand. "I saw you this morning when you got Austin ready for school. Thank you, by the way."

"You don't need to thank me." Amber smiled as kindly as she could. It broke her heart to see her sweet friend so completely broken. She'd been strong throughout her husband Eric's cancer, handling everything in stride. It seemed to everyone that Drew had everything completely under control and was dealing with her husband's illness with more grace than anyone ever could have imagined.

The truth was, that despite the outward appearances she'd been working so hard to keep up, on the inside she was having a complete meltdown. In the days following Eric's passing and his memorial service, Drew started to struggle more and more.

Which was exactly what Amber had hoped wouldn't happen, but that she'd guessed would. She knew her best friend well enough to know that Drew would need her. And that's why she was there.

It's not the only reason.

Amber forced the thought from her head as she slid the plate of salad in front of her friend. "Seriously," she said. "You don't need to thank me. I'm happy to be here to help you guys. And you should have seen Austin. He was so brave about meeting the new kids. I think it's going to be really good for him. Look, I even took a picture for you." She passed Drew her cell phone with the picture of Austin in his new class.

Her friend stared at the picture, fresh tears pooling in her eyes. "I should have been there."

"It's fine. He hardly even noticed that *I* was there," Amber said kindly. "Eat something."

"Send me that picture, please." Drew handed the phone back and looked at her plate for the first time. "Salad again?"

She picked up her fork and pushed the leaves around the plate. "Do you think I need to be on a diet or something?"

"Not at all." Amber slid into the seat across from her. "It's kind of all I know how to make. Besides shaking chicken fingers out of a bag and putting them in the oven, but I thought I'd save that for dinner." She grinned, but Drew didn't look impressed.

"Seriously? You don't cook?"

Amber shrugged. "When would I ever have learned how to cook? Dad always made dinner or brought home frozen dinners, and ever since then it's just been easier to order in."

"What about the lasagna and the shepherd's pie we had the other night?"

"Pretty much everything we've been eating has been thanks to the kindness of your family and friends," Amber explained. "They did a good job filling the freezer, but supplies are starting to get a little low."

"So, we get salad?" Drew lifted her fork and held a cucumber aloft.

"Don't forget the chicken fingers." Amber winked and stuffed a forkful into her mouth. "But if you don't like it," she said after a moment, "maybe you could cook something? What's Austin's favorite meal? It might be nice to surprise him with that on his first day of school, don't you think?"

The instant Amber suggested it, she regretted it. Drew's eyes filled up with tears and she dropped the fork and buried her face in her hands.

"What did I say? Drew?" Amber prodded gently.

"My spaghetti is Austin's favorite."

That didn't seem like a reason to burst into tears, but then again, Amber was definitely not an expert in grief. "That sounds good," she said. "Why don't we make that? I'll get the ingredients at the store and—"

"It was Eric's favorite, too."

Ahhh.

"Okay," she said cautiously. "How does chicken fingers sound?"

Drew lifted her head and even managed a small smile. "Perfect. Thank you."

Amber reached across the table and squeezed Drew's hand. "It's nothing."

Thankfully, they were able to finish lunch without any more tears and Amber even got Drew to smile again when she told her about all of Austin's questions before they went into the school. But despite her best efforts, she couldn't convince her friend to leave the house to pick up her son with her.

Baby steps, she reminded herself later that afternoon when she made her trip to Timber Trade to pick up the supplies for dinner, including a bag of frozen French fries and a pint of ice cream for dessert. It was his first day of school, after all; they should celebrate at least a little bit.

It had only been a few weeks since Eric died. Amber needed to remember that everyone went through the grieving process differently. She'd just turned thirteen when her mom died from breast cancer. It was a short-lived battle, as her mom had ignored all the signs and symptoms, pushing them off as "just feeling under the weather." By the time she saw the doctor, there wasn't much that could be done. And even though she'd only been a kid and everyone around her expected her and her father to fall apart, the opposite had happened. Amber only remembered seeing her dad cry the one time, the day he told her that her mother had passed in her sleep. After that, he'd been strong and stoic.

She herself *had* cried.

Secretly, in bed, after all the friends and relatives who meant well had gone home. It was important for her to keep her feelings in check, because if she lost control, if she let her hurt show through, even a little, her dad would start to worry about her. And he had enough to worry about. Everyone kept saying that. How much Joseph had to worry about now.

When they thought Amber wasn't listening, the adults would huddle their heads together and talk about how much pressure was on his shoulders now to raise her all on his own and they didn't know how he was going to do it.

The last thing Amber needed to do was add more worry to his stress load. Which was why, after crying herself to sleep for the first few nights, the tears dried up and she vowed to keep the promise she'd once made to her mom.

She'd never lose her drive to be successful. No matter what, Amber was going to achieve all of her dreams. Not only for her, but for her mom.

And she had, too. Mostly. At least for a little while.

Would her mom be proud of her now? She was pretty sure she knew the answer to that question.

Amber shook her head and was about to do what she always did, which was make a mental list about what she could do to get back on track, when her phone chirped with an incoming text message.

It had once been such an ordinary sound in her daily life, almost like a soundtrack to her day, but that was before. Now the sound was jarring, snapping her back to her current situation, which was anything but ordinary.

She grabbed at her phone and clicked it open, eager to see who'd finally reached out.

How R U? You missed the meeting again last night.

The second she read it, guilt flooded through her. She should have known that Cody wouldn't let it slide that she'd missed her meeting yet again. That was the point of a sponsor. To hold her accountable and make sure she stayed on track. It didn't seem to matter that she *was* on track. There just weren't any meetings that she knew of in Timber Creek and even if there were, it's not as if she could go to them. It was a small town, and despite the fact that they were supposed to be anonymous, she wasn't stupid enough to actually believe that it wouldn't get out. And the last thing she needed was for anyone, especially her best friends or her father, who'd give her that *look*, to know that, despite the fact that she'd tried so hard to have it all, instead she'd ruined everything.

Read the rest of Amber's story in *When We Began!*

About the Author

Elena Aitken is a USA Today Bestselling Author of more than forty romance and women's fiction novels. The mother of 'grown up' twins, Elena now lives with her very own mountain man in the heart of the very mountains she writes about. She can often be found with her toes in the lake and a glass of wine in her hand, dreaming up her next book and working on her own happily ever after.

To learn more about Elena:
www.elenaaitken.com
elena@elenaaitken.com